Our lunches arrived and we ate in silence for a couple of minutes. I was already excited about this sudden opportunity, but then a dark thought came to mind. What would Andrea think? She already thought I was starting to take the 'weirdo stuff,' as she called it, too seriously.

One day she asked me what I was reading, and I told her the book was about the works of mystic Rudolf Steiner. He wrote that there was an invisible spirit world nearby that could be accessed and studied by those who developed certain latent abilities. Andrea stared at me a moment, as if seeing me for the first time. "Are you losing your fucking mind, Jake? I think you're starting to believe that shit. Maybe you should drop that course."

I0545570

Copyright © 2019 by Trish & Rob MacGregor
ISBN 978-1-950565-72-6
All rights reserved. No part of this book may be used or reproduced in any manner
whatsoever without written permission except in the case of
brief quotations embodied in criticalarticles and reviews
For information address Crossroad Press at 141 Brayden Dr., Hertford, NC 27944
A Mystique Press Production - Mystique Press is an imprint of Crossroad Press.
www.crossroadpress.com

First edition

THE OUTLIERS

BY TRISH & ROB MACGREGOR

CONTENTS

FOREWORD

WHO ARE THESE OUTLIERS?

For writers, outliers are often isolated scribblings. They may be ideas that wake you in the dead of night and they're so vivid you feel compelled to jot them down. They can be condensed from novels or may be events taken from your own life that you've embellished in some way to fit a particular genre of writing. They usually follow your interests and passions.

What they have in common is they often reflect a creative theme that works best as short fiction. In this collection of short stories, the outliers are people who don't fit into our consensus reality. They're anomalies, weirdos, individuals whose experiences are vastly different from the rest of us. And yet, they *are* us in their humanity, their emotions, and in their curiosity that asks, *What if?*

By definition, an outlier is something or someone that lies outside of the main group that it's a part of. Think of a crow that flies separately from the flock to which it belongs. It could be out in front, leading the way, flying off to the side, or trailing far behind the others. For better or worse, outliers stand out from the crowd but aren't always as obvious as that rebellious crow.

Spinning Out, a novella that sets the pace, began with Rob's initial interest years ago in lucid dreaming and out-of-body experiences. However, the idea for the story didn't come about until he met a man who, at face value, seemed an unlikely outlier. He was a retired police officer from Midland, Texas, who works in hospital security. He wanted to talk about his out-of-body encounters with someone who would listen and not consider him insane. His experiences exceeded anything Rob had ever heard, and he knew that the man's apparent ability to manipulate matter while out of body would make for an unusual fictive tale.

Rivereños was born during a trip to the Peruvian Amazon, when we used to lead trips to the area for travel writers. The jungle's lush richness, its heat and exotic animals, its myths and legends, have a way of swallowing the life you left at home and transforming it into something that isn't necessarily wonderful. It was originally published in *Stalkers*, a collection of short stories edited by Ed Gorman and Martin Greenberg and published by ROC.

The Unit, originally published in *Ellery Queen*, deals with dementia/Alzheimer's. It came about because Trish's mother suffered from Alzheimer's for several years before her death. The 84-year-old protagonist in the story, though, outwits her "handlers" in a dementia unit.

A Very Thin, Thin Line came about during a trip to Colombia. We received an email from our agent that Apple was reviving Spielberg's *Amazing Stories* and was looking for stories that take place in the 1980s, have elements of magical realism, and an uplifting ending. Check, check, check. Our agent approved the co-authored story, submitted it, and months of radio silence followed. Eventually, we decided to include it here.

A Gambler's Superstition evolved from an embarrassing personal experience. One day Trish bought a scratch off lottery ticket, didn't read the fine print about what constituted a win, and thought she'd won a thousand bucks. Rather than going to the grocery store or to a convenience store to collect, she drove to the county lottery office.

Trish got in line with half a dozen others who held winning lottery tickets. When she reached the window, the clerk ran the ticket through the machine that validates a win and instead of making a happy sound, the machine made a noise like a burp.

"Sorry, it's not a win," the clerk said, and explained that the ticket lacked one necessary number.

In the story, the lack of attention to details proves to be a woman's undoing. The story was originally published in *Ellery Queen.*

The Works first appeared in *Sisters in Crime 2,* edited by Marilyn Wallace and published by Berkley. It's set in Miami Beach's Deco area and is told by an eccentric woman, a former nurse, who tends to the "old ones." It's been revised and updated for the 21st century.

The Devil's Chair is a story based on an urban legend about a brick chair that faces two gravestones in a cemetery in central Florida, north of Orlando. The cemetery is located outside the spiritualist community of Cassadaga, which offers weekly ghost tours of the town. In this story, the spookiness is enhanced when a reporter looking for a Halloween story visits the cemetery at midnight as he investigates the urban legend.

Wild Card evolved from a personal experience. In May of 1984, 8-year-old Christie Luna disappeared while walking to a convenience store in Green Acres, Florida, to buy food for her cat. The police investigation was intense and included help from psychic empath Renie Wiley. We accompanied her to the Green Acres Police Department one night and watched her work with Christie's toys that her mother had brought over.

In the story, the missing girl is found. In real life, the disappearance of Christie Luna remains an open case.

Portal came about because of Trish's interest in Mary Todd Lincoln's alleged psychic experiences. It was originally published in *The First Lady Murders,* edited by Nancy Pickard and published by Pocket Books.

Finally, we've finished our tales with two teasers from our newest novels, available now. The first one is the prologue for Trish's newest, *Skin Shifters.* The other one is the prologue from Rob's latest novel, *Tulpas.* We hope you enjoy all the stories.

Trish MacGregor & Rob MacGregor
September 2018

SPINNING OUT

BY ROB MACGREGOR

*G*et in, do it, get out.

That was his mantra. Bill Waters had said it over and over as he'd prepared for the journey. But now that he was here, inside the beehive, he struggled to maintain his focus. He felt stymied, unable to act, overwhelmed by a desire to flee. He stood in the dayroom at the center of the pod, surrounded by twenty-four single cells, twelve on each level. His target was locked inside cell 9 of cell block #3, pod 4, Unit III of Central Prison.

Get in, do it, and get out.

He forced himself to remain calm in the midst of the hive, all these cells containing death row inmates. Again, he told himself that he could do it by himself, do it and get out. They were here for life...and death. If all went well, he was here for minutes... and gone. But why was he feeling so oppressed? Was he picking up the dark energy in this pod, in this cell block, in this prison? Or was it because he was alone, abandoned by his partner? There was more than double the energy with a partner, and he couldn't ignore the absence, the loss.

He suddenly sensed movement, another presence. Someone was here, watching. He scanned the dayroom and glimpsed a figure move out from the shadows, coming toward him. Danny. "So you changed your mind?"

"I'm here."

He sounded surly. They would talk later. "Let's get it over with. I want you to do it." It was the best way to get him firmly entrenched.

"I knew you were going to say that."

Waters laughed. "You know me all too well, Danny-Boy. C'mon."

He led the way to the cell door. "Ready?"

Danny shrugged. "I guess."

A moment later, they were both inside an eight-by-ten cell. Nice and roomy, Waters thought. Must be a real blast spending thirty-one years here, most of it in this hole, as this poor fucker had done. But he wouldn't have to wait another minute for his execution. His time was up.

Darrell Jacob Everett lay on his side under a thin blanket. His narrow bed was about the size of a cot. The only other furnishings were a writing table attached to the wall, a toilet, and a sink. Danny approached the bed, stared down, then leaned over and put a hand on Everett's shoulder.

What was he doing? Saying good-bye or trying to wake him? What the fuck! Waters nudged Danny in the back at the same moment Everett bolted upright in bed and jerked his head around, shouting, "Who's here?"

Danny's hands clamped like a shark's jaw onto Everett's throat and shoved him back onto the bed. Everett's arms flayed about. He kicked his legs frantically, his body bucked, hips and back rising off the bed. Danny kept throttling him. But Everett managed to roll onto the floor, and Danny lost his grip.

Everett emitted a chilling banshee howl that probably echoed through the cell block like an alarm. Waters lunged for his throat and banged Everett's head against the floor again and again. Danny clung to Everett's lower body, holding him in place until the man went still. Waters kept clutching his throat and pressing his thumbs against Everett's larynx and trachea.

For a moment, Waters thought he was back in Afghanistan fighting for his life, under attack from behind. Danny shook his shoulders. "Billy, c'mon. Let's get out of here."

He released the dead man's throat, stared down at the crumpled figure, and was overcome with a sense of relief and elation. Everett was number 3. One more to go, then mission accomplished.

2

SIX WEEKS LATER

I glanced up from my notes on the lectern and looked out over two dozen youthful faces, some curious and waiting to hear what I would say next, probably hoping for hints about their upcoming final exam. I wanted to finish with something significant, something they might remember. But nothing came to mind, except something I'd already talked about.

"Does anyone remember the first thing I said to you on the first day of class?"

Silence.

Finally, Tracy, a bespectacled redhead who always sat in the first row, spoke up. "I think I remember, Professor Harrison. It was about randomness, and how given enough time some monkeys could type the great American novel."

Laughter rippled through the class. "That's it?"

"Well, then you went on to say that was bullshit."

The class guffawed. "Did I really say that?"

Several heads bobbed.

"I guess I did. Let me rephrase that. Let's face it, folks, we were all born into a random universe where human existence, and life itself, is the result of a vast number of accidental combinations of molecular soup." I paused and watched several students typing rapidly on their devices, as if I'd just revealed the secret to the universe. Others simply waited for the flip. "But hold on, it only appears that way. According to theoretical quantum physics, at a deeper level of conscience, the universe is a vast, interconnected web, where everything is entangled, vibrating together, resonating energetically with everything else. This dovetails nicely with Eastern notions of nonduality."

I noticed Tracy nodding in a knowing manner. "Do you want to explain what nonduality is, Tracy?"

"Sure. It's the mystical perception that unity is the underlying reality, and that there aren't opposing sides, and that individual consciousness is an illusion. It's all consciousness and all interconnected."

Tracy was a junior carrying a heavy credit load. She was on track to earn bachelor's degrees in physics and political science. When I'd asked her why she had taken a parapsychology course, she said she had an experience that she couldn't explain. Her grandmother had appeared to her in a dream and held up her hand showing an eye in the center of her palm. The next day Tracy was looking online at courses for the next semester, and there was the eye in a palm next to the description of my class. I didn't know who had selected that image to promote the class, and I never knew what to say when I was asked about it. But it has remained there semester after semester and seemed to work since the class was always filled to capacity.

"Well put," I told her. "So rather than our existence being the result of mere chance, it's synchronicity or meaningful coincidence. Consciousness at play."

"What's the meaning?" someone called out.

"That's for you to figure out. In fact, that sounds like a possible subject for an essay on your final."

The comment was met with groans. I stuffed my iPad in my leather satchel. "Speaking of, your final exam is Saturday at ten. I'm out of here, but my trusty assistant Roger will be in charge."

"Any hints about what we need to know, Professor Harrison?"

I was looking into my satchel at the remains of a sandwich I'd forgotten about, but I recognized the accented voice of Barbara Morales, a raven-haired Latina who hailed originally from Colombia. One day when I randomly paired students and had them attempt to give each other ten-minute psychic readings, Barbara was astonishingly accurate in the three readings she gave. She later told me that her mother and aunt were mediumistic and she'd inherited the ability.

"Sure, you need to know about telepathy, precognition, clairvoyance—a.k.a. remote viewing, PK—psychokinesis, mediumship or spirit contact, OBEs and NDEs, and finally, synchronicity. Be prepared to write at least 500 words on any or all of them, emphasizing related scientific studies, pro and con. That should about cover it."

Another collective groan. "Good luck to all of you, and don't forget extra credit essays about your personal psychic experiences must be turned in before the final."

With that, I headed toward the door.

"Wait, Professor Harrison. Can I ask a personal question?"

I shrugged. I knew what was coming. "Go ahead, Tracy."

"Is it true that you're not teaching here in the fall, that the department is cancelling your class?"

"Yup. I'm really out of here, and I doubt that there will be a parapsychology course in the fall."

"It's unfair, that's what I think," Barbara interjected. "Your class is like one of the most popular on campus. Even the skeptics admit that."

"Ha, maybe a little too popular."

"We won't diss you, but we'll miss you, Prof Harrison," Purple Hair George shouted out. "Your class was totally lit, you woke us up." Everyone stood and applauded.

I waved a hand. "I think I can translate that. Have a good summer everyone." With that, I slipped out the door and hurried down the hall. I had a lunch date in twenty minutes. In spite of my rush, I couldn't help musing over my history here.

Parapsychology 101 at Blue Ridge-Henson College was one of several classes, including the History of Comics and Science Fiction Classics, that were instituted three years ago in the hopes of attracting new students. They were lumped together as pop culture courses. I'd taught two semesters of entry level psychology at the college when I was asked if I could teach such a course. Personally, I thought it was a cool idea but said I wasn't qualified.

Algernon Warren, the head of the psychology department, didn't care about my qualifications. In fact, he thought the idea of the course was nonsense but that it wasn't worth fighting the administration. I was given free rein to create a syllabus. But as I read the most recent books on the subject, I realized my preconceived notions about the paranormal had been distorted by skeptics, who were often dismissive based solely on personal biases. In spite of that, I emphasized skepticism about the paranormal throughout my first semester. By the second one, I spoke of the value of skepticism, but not the point of view of hardcore skeptics and debunkers.

As I read more and attended a couple of conferences, my perspective shifted further. During the past two semesters, I criticized mainstream science's views on the paranormal as stagnant, outdated, and simply wrong. While the standard point of view was that one's own experiences in these realms could not be trusted, I told students that everyone had psychic abilities to some extent, and these talents could be enhanced with practice. I also emphasized that we should never deny the validity of our own experiences.

After the Asheville newspaper did a lengthy article on the study of the paranormal and featured my class, Warren took a greater interest in what I was teaching and how I was teaching it. Two weeks ago, I got an email informing me that my contract wouldn't be renewed and the class would be dropped from the curriculum.

The next day I confronted him in the hall outside of his office and asked if there had been complaints about the class. "I've got a major complaint," he'd responded. "You're entertaining students with unprovable anecdotes and suggesting that they could become psychic themselves. That kind of class is more fitting for the adult-ed program at one of the high schools than an institution of higher learning." His comment virtually mimicked that of an Asheville area skeptic, Max Owens, who was quoted in the article.

If I were a tenured professor teaching a popular course, Warren would've been virtually powerless to fire me. As it was, there was no hearing for an adjunct professor, no chance for an appeal. I still had two other classes at another college a few miles away, but those were about to end, and I didn't have any summer session classes scheduled.

I moved swiftly across campus toward the parking garage, breathing deeply of the fresh air and enjoying the warm spring sun on my face. I glanced at my watch. If I found a parking spot near the restaurant, I might even make it on time. I found my car on the second level and quickly made my way out of the parking garage.

My lunch date was with Jamie Horner, a former social worker and psychic counselor, who had written three wildly popular humorous self-help books that emphasized developing your intuition to achieve your goals. In the past decade, she'd gone from living on a survival economy, never certain whether she would be able to cover her rent, to a multi-million dollar author and popular cable TV personality. She was the first psychic to break into cable politics and make on-air predictions. She was a controversial guest, but in frequent demand.

I was fortunate she lived in Asheville and had taken an interest in my course. She'd served as a guest speaker once every semester. Not only did her national status bolster the popularity of my class, but she was a great resource on research about psychic abilities. Over the past couple of years, several of my students had taken part in research in psychic phenomena at her ranch. To that end, she was director of the Institute of Mind Technology.

She'd called yesterday to arrange the lunch to tell me about her new project. When I asked what it was about, she said, "Just wait. It's something I think you'll find very interesting."

In spite of my best effort, I still arrived at Yucas a few minutes late. I perused the outdoor tables but didn't see Jamie. The pleasant weather had attracted a throng of lunchtime diners at all of the restaurants with sidewalk seating along Broadway. Yucas was unique for western North Carolina, an authentic Cuban restaurant. I'd gone to graduate school at the University of Miami, so I was looking forward to arroz con pollo with plantains and black beans.

I was about to go inside when I felt a tap on my shoulder and turned to see Jamie. She was a petite woman in her late thirties or early forties with straight dark hair that reached her jaw and framed her face. Dressed casually in jeans and a blouse, she had a red scarf draped over her shoulders. In spite of her size, she radiated a sense of power, and I knew she had a black belt in some form of martial arts. She'd told me that her ex-husband ran a martial arts school in Fort Lauderdale, where she was from.

"Glad you made it, Jake."

"Sorry I'm late."

"I just walked up a minute ago, got a table in the corner. You don't mind eating out here, do you?"

"Not at all."

We settled in and chatted a few minutes about the demise of parapsychology at Blue Ridge-Henson. Jamie seemed more annoyed by my dismissal than I was. "My god, I know it's a cliché, but they don't know a good thing when it's looking them right in the third eye, for chrissake."

"Good one," I laughed. "And thanks again for talking to my students. You're the hit of every semester. You made the kids not only think about the practical applications, but to try to apply them in their own lives."

"I feel a certain duty to get out on college campuses when I can. It's important for students to hear the other side from the standard academic response to anything metaphysical. I also appreciate that you always mention that I have an advanced degree in psychology and that you don't just refer to me as a psychic who hit the bestseller's list. That's how the talk show hosts like to label me."

"Most of my students were already on board, largely because of personal experiences. They were much more interested in your techniques for exploring these abilities than establishing a rationale for the existence of such so-called powers."

"Yeah, I noticed that. I remember last year that you were trying to get out of your body. How's that going, Jake?"

It felt odd talking to someone about out-of-body travel. It sure as hell wasn't a topic broached at a cocktail party of academics. "When I lay down to practice, I tend to fall asleep within a minute or two. But I've actually had some luck when I'm able to maintain my conscious awareness as I start to drift off."

The server, a guy in his twenties with an abundance of tattoos and piercings, came over and immediately gushed about the honor of waiting on Jamie Horner. He set down menus, glasses of water, and a basket of warm Cuban bread. I already knew what I wanted and ordered. Jamie ordered the same thing. When the server left, she leaned forward, elbows propped on the table, fingers laced together. "Tell me about it. I'm interested."

"The first time, I rolled out and just sort of hovered next to the bed. I got really excited and fell right back into my body. But the second time, I managed to hold my awareness outside of my body for about thirty seconds. I didn't go more than a few feet from the bed. Then, just last week, I got out for four or five minutes and moved around the house and right through the locked back door and out into the yard. I saw one of Sam's favorite toys that had gone missing behind an oak tree, and in the morning went out and found it right where I saw it."

"Very interesting. Sam is...?"

"My bloodhound."

She smiled. "That's a great start. You verified that it wasn't a dream when you found the toy in the same spot." Jamie rested her forearms on the table and leaned forward. "So, you're not teaching any summer session courses?"

"No, I cleared my schedule because Andrea and I had talked about going to Greece and Turkey for six weeks. But that's not going to happen."

"Why not, if you don't mind me asking?"

"Andrea left the academic world in January to take a corporate job. You know, more money and new opportunities."

"She's a lawyer, right?"

"Yeah, she taught at Blue Ridge-Henson's law school for eight years and had enough. But now she's working twelve, sometimes fourteen-hour days. I hardly see her, and a couple of weeks ago she said there was no way she could leave for a six-week vacation. I tried to get her to commit to at least to two weeks, but we got into an argument and that was that. No trip."

"Have you ever thought of doing something else?"

I shrugged. "Not really. I kind of like being an itinerant prof. I taught in Oregon, New Mexico and Massachusetts before arriving here."

"But you've been here, what, three years?"

"Four actually. Thanks to Andrea. She domesticated me, and I like Asheville."

Jamie leaned forward again. "What would you do if you weren't teaching?"

"I don't know. I've never really thought about it."

"C'mon, humor me."

"Okay. Maybe I'd be a private eye."

"You mean like Sam Spade, Phillip Marlowe, Columbo?"

"How about Shylock Holmes?"

"What, Shakespeare meets Arthur Conan Doyle?" She laughed and sat back in her chair.

"You know, I don't think I would ever mistake you for a private investigator. Jeans, rumpled shirt and sandals, unkempt hair, the hint of a beard. Well, maybe that's a good cover." She frowned, but I could see by the glint in her eye that she liked what she saw. "And a crooked smile," she added as an afterthought.

"So, what would you do if you weren't a psychic counselor and best-selling author?"

She surprised me with a ready response. "I'm already getting nudged in that direction. I have an opportunity to become the host for a new cable documentary series on the paranormal on the Vision-TV channel."

"Really? How do you find the time?"

"Ha. I had to give up Words With Friends."

"Oh, that's a hardship."

"Listen, the reason I asked you to lunch is to find out if you would like to work with me on the series."

"Doing what?"

"Co-producer."

I was flattered, but... "What the hell does that even mean?"

"Look, Jake, I'm being given a lot of leeway in shaping this show, and I trust your judgment. I think we could make a good team. I want you to serve as my lead researcher and investigator. You know, kind of like a private eye, but looking into the paranormal."

"Ah, a private third eye."

"Touché."

The opportunity intrigued and confused me. "What about the film crew and the mechanics of running the show? I don't know anything about any of that."

"If this comes through, Vision-TV will hire a local

documentary film crew and provide a director. We'll have the freedom to select the topics and find subjects for interviews."

"It sounds great, but when would we begin?"

"The Vision-TV execs want to see an outline for at least six episodes before they commit. I'm in the midst of writing my next book. I've got a contract and a deadline. I'd want you to step in and put some ideas together not only about the subjects, but how we would approach them."

"But if you don't have a commitment, would I get paid?"

"You would be working for me, at least in the beginning. If they go for what we come up with, then we'll both be on their payroll. Meanwhile I should be able to get you the monthly pay for a full-time adjunct professor while you're working for me."

"That sounds fair. I've already got an idea about the approach for the series."

"Really? Tell me."

"Well, there are lots of cable shows that look into these mysteries, but there's one thing none of them do."

"What's that?"

"These shows usually focus on the extraordinary, the unusual, the wow-factor, which is fine. But none of them bring it down to the level of the average person. How about if you get a group of people—skeptics and believers—and train them to develop their skills. You see their progress from week-to-week."

She thought about it, but not for long. "What a cool idea—a psychic reality show. You could make it a contest to see who advanced the farthest, and viewers could play along at home, following the same instructions. I love it. I knew you were the right person for this show. What made you think of that?"

"Participation has been the taboo area of teaching parapsychology at Blue Ridge-Henson. It's what I'm not supposed to do. My class was an overview of the paranormal, research, but not about displaying or developing abilities."

"Break out time. Perfect. Let's go for it."

Jamie was about to say something more when the server arrived with two iced teas. "Sweet and unsweetened," he said, setting the latter in front of me. "You're Professor Harrison, aren't you? My girlfriend Tracy is taking your parapsychology class. I remember seeing you when I met her one day outside of your classroom. She talks about your class all the time."

"It was a pleasure having her in class. I think she could teach it herself."

"I'll tell her that."

Jamie smiled as the waiter walked off. "See, you've already got fans. Wait until you're on TV."

"Tracy put me in touch with her uncle a few weeks ago. He told me a fascinating story about how he and a woman companion had a time travel experience years ago. He said they actually walked into a small village in Bermuda and later found out it had been destroyed by a hurricane two hundred years ago and was never rebuilt."

"Wow." Her head bobbed. "I like that. It's a possible story to explore down the road, especially if they're both still alive and willing to talk about their experience on-camera. We could take them back to Bermuda to see if they could reproduce the experience."

"He told me that a few years ago he located the woman who shared the experience and they've stayed in contact. He thinks that he and the woman lived in the village in a past life."

"Definitely sounds worth pursuing. We could do that one in an episode on past lives and do past-life regressions with our group, if we go that route."

Our lunches arrived and we ate in silence for a couple of minutes. I was already excited about this sudden opportunity, but then a dark thought came to mind. What would Andrea think? She already thought I was starting to take the 'weirdo stuff,' as she called it, too seriously.

One day she asked me what I was reading, and I told her the book was about the works of the mystic Rudolf Steiner. He wrote that there was an invisible spirit world nearby that could be accessed and studied by those who developed certain latent abilities. Andrea stared at me a moment, as if seeing me for the first time. "Are you losing your fucking mind, Jake? I think you're starting to believe that shit. Maybe you should drop that course."

No need for that. The next day I got that email about my class being cancelled.

"So a couple of weeks ago, a new client came to my office," Jamie said, interrupting my ruminations. "I'm only doing my counseling one or two days a week now and don't take many appointments. But I had an inkling that I should sit down and talk to this guy. I immediately picked up that he travels out of body, which was an odd thing to tune into right away. But I also realized he was involved in something really strange and dangerous. After the reading, he spelled it all out in detail. I knew that what he was telling me was important, that I couldn't just let it go."

"He came to you for a reading?"

"Initially. I think he was testing me. But really, he was there as an informant. He wanted to tell his story to someone who would understand it. I suggested he go to the *New York Times* or the *Washington Post*, but he was sure they would twist it into a story about the foolish waste of taxpayer money and wouldn't accept the reality of what was actually going on."

I scooped some black beans onto a slice of Cuban bread. "What *is* going on?"

She hesitated again, her eyes darted over my shoulder, as if she was looking at something or someone. Oddly enough, as we'd been eating, I'd felt as if someone was staring at me from behind, a sensation that registered as a prickly feeling from my neck to the middle of my back. She focused again. "If I had to summarize what my informant told me, I would say this: Out-of-body cops...out of control."

I snapped upright. "What?"

"Well, they're not exactly cops, more like intelligence agents who travel out of body, but a couple of them were actually cops."

"Seriously?"

"If we're to believe him, and I think I do, there's a black bag operation buried in the defense department that involves both members of the military and civilians, who were selected because their psychological profiles suggested they were either out-of-body experiencers or had a strong potential to learn the ability. According to our informant, they're working cases as a unit in the out-of-body state."

"Is that even possible?"

She smiled. "I think you're the ideal person to investigate this man's story, Jake, and find out the answer."

"What do they do with their abilities?"

"Apparently, they do whatever their handlers want. On the surface, it's a great deal for law enforcement. They can obtain information in ways that would be otherwise illegal or impossible to gather."

I thought about that for a moment. And I thought about how the scent I associated with Jamie was dark chocolate. Whenever I could connect a particular scent to a person, it usually meant that individual was or would be significant for me in some way.

"You mean they're like flies on the wall," I said. "They can hear and see people incriminating themselves behind closed doors."

"Exactly. But it's more than just observing. It's much more."

"What's the informant's story? Who is he?"

"He's one of them, but he doesn't like what they're doing."

"So why doesn't he quit?"

"Why don't you ask him? He's sitting at the corner table behind you. He flew in again last night at my request."

I frowned, slowly turned, and scanned the tables until I spotted a broad-shouldered man in his early thirties wearing a tight blue t-shirt that accented his barrel chest and prominent biceps. Short, dark hair. A full, thick beard that climbed up his cheeks, hiding much of his face. He caught my eye, nodded.

"Wait a minute. Are you telling me that you think this guy's story should be part of the TV series?"

"Maybe, maybe not. Talk to him and tell me what you think. It could be something more important than the TV show."

"I don't know what that means."

She guffawed. "We'll talk about that later. Go ahead. Introduce yourself. I'll get the check. I've got to scoot."

I got up, wondering what exactly I was stepping into. A few minutes ago, Jamie's offer sounded like a dream job, but now I felt like it could turn out to be a dangerous folly. It was one thing to be lead investigator in a ghost story or a reincarnation drama. It was something else altogether when a secret government operation was involved and the questionable activities were highly unusual as well.

I wasn't too pleased with her right now. I could walk away and be done with it. I would be turning down a promising project, but I wouldn't have to worry about spooks—the living kind—screwing up my life. I glanced at Jamie, who was watching me with a curious expression.

What the hell. I could at least see what he had to say. Maybe he was just nuts and there was nothing to his story or it was just a rumor he'd heard. Then again, if either of those possibilities were true, Jamie wouldn't be dealing with him, at least, not as a source for a potentially explosive story.

I threaded my way through the tables and sat down across from the stout, bearded man. I didn't say a word to him and he just looked at me, his expression blank.

"Jake Harrison." I extended my hand.

He hesitated, staring at my hand as if he expected it to change shape, to come alive, then held out his own. "Danny. Just Danny for now."

A quick but firm grip. "Okay. So what's your story, Danny?"

"Do you get out? She said you did. She thought you did. That's why I came back." He spoke in a raspy whisper, the voice of the paranoid who believed the walls had ears.

"Out? Of body?" Of course that was what he meant. "I'm learning. I'm a beginner."

"But you do get out, right?"

"Yeah, a few times." Now I was whispering, and that annoyed me.

"Great, that's great." He nodded enthusiastically. "It means we can move right past the belief issue. That's why I went to Jamie Horner. She knows what's what."

I glanced back and saw that Jamie had already left. "You're a cop?" I asked. "Or a former cop?"

"Shit, no. Military." He talked fast—but still in a soft voice— as if he'd been waiting a long time to give someone the inside scoop. "I was a Navy warrant officer until I got reassigned into a Navy intelligence unit that sent me to CIA headquarters, where I joined other candidates being trained for a secret project called

Fliers. I can thank my brother for that. He's a CIA shrink and runs the Fliers. He's one himself, of course. At first, we were from three services—Navy, Army, Marines—and civilian intelligence—FBI, CIA, DIA. Later, a police detective and a sheriff's deputy tried out."

He talked so rapidly it took me a bit to absorb everything he said. Then it struck me as inconceivable and fascinating. "How many altogether?"

"Fifteen or sixteen, but that was whittled down to seven by Dr. Bill, my bro." He laughed as if it was a joke. "If we weren't brothers, he would've dumped me along with the others."

"But they all knew how to get out of body?"

"Damn straight. It's more common than you might think. But when you're working in a team and following a protocol, it's something else. I can show you."

I wasn't sure what he meant by that. "What's this about? Why are you talking to me and Jamie? She said you're still involved."

He looked around, paranoid again that someone might be eavesdropping. "I'm still one of the Fliers, but I don't like what's going on now."

"Have you complained?"

"I've made my opinion known."

"To your brother?"

"Yep, the shrink. He told me to get my head straight or get out."

"Why don't you?"

"I entered the Navy when I was eighteen. I've got only got three months left to reach twenty years and qualify for a retirement pension. There's a chance I would be discharged early for not cooperating, and I could lose everything."

"Seems like you should've just ridden it out and kept your mouth shut."

"Yeah, you would think so. But you don't know what's going on."

"What did you complain about?"

"Mission drift. I'm military, and yet I'm working domestic investigations. At first everything was tied to terrorism, and it didn't matter where the terrorists came from or if they were tied to ISIS or any other foreign terrorist group. That was all right by me. But our domestic targets expanded, and we weren't just spying. We were assaulting and taking down."

I was confused. "I thought you were working out of body."

"That's right. You need to realize, Jake, that we can do much more than simply observe. We can manipulate matter."

Was he bullshitting to make his story more dramatic? "Did Jamie tell you about the documentary she wants to make?"

"Yeah, she did. But that's not the point, man. The Fliers need to be stopped. It's gone too far already, and it's going to get worse. I'm sure of it."

"Tell me about manipulating matter. What does that mean in practical terms?"

"Ever see *Ghost?* With Patrick Swayze?"

"Who hasn't?"

"That scene in the subway, where the old fart spirit is teaching him how to manipulate matter in the world of the living. It's like that, except we're OBE, not dead."

It made things clearer but didn't explain what was really involved. "Give me a personal example."

"Okay, but then I've got to go. We went into death row prisons. They're in thirty-one states in this country, with nearly 3,000 prisoners on death rows somewhere. We can move through walls and bars and get into any locked down facility with ease. We would go in pairs. A particular prisoner was our target. We would get into our target's cell, and that's when we would apply 'enhanced contact.' That's our term for any kind of manipulation of physical matter. There's a protocol you learn. In these cases, enhanced contact was fatal."

Huh? "You killed death-row inmates while out of body?"

"That's exactly it."

Yeah, sure you did, dude.

The incredulity I felt just then must have shown on my face, because Danny rushed on. "Hey, man, look it up on Google. You'll find four death-row inmates died in their cells in the last four months, and there's no known cause of death. Unless they've made up something by now."

Danny abruptly stood, then I pushed back from the table and got to my feet too. I noticed I was several inches taller. "Are you willing to tell this story in front of a camera?"

"Fuck, no. Like I said, I'm still part of it."

"Would you be more willing to talk on the record after you're out of the navy?"

"That'll be too late. Bad stuff is coming soon. I need your help and Jamie's." He glanced around, uneasily. "I'll be in touch."

With that, he walked quickly away, and I just stood there, staring after him, stunned and confused. What did he want from us?

3

I glanced at my bedside clock and saw that I'd been lying awake for more than an hour. Sam lay puddled nearby on the floor, emitting soft snoring gurgles as he slept soundly, his floppy bloodhound ears splayed out like wings. I patted Andrea's side of the bed, for a moment forgetting that she'd left this afternoon for a conference in Atlanta. I was done with classes for the semester and should have been relaxed and thrilled about the new opportunity that was unfolding. Instead, I felt only unease.

I'd called Jamie from my car and left a brief message telling her we needed to talk. She hadn't responded yet, and now I wondered if she wanted to give me time to process what I'd heard. If Danny's story was true, then the Fliers had discovered the nuclear weapon of paranormal research. Once exposed and verified, the ability to kill while out of body would be sought after by other governments. Civil rights and rule of law would be obliterated, murders would be undetectable. I couldn't even imagine the fear and havoc that would result.

So here I was thinking about Danny and his fellow Fliers instead of sleeping. Danny was the only source so far, and he was unwilling to go on the record. Maybe that was for the best. Revealing the existence of this incredible ability—if it truly existed—might be more dangerous than keeping it hidden. Danny was right that the Fliers needed to be stopped, but not exposed. If Jamie was intent on pursuing this story, I would argue against it and tell her that she would be doing it without me.

I rolled over, and my thoughts drifted to Andrea. She and I were no longer a free and easygoing couple who complemented each other. In fact, I sensed our three-year relationship was coming to an end. I hadn't told her about my opportunity to work with Jamie on a documentary series because I already knew how she would react. She would express concern for my mental stability rather than offer congratulations.

She would want to know about my relationship with Jamie Horner, and I would remind her that Jamie had been a guest speaker several times in my classes. I'd mentioned it the first couple of times that she'd appeared, but Andrea had been unimpressed. I'd stopped saying anything about her after Andrea told me she'd heard Jamie was a fraud and wondered why I would want her to speak to my class. She probably would want to know if this new career turn was going to mean that I wouldn't be teaching in the fall, and I had no answer on that one. I had two classes pending and would have to decide whether to drop them.

If Jamie's project didn't work out and *if* my relationship with Andrea skittered down into nothingness, it would be a signal that it was time to move on. I hadn't pondered such a shift in my life for a long time. Where would I like to move? Live? Maybe Charleston, Gainesville, or Boulder.

For the umpteenth time, I attempted to relax and let go of the tumult of thoughts and nervous tension. I rolled over onto my side, took a few slow, deep breaths, and imagined I was falling asleep. That usually worked. I started to drift off, then sucked in my breath, coming fully awake again. But now I felt the vibrations, a rippling sensation that coursed through my body, around it, and knew what this was and what it could lead to.

I recalled the method that Jamie had taught my students for entering an OBE, the same one that I'd practiced from time to time with mixed success. I moved the vibrations up and down and around my body and smoothed them out. I imagined a silver cord extending from my solar plexus, clutched it, and climbed hand over hand, pulling myself out of my body.

I felt dizzy and disoriented but only had to look down to get my bearings. There, below me, lay a reclining body in black drawstring pants and a white t-shirt. Me. It was me. Sam remained stretched out right where I'd last seen him a couple feet from the bed. My awareness was *out* and I was hovering just below the ceiling. I fought off a mounting panic and told myself that I could easily snap back into my body at any time.

I glided out of the room convinced that this time would be different. I drifted across the living room, paused. I felt a chill and an odd sensation that I wasn't alone, that someone or something was watching from a dark corner of the room.

Come out and play.

I dismissed the thought. It was a manifestation of my own fear, the fear that had kept me from exploring the out-of-body state beyond my backyard. I focused on remaining out and getting accustomed to directing my movements. I'd never felt so free and fearless while out of body. I wanted to go somewhere and do something. But where and what?

Maybe I could find Andrea in Atlanta. It would be a bold move, but why not try it? If it worked and I saw her, I would have an opportunity to verify the experience with her. I tried to remember the name of the hotel where she was staying. Maybe it didn't matter.

I want to go to Andrea, wherever she is.

I heard a whoosh, felt a sensation of enormous expansion and rapid movement. I actually felt air rushing against my face. How could that be if I was out of body? Abruptly, I found myself in the lobby of a hotel with spotless tile floors and colorful art on the walls. I saw a man behind the check-in counter and a couple of people in the lobby. A door opened off to one side, and I heard music. I knew I couldn't smell anything while I was out, but a particular scent came to me, of booze and hormones.

I moved over to the door, paused, then walked right into it, and through it. That was easy. I stood in the entrance to a night-club. Cautiously, I stepped forward. The tile floor felt soft, like cork, and my bare feet seemed to sink slightly into it.

The place was crowded, noisy with laughter, shouts, and music. The dim lighting was tinged blue from the follow-spots that played out over the tiny stage nestled beyond the open end of the horseshoe bar. A banner in front of the stage read: FreeDaJazz. But the band must've been on a break.

I moved carefully between tables, making my way toward the bar. I stopped and backed up a step when a man, beer bottle in hand, came my way. I let him pass and felt a slight tickling sensation when his elbow brushed my bicep. He didn't seem to notice. I moved ahead, then stopped abruptly.

Andrea was seated directly across from me, maybe fifteen feet away. Her focus was on the man next to her, whom I recognized as her boss, a guy named Chad. I recalled Andrea saying he was recently divorced. And his hand was on her thigh. Nice. Real nice.

I stood between two men seated at the bar who jabbered on about fantasy football. They weren't aware of my presence. No one was. The bartender looked my way, and I glanced back to see another man closing in on my space, a hand raised. I scuttled aside and moved around the bar for a closer look at Andrea. I'd sensed for some time that she was bored with our relationship, that I was the past not the future. She'd denied it, said she loved me. But now the truth was evident.

I danced around two women, then carefully avoided a group of people milling near the bar. I was only a few feet away from Andrea when the band members started returning to the stage. I recognized her laughter, a high trill, and eavesdropped on their conversation. They were talking about one of their colleagues and laughing about his odd habit of looking down at his feet when engaged in conversation.

"Andrea, I think he's admiring his $300 wing tips," Chad said in a slurred voice.

"He doesn't do that in court, does he?"

"Who the fuck knows. He hasn't been in a courtroom in a dozen years."

She smiled coyly and leaned closer to him. The bass player struck a few warmup notes. "Let's get out of here, Chad." She looked over her shoulder at the stage. "I've heard enough of these guys. Let's go to the room."

They both slid off their stools simultaneously, and I tried to stiff arm Chad, who was about to walk into me. It felt as if I'd struck a bag of marshmallows. He casually brushed off his shoulder and the couple moved on hand-in-hand.

"Andrea!" I shouted, but of course she didn't hear me.

"A friend of yours, that deaf one?"

My head snapped around. A man nearby stared at me like he could see me. He was about thirty, with a square jaw, blue eyes, blond hair tied in a ponytail. Dressed in a silver and black workout outfit, he looked like he'd just come from the gym. His feet, like mine, were bare. "You can see me? Hear me?"

"I've been watching you stumble around, Jake. I can tell you're a newbie, at least among crowds."

"Who are you? How do you know my name?"

"What a short memory you have. We met today."

"Danny?"

Abruptly, his features blurred and shifted into the muscular, barrel-chested, bearded man I'd met at the restaurant. "That's an ability you can learn. You can change your appearance to remain anonymous when other free fliers might be around."

"How did you find me?"

"Another trick of the trade. I locked into your energy when we met. I got out tonight, traced you, and helped you get out."

"How? How did you do that?"

"I made sure you didn't fall asleep and gave your second body a nudge."

I jumped aside as a man walked right toward me. Danny shook his head. "Don't worry about people bumping into you. You're not going to feel anything and they aren't either. Not unless you put your mind to it."

I realized there was an entire language, a lexicon, in this out of body state that I would have to learn quickly. "What the hell does that mean?"

"It's what we were talking about earlier today. With practice you can learn to manipulate physical matter much better than that butterfly slap you gave that other guy. Now watch."

He leaned in toward the bar where a young couple were deep in conversation and ignoring their drinks. Danny tapped the neck of the man's half-empty beer bottle. It fell over, rolled across the bar, and into his lap. He snatched it, setting it upright. "What the hell. Did you see that? I didn't even touch it."

"You must've hit it with your elbow," the woman said, pressing a handful of napkins over the spilled beer. The man brushed off his pants, shaking his head.

Danny reached over, hooked his index finger over the rim of the woman's wine glass, and knocked it over. "Shit, what's going on!" she shrieked and grabbed for the glass. "Mine fell over, too."

They both jumped up as wine and beer dripped over the edge of the bar. "Let's get the fuck out of here," the man said. "The bar is tilted or something."

Danny moved back as they hurried past him. "I know. I know. That was mean of me, but I wanted you to see it for yourself."

"Shit, I'm impressed. That was amazing." I started laughing. "He thought the bar was tilted. That's hilarious."

"Yes, but no more bizarre than the real reason those drinks fell over."

An impressive display, I thought, but knocking over drinks didn't necessarily mean he had the ability to strangle someone. "Do you trick people like that often?"

Danny looked amused. "Only for your benefit. Jamie was right about you, Jake. You have the ability, more of it than you realize. You're the perfect person to work with us."

"With who?"

"With me and Jamie, taking on the Fliers."

I started to ask him how we would do that, but his hand shot up and he hissed, "Not another word about it."

"Knocking over drinks. Shame on you, Danny." I turned to see a tall slender man with high cheekbones and a constipated mouth moving toward us. His black silk outfit looked like pajamas. He regarded me with open curiosity.

"You can see us?" I asked.

He smirked at me, then turned to Danny. "You left yourself open, little brother. Very easy to trace you. I see you're showing off your talents to someone who doesn't have a clue."

"He's got a lot of potential." He laughed. "I like your new look, Billy. I mean, c'mon, dude, black silk PJs?"

I realized I was looking at Danny's brother, Dr. Bill, who gave me another condescending look. He shifted his gaze toward a server who approached with a tray of drinks. "Watch this and learn."

He swiftly reached out and slipped a finger inside the waist-band of her shorts, and jerked them and her underwear down to her knees. She screamed, stumbled, and dropped the tray of drinks. Her tray clattered against the floor, glasses shattered, people were splashed with beer and wine, vodka and gin. She quickly pulled up her shorts and scrambled away, darting between tables, and vanished through a door on the other side of the room.

The whole thing appalled me, left me speechless.

"That's nothing compared to what Danny-boy and I have done."

Before I could respond, Danny was gone. I quickly scanned the crowd, thinking he'd shifted instantly to some other spot, but didn't see him anywhere. A cleanup crew arrived and went to work on the broken class and spilled drinks. My surround-ings started to fade. I was losing contact and abruptly found myself in bed. I bolted upright, looked frantically around, and realized I was home in my bedroom. A thin film of sweat cov-ered my face.

Did that really happen? It wasn't a dream, I was certain of that. I'd been awake, alert and out of my body, but in a second ephemeral form, a duplicate of my physical self. I felt a strange combination of emotions spinning like a dust devil around me. I was energized by the experience, wary, but confused by Danny and the man who was apparently chief of the Fliers. Simultaneously I was deeply disturbed, saddened and disap-pointed about Andrea.

I pushed the Fliers out of my mind for the time being. I wanted to prove to myself that I'd really seen Andrea and her boss romancing their way out of that bar and up to his room. I reached for my phone on the bedside stand and searched online for a band called FreeDaJazz. In spite of my certainty, I was still astonished to find the band's website. I quickly located their schedule, and yes, they were playing tonight. But they were at the Ritz Carlton bar in Charlotte. Not Atlanta.

But if they were in Charlotte, were Andrea and Chad there? How could I prove that? I thought a moment and realized I could verify her location. I flipped through the apps on my phone until I located Find iPhone. Andreas' phone was the only one listed. I touched it and immediately a small blue ball move across a map of Charlotte and stop within the city limits. Adjacent to the blue ball, orange letters read: *Ritz Carlton.* Damn.

So it was real. But I still wanted to see if I could prove that Chad was staying at the Ritz Carlton. I went to the law firm's website and found his last name, then looked up the number for the hotel.

"Ritz Carlton," said a woman who sounded abnormally perky for this obscenely late hour.

"Could you please connect me with Chad Chastain's room? He's not picking up his cell. He's expecting a call from me." When the night clerk didn't respond right away, I added: "You do still have room phones, don't you?"

"Yes, of course. Now it's mostly for connecting with the desk or kitchen. But let me check. Spell that name, please."

If he didn't use his real name, I was out of luck, I thought, then spelled it.

"Sorry, I'm not able to complete your request. Mr. Chastain doesn't want any calls to the room. Would you like me to leave a message for him?"

That confirmed it. The band was there. Andrea's phone was there. Chad was there. But were they together? "No thanks. Could you try Andrea Blake's room?'

"One moment." A couple of beats passed. "I'm sorry, sir, there is no one named Andrea Blake registered here."

"Oh, that's interesting. Is the law conference that Mr. Chastain is attending being held there at the Ritz Carlton?"

"There are no conferences here this weekend, sir."

I thought a moment. "Well, I know his wife loves the Ritz Carlton. I bet that's why he's staying there."

"Could be. She looked very happy when they walked by a few minutes ago."

Under different circumstances, I would've felt elated that I'd actually traveled out of body and verified my experience. But the reality of it left me feeling empty and lost. I'd hoped I was wrong. The fact that I wasn't spelled the end of my three-year fling with Andrea.

I flopped down heavily on the bed. I felt like I weighed three hundred pounds, that I was some high school fat boy whose life was spinning out of control. No wonder Andrea and I didn't seem compatible any longer. I suddenly just wanted to sleep, but my thoughts invariably turned back to the other scene at the Ritz-Carlton. I never had considered the possibility that out-of-body travelers could actually push and pull things. If the Flier chief could assault the server the way he did while out of body, then Danny's contention that they killed death row inmates wasn't as crazy as it sounded.

4

After last night's revelations, I felt like I was living in a void. I didn't belong here anymore. I felt like an intruder in my own home, which wasn't even my home. It was Andrea's place, and I was her in-house lover. But that was over. I needed to pack and get out. But first I needed to talk to her and find a place to stay.

"Where are we going to go, Sam? You got any ideas? Can you sniff out a new home for us?" I bent over and opened the cupboard below the granite counter and pulled out the bag of beef deli sticks, his favorite morning treat. I held one out and he looked up at me with his sad eyes, then sniffed the treat, doing his quick chemical analysis like he did every morning. Satisfied that the treat was unaltered by the insertion of a pill, he took it from my hand.

I waited until 8:30 before I called Andrea. She didn't pick up, and I left a message, asking her to call me. I'd spoken in a normal voice but couldn't avoid the slight catch in my throat. Now I imagined her preparing a story about the non-existent conference, a clever coverup. Or maybe not. Maybe she was ready to call it quits.

On reflection, it was pathetic how little I knew about her feelings, and I shared the blame in the disintegration of our relationship. I liked to think that her move from the academic world to the corporate world was the turning point. She said she felt a fresh sense of power in her new role and that the academic world, where I remained, had become cold, stale, and stifling.

For my part, I'd pined aloud from time to time about how I was losing my wanderlust, the opportunities to explore new horizons as an itinerant prof, and she probably took that as an indication that I didn't consider her more than a temporary convenience. Yet, clearly, I'd enjoyed the safe comfort zone of our relationship that included a regular sex life, a home that I couldn't afford on my own, and an attractive, intelligent partner. Our tastes were similar, and we agreed on most everything.

The notable exception was the paranormal, which didn't interest her in the least, and was a topic she wasn't comfortable talking about. She'd once told me that the psychology department was devoid of ethical standards because it continued to allow me to teach a class that entertained and distracted students from the true pursuits of higher education. For my part, I'd always been open and curious about the paranormal, and the course had given me an opportunity to expand my knowledge and even test my own psychic prowess.

I would miss living in this tranquil bucolic setting with the floor to ceiling windows looking out on mountain vistas, the rich oak walls and high beamed ceiling. And I would miss driving Andrea's Porsche 911, which she'd leased the same week she stepped into her new corporate career. But the sooner I left, the better. So I made a second call, one that I hoped would result in the offer of a temporary abode. Again, I left a message that sounded casual and now waited for the return calls.

Meanwhile, I sat at the kitchen table sipping coffee and perused online articles about death row inmates who had died while awaiting execution. A grim subject, but one with a surprising number of entries from the past few years. Most of the deceased inmates had spent decades on death row, including one man who died of lung cancer in a Louisiana prison after waiting thirty-five years for his execution. He'd spent twenty-three hours a day in his cell, and his lawyer had been trying to get him released, citing "lengthy and unusual punishment."

But the article that caught my attention was one from the *Minneapolis Star-Tribune* from three weeks ago. Keene Larson, chief investigator for the Minnesota Attorney General's Office, had flown to Durham, North Carolina, to meet Darrell Jacob Everett, the man he believed had killed his younger sister. He said he was following up on a tip from a former prison guard who told him that he'd overheard Everett bragging to another prisoner that he'd raped and murdered a twelve-year-old girl in a small Minnesota town twenty-five years ago.

He said he would know when he looked into Everett's eyes if he'd killed Julie. He'd waited several weeks to win approval to meet the death-row inmate, who had been convicted of other murders, only to be told that Everett had died in his cell just hours earlier.

No mention of the cause of death, but Everett's demise fit in the right time frame for Danny's scenario.

Another article from the Associated Press listed five deaths on death row in the past six months—two in Alabama, one in Texas, another in Louisiana, and Everett's in North Carolina. The men ranged in age from forty-two to fifty-seven. I scribbled down their names and looked them up. I quickly noticed that all but one had been convicted of murdering or raping children. The exception was a man who had killed his parents and an adult cousin, and he'd died of cancer.

The death of the inmate in Texas four months ago was attributed to "compression of the throat," an odd way of describing strangulation, and the case was under investigation as a possible suicide. No cause of death was listed for the other two. Danny could've looked up this information, just as I had done, and created the entire scenario about those four deaths. But after my experience last night, I tended to believe his story, outrageous as it sounded.

I had an inkling that the Minnesota investigator might've followed up on Everett's death and could tell me how he'd died.

Of course, I would have to tell him what I was doing. I quickly found the number for the Minnesota Attorney General's Office and called it. After listening to a recording, I got through to a receptionist who said that Keene Larson wasn't available, but she would transfer me and I could leave a message.

I introduced myself as a documentary TV producer and explained we were investigating a series of unusual deaths of death row inmates and that I'd read the story about his experience in Durham. "I'd appreciate it if you could call me back. I have a few questions I'd like to ask you." I disconnected and figured I had a 50-50 chance of hearing from Larson.

I next turned my attention to articles and blog posts about out-of-body experiences. Specifically, I looked for stories of astral travelers who could manipulate matter, but all I found were tips for beginning explorers, personal stories, or the skeptical perspective pointing to inner ear issues or neurological explanations—essentially, the brain going haywire and creating the sensation of floating outside one's body. There were tales of travel throughout the cosmos but a dearth of stories about tipping over beer bottles or any other physical machinations.

I was about to give up when I found an intriguing reference mentioned on a blog. Supposedly, Robert Monroe, author of *Journeys Out of Body* and founder of the Monroe Institute, once pinched his wife in the side while he was out of body. She felt it, and a bruise appeared at the spot.

That, it seemed, was about the extent of what I was going to find. If other astral travelers were moving objects or manhandling people in any way, it looked like they were keeping it to themselves.

My iPad dinged, an e-mail from Jamie. I clicked into it and read her brief note. *Jake, I'm attaching an article that appeared last year on the Charlotte Observer's website. It caught Danny's attention and led him to contacting me.*

I opened the file, and the first line hooked me: *She's a best-selling author of tomes on the paranormal, makes frequent media appearances, and now she's teaching her second summer program for children interested in horseback riding and developing their psychic abilities. But critics are tossing their lassoes at Jamie Horner from all sides.*

I remembered that Jamie had once mentioned that summer program during one of her guest appearances. I had no idea that the program had been controversial. Apparently, Jamie had attracted the wrath of a hard-core skeptic and an evangelical minister. Both were convinced that she was misguiding children and teaching false concepts. Max Owens, editor of a skeptics' journal, said Jamie was tricking children into believing in the impossible and ignoring scientific truths. Meanwhile, Avery Aimes, a TV evangelist based in Charlotte, repeatedly targeted Jamie for doing the devil's work by twisting the minds of children.

I'd heard of Reverend Aimes and his TV ministry known for promising salvation in exchange for donations, but I was more familiar with Owens. He lived in Asheville, knew about my parapsychology class, and had complained about it to the president of Blue Ridge-Hensen.

He'd also mentioned it in a column in his journal in which he said the class was an example of the dumbing-down of America's education system. Owens was an amateur magician and outspoken atheist known for setting up mediums and psychics to make them look foolish. One of his favorite tricks was to create a fake dead relative and see what the reader would pick up from the non-existent person.

I was halfway through the article when my phone chimed. I felt a momentary sense of relief when I saw it was Casey Foster and not Andrea. "Hey, Casey. Thanks for getting back to me."

"What's up, Jake? You haven't left for Greece yet?"

"Guess we haven't talked for awhile. That's not happening." Casey, a fellow adjunct professor, taught in the criminal justice department at Buncombe State College, and I taught criminal psychology in the same department. He'd stayed in our spare bedroom here for four months when he first arrived in Asheville two years ago. Andrea had been against renting the room, but she and Casey had gotten along well and we both missed his company after he left.

"Sorry to hear that. I know you were looking forward to it."

"That's only half the story. I'm leaving Andrea and need a place to stay, at least temporarily."

"Oh, wow. You two seemed so good together, Jake. At least when I was staying with you. What happened?"

"She found someone else more interesting, another lawyer."

"Oh, really. May she always be surrounded by lawyers. That's a Colombian curse, Carlos tells me. I don't know if it applies to lawyers, though, come to think of it."

"Probably not. Is your spare bedroom available for a few days?"

"Jesus, I wish I could help you. But Carlos's brother is coming in tomorrow, visiting from Miami for a week."

I walked into the kitchen for a second cup of coffee. "Oh, I thought you and Carlos had called it quits."

Casey laughed. "Yeah, we do that every few months, get everything off our chests, then make up."

"That's cool."

"I guess. Hey, I'm sorry I can't help you out right now, but check back in a week. I owe you for all you and Andrea did for me when I got here."

I sat down at the kitchen table with my coffee after ending the call and tried to think of another alternative. A series of beeps interrupted my thoughts, and I saw Andrea was calling.

Okay, here comes, I thought grimly. "Hi, how's it going?"

"Oh, just boring law and lots of lawyers."

"May you always be surrounded by lawyers."

"What?"

"Never mind. I'm sure there's at least one special lawyer there."

She paused a moment. "Yeah, me. So what's up, Jake? I'll be home tomorrow afternoon."

"I won't be here."

"Why not? Where're you going?"

"Look, I know you're not in Atlanta and you're not at a conference. Don't ask me how I know. It doesn't matter. You're in Charlotte with Chad. Good luck to both of you. I'm outta here."

"Wait a minute. Don't hang up. I am in Atlanta at the conference. Chad Chastain, if that's who you mean, is speaking later this morning, and I'm on a panel this afternoon. Look it up online."

"Hang on." I wasn't about to look up the conference schedule. I went again to the Find iPhone app.

"You're actually looking it up, Jake, checking on me? Wow, you really don't trust me?"

I stared at the map in disbelief. She was in Atlanta. What did that mean? Then I knew. "You two must've caught a red eye early this morning out of Charlotte. I guess you didn't get much sleep last night."

"What're you talking about? Is this some psychic bullshit, far seeing or whatever you call it?"

"Remote viewing," I snapped. "No, actually, it's technology, Andrea. Your phone was in Charlotte last night and Chastain registered at the Ritz-Carlton under his own name. How was that jazz band?"

"You don't have to raise your voice, Jake," she calmly replied. "Look, I've got to go. I'll see you tomorrow. We can talk."

"Sure. You can tell me all about your new relationship. Lawyers in love."

I disconnected and got up from the table. Sadness overwhelmed my anger. Burning bridges, no matter what the reason, was no fun. I felt alone and burdened. Where could I go? I walked over to my closet in the master bedroom and dumped all of my clothes onto the king-size bed. I started separating the clothes I would keep from the rest destined for Goodwill.

My phone resounded with the familiar tinkling of a text from Andrea. Would she actually make a plea for me to stay, vow to break it off with Chad? Was that what I wanted, what I was hoping? I didn't know. I tapped into her message.

So you're running away again. Off on another macho adventure. I figured that was coming. Surprised you stayed as long as you did. And, you know what, it's kind of sad that you couldn't even tell me face-to-face. You had to call it in. You coward!

That didn't take long for her to adjust to my departure and turn it around so it was my issue. The phone chimed. Casey again. "Hey, what's up?"

"Hey yourself. You sound a little down."

"Yeah, I told her it's over."

"Good for you. Listen, I just talked to Carlos. You can sleep on the couch until you find a place."

"Thanks, I really appreciate it. I'll find an apartment as soon as I can. It shouldn't take long. I'm not real busy right now."

"The only thing is that you'll have to find a kennel or something for Sam while you're here. Carlos has issues with big dogs."

"I understand. I think I'll stay here another night since Andrea won't be home until tomorrow. I'm taking all my stuff to my storage unit. That's where I've kept my furniture since I moved in with Andrea."

"I'm sorry I can't be more accommodating, Jake. You're staying in Asheville, aren't you?"

"At least for now. I've got a new project I'm starting. I'll tell you about it later."

"Tell me now."

"Not too much to tell now. I've been asked to work on a TV documentary series about the paranormal." I wasn't about to try to explain Danny and the Fliers.

"Sounds fascinating. A TV star staying on our couch. Wait till I tell Carlos."

I rang off and headed to the bedroom, back to packing and getting out of here. Luckily I still had my old pickup, which was always handy on my moves, and my storage unit was only five miles away.

A couple of hours later, the pickup was packed to the max and I still had stuff strewn around the house, on the bed, the kitchen table, in the garage. I was going to need a second trip. Sam was sitting by my feet watching me. "Yeah, it's time to hit the road again, buddy. But we're staying in Asheville for now."

I got a marrow bone out of the freezer and set it on a paper towel on the kitchen floor. Sam knew that was a sign I would be leaving him for awhile. "Don't worry. I'll be back in a little while." He slumped to the floor and rested his chin on the tile, his eyes accusing and sad. I patted his head and made my exit.

I was within half a mile of my destination when I got a call from Jamie. I definitely wanted to talk to her about Danny, but I let the call go to voicemail. I would call her after I got to the storage unit. A couple of blocks later, I stopped for a red light and played her message. Her breathless tone immediately caught my attention.

"Jake, Jamie here. Please call me back as soon as you get this message. Something strange has come up. I need to talk to you right away."

Something strange. What else is new, I thought. However, she sounded nothing like the confident, composed woman I'd met for lunch yesterday. The light changed, and I hit the call button and turned on the speaker. I had barely gotten through the intersection when Jamie answered.

"Thanks for getting back to me. Jake, I hate to sound crazy, but something has happened and I'm very concerned. Could you come here right away? I can't explain it. You've got to see it for yourself."

"Sure." I pulled over. The gate to the storage facility was about a hundred yards away. "Give me your address. I'll come right over."

What the hell could this be? And what the fuck was I getting myself into?

5

My overloaded twenty-year-old pickup rattled its way up the winding mountain road. Even though I was eager to see what Jamie was talking about, I was barely approaching twenty miles an hour when another sharp curve appeared. Although Jamie's place was only seven or eight miles from the outskirts of the city where my storage unit was located, the winding road with its perilous turns and steep drops forced me down to fifteen miles an hour. I rounded another curve, the road leveled, and a pristine valley opened up below me.

I glanced at my digital map and turned onto a dirt road leading to the property. A sign at the entrance read: Welcome to M-O-M Ranch. Odd name for a ranch, I thought. At least half a dozen horses grazed on the grassy field. On the far side of the valley, a two-story log cabin was nestled against a pine forest on a raised outcropping. As I drove closer, I noticed another two-story building at the bottom of the valley a few hundred feet from the house. No doubt the barn. It was long and narrow and I could see a series of open stall windows on the first level. The second level featured a balcony that overlooked the valley, probably an apartment for a groom or a storage area.

After crossing the valley, I drove slowly up a steep drive to the house. Everything shifted positions in the bed of the truck, sliding back toward the gate. I parked next to a Toyota 4Runner, a four-wheel drive vehicle capable of ascending the driveway in icy conditions. I climbed out and gazed over the valley.

The setting was rustic and appealing, and there were no other houses in sight. Whatever Jamie was calling about certainly wasn't apparent in this bucolic scene. I checked my belongings to make sure everything was intact. Piles of loose clothing, two suitcases, a duffel bag and a backpack, boxes of books, a couple of file cabinets, and an antique dresser—the only piece of my furniture that Andrea had allowed in her house. All good.

I was about to approach the house when my phone jangled. Just as I pulled it out of my pocket, Jamie stepped out the front door and greeted me. She wore jeans and a snug-fitting t-shirt. She looked great, a pioneer at the top of the mountain. But I could see the concern on her face.

"Hey, Jamie." I gave her a wave, phone in hand. "Let me just see who this is."

"Go ahead."

I glanced at the screen: Keene Larson, the investigator from Minnesota. "Oh, I better take it. You might want to listen." I answered and turned the speaker on. "What can I do for you, Mr. Harrison?" Larson's friendly voice sounded like a character from the movie *Fargo*.

"I'm working on a documentary dealing with some unusual deaths of inmates on death row. Unusual in that they weren't executed. At least not in the traditional sense."

"Are you recording this conversation?"

"No, I'm not."

"Well, I am," Larson responded. "Standard procedure. I'm

most familiar with the death of Darrell Everett, who I believe murdered my sister. But I have looked into a few other recent deaths of inmates. However, my assessment, Jake, will have to be off the record. I hope you agree to that."

"Yes, of course. Would you be open to a formal interview at a later date?"

"Hey, that's my line. Possibly, it depends. For now, don't quote me beyond anything that I've already said in the press. I'm sure that's where you heard about my interest in this matter."

"Understood."

"I'm only going to talk about Everett's case. The simple explanation is that he was poisoned, but with a substance that so far defies detection."

"What about the bruises on his throat?"

"That could be self-inflicted, a reaction to the poison."

"Is that what you believe?"

"I guess it's the most likely answer, but thanks to a contact in the Justice Department I've seen videos of three other recent deaths on death row, and they're very disturbing. It appears the inmates were struggling with someone who isn't visible to the camera. In one case in particular, it appears that the victim is being held up as he's choked. Maybe an acrobat could bend over backwards and not fall down, but that guy was not in very good physical condition. But who knows what the body can do under dire circumstances."

I glanced at Jamie, who was listening closely. "Do you have an alternate explanation?"

Larson laughed. "Just wild speculation. Do you know about the articles and videos that claim the U.S. military possesses cloaking capabilities for fighter jets so they can avoid detection?"

"I've read something about that."

"Maybe it's possible to cloak humans so they don't appear on video."

"How would they get to prisoners on death row?"

"Well, it would have to be an inside job. So what direction are you going?"

"For the truth."

"C'mon. You must have some perspective if you've been looking into these deaths."

I turned to Jamie and she shrugged. "We're looking at the possibility of a secret government program involving out-of-body travelers who have harnessed the ability to manipulate matter, including strangulation."

Larson was quiet a moment. Then laughed. "That's a good one. You had me going there for a second. Out-of-body travel might be a real thing, like near-death experiences. But if those travelers can glide through walls like they say, they're surely not strangling anyone."

"You would think not." I thanked Larson for his time. We chatted a few moments longer, and I told him I would get back to him pending further developments. I put my phone away. "Sorry about that, but I didn't want to miss that call."

"That was interesting, if only because he verified Danny's story about the string of unusual deaths. I see you're right on top of this story."

More than she realizes, I thought. "We need to talk, but what's going on?"

"Believe me, there's a reason I asked you to come on short notice. Did you have any trouble finding us?"

"Nope. But your M-O-M Ranch sign surprised me."

"Oh, yeah. Everyone thinks, 'Hey, it's Mom's ranch,' but actually the M-O-M stands for Mind Over Matter."

"Interesting, considering what we've been talking about."

"I guess. C'mon, this way."

Without further explanation, she led me around the far side of the house. I had no idea what she was about to show me. The only thing I saw was a golf cart parked on a gravel-covered path. "Hop in and hang on."

I clutched the frame as Jamie sped down the steep driveway. If she made a sharp turn, I was certain we'd flip over. But she maneuvered the vehicle expertly, turned off the drive, and headed toward the barn, bouncing over a rutted double track.

She stopped about fifty feet short of the building. I could see eight or nine stalls on either side of a central corridor open on either end, and three horses were peering out. "Do all the horses belong to you?"

"No, only two of them are ours. The others are boarders. We feed them, turn them out, provide farrier and vet service. All for a price, of course."

Instead of going inside, Jamie led me around the side of the pine green-colored barn. She stopped and pointed at the wall. Someone had spray-painted a message that extended over fifteen feet of the wall. It read: *God save the children.* Below that was a longer message: *Devil worshippers Jamie and Jake burn in Hell!!!*

"What?"

"Now do you understand why I wanted you to come right away?"

"Yeah. It sounds like the good reverend, the one in the article you sent me."

"Avery Aimes. It certainly does, except it doesn't make sense."

"It probably makes perfect sense to him."

She shook her head. "No, that's not what I mean. Think about it. Whoever did this apparently doesn't know that I'm not holding a psychic development program for kids this summer. Yet the perpetrator knows who you are and that you're somehow associated with me."

I nodded. "You're right. Which means the person must've seen us at lunch."

"Any ideas who it might be, Jake?"

I shook my head. "There were at least six or seven tables with diners outside. It was busy. Plus there were people inside."

"It's puzzling. Even if Aimes was at Yucas, how would he know who you were?"

"Well, whoever it was will be happy to find out that you're not teaching any kids to be psychic spies or read minds."

She laughed. "Or travel out of body. I talked to Danny this morning briefly while he was waiting for his plane. He said I should ask you about what happened last night."

"I met him out of body while I was looking for Andrea, who was definitely in her body and in Charlotte."

"Hold on. Let's go to the house. It's lunchtime. I'm going to fix a grilled cheese sandwich for my niece, Iris, who's visiting.

Would you like one, too?"

"Sure, why not. I haven't had a grilled cheese sandwich in years."

"Good. We'll talk about Danny and the future of the project after lunch." We climbed back into the golf cart, but before she put it into drive, Jamie said: "I should tell you a little about Iris. She's an unusual girl. She had some brain damage at birth that resulted in an awkwardness in the way she walks. She stutters and is very shy because of her disabilities."

"Sorry to hear that."

"The trauma she experienced at birth actually resulted in some peculiar traits, as well as disabilities. Since she was three or four years old, she's had invisible friends, who she thinks protect and help her. At first, Sarah, my sister, considered it a form of childhood escapism that she would outgrow. But Iris has maintained contact with these...friends."

"Could it be compensation for her shyness among kids her age?"

"Possibly, but it's more than that. She learns things from them that she couldn't possibly know. She also has an uncanny ability to see things that are going to happen. Usually little stuff, but she's very specific. For instance, when she stayed here two years ago, she told me my car was going to get a flat tire on the front left side and that I would be at the grocery store. Two days later, it happened, just as she said."

"Wow. Was she with you?"

"No, she was at the house, and she wouldn't play a trick like that, if that's what you're thinking. That was just one of many things she's predicted. It's part of the reason that Sarah sends her to me every summer. Sometimes, she sees things that were going on somewhere else right at that moment. Stuff that could be verified." She pointed at the wall. "Like that!"

"What? She told you someone would paint our names on the barn?"

"Not exactly. But last night just as she was falling asleep, she asked me who was writing on the barn. I thought she meant writing about the barn. I just told her no one that I know of, and that was that."

Jamie put the golf cart into gear, and we bounced over the rough terrain and drove up the steep drive. We came to a stop next to my pickup, and she surveyed the clutter of my belongings. "What's all this? Are you a junk collector on the side?"

"One person's junk, another person's treasure. Actually, this is my stuff. I was about to put it in my storage unit when you called."

"Oh, sorry. That was rude of me. I didn't mean to call your stuff junk. C'mon."

I followed her inside and paused to admire the interior, the wood walls and floors, stone fireplace, the open floor plan with high ceiling, a stairway to a loft, everything neat and orderly. Instead of a panoramic mountain view like Andrea's, Jamie's expansive windows looked out on the valley. "How far does your property go?"

"I've got twenty-eight acres. The rest of the valley is a nature preserve."

"Very nice."

"Why don't you go out on the back porch? We can eat out there. I'll get Iris."

Jamie opened the sliding glass door, and I walked over to the porch railing. The back side of the house looked out onto a forest of tall pines, and a creek flowed by just a few feet from the porch. The gurgling water made me think of one of those relaxation CDs featuring sounds of nature. I noticed a gate and three stairs leading down to the creek and was tempted to take a closer look, but I heard voices coming from inside the house and sat down at the porch table.

When no one appeared, my thoughts drifted back to my predicament. I'd just ended a long-term relationship. My truck was full of my stuff and I had more to clear out, and here I was waiting for a grilled cheese sandwich and wondering why my name was painted on Jamie's barn. You can't make up this stuff.

A couple of minutes later, Jamie opened the door and ushered out a slender girl in workout pants and a t-shirt. Iris paused in the doorway and met my gaze, a curious expression on her young face. She looked like a typical pre-teen in that awkward stage between childhood and becoming a young woman. She moved awkwardly, as if she were off-balance. She reminded me of a newborn doe just discovering how to use its legs. For a moment, I thought she'd stumbled. Then I realized one of her legs appeared twisted and that her gait was ungainly.

The door closed and Jamie retreated to the kitchen. "Hello, Iris. How are you?"

She clamped her hands on the back of the nearest chair. Her lips moved, but the word she wanted to say was stuck. "I'm fa-fa-fa-fa-fa-fa-fine." She worked her way around the chair and cautiously lowered herself to the chair as if she expected me to pull it out from beneath her.

She dropped her chin, looking down at the table. I sensed her shyness and felt sorry for her. It as obvious she didn't want to be here right now, but Jamie probably had asked her to go sit with me.

"Iris, my name is Jake. Did your Aunt Jamie tell you anything about me?"

Her gaze strayed side to side as if she were looking for something. "She said you're a pa-pro-pro-pro…"

"Professor?"

She shook her head. "Pro-producer."

I laughed. "That's a new one. Do you know what producers do?"

She shook her head.

"I don't either. But I guess I'm going to find out. It's very beautiful here. Do you like it here on the ranch?"

Her eyes widened, her lips parted, and she attempted to form a word. "Ba-ba-ba-bears!"

"Bears? There are bears here?"

"Ya-ya-yes." She paused, then spoke in a nearly normal voice. "They…they come up on the porch, and…and they look in the windows."

"Big bears?"

She shook her head. "The cubs."

"Are they cute?"

"Adorable, but they told me to stay away from them, that the mother is watching."

She seemed to be getting more comfortable talking to me.

Her words flowed more smoothly. But I was puzzled by what she'd just said. "You mean your aunt told you to stay away from the cubs?"

"No, Jamie didn't have to. She knows they warned me."

"The cubs warned you?"

Iris frowned and shook her head. She gave me a look that suggested I must be dense not to know what she meant. "Friends, my special friends."

Of course, her invisible friends. Although I wasn't a child psychologist, I was aware that such friends usually fell out of favor by the time kids turned four or five. But then Iris was an unusual girl, one with brain damage at birth. "Your friends warned you about the cubs. That was very smart of them."

"They are very smart."

"Are you able to see them?"

She stared coolly at me again. "Invisible friends are difficult to see." She tilted her head sideways as if listening, then laughed.

"What's the joke, Iris?"

"They are funny." She spoke now without the hint of a stutter. "They said to tell you that you might be able to see them when you are out of your body."

Holy shit. "Tell them I'll look for them."

She dropped her chin as if she were thinking. Or listening. "You won't see them unless I'm nearby. They are here for me."

Maybe they were more real than I wanted to admit. After all, to most people my OBEs would be every bit as strange as her friends. I was about to prod her about her comment last night about the barn, but Jamie appeared, balancing a platter holding three plates of grilled cheese sandwiches and potato salad and three glasses of milk. She carefully set the platter down. "I hope you don't mind drinking milk. It's low fat."

"No problem." It was more dairy than I typically consumed in a week, but what the hell.

"I'm sorry I took so long. I got a phone call I had to take." She met my gaze and was about to say something when Iris spoke up.

"Aunt Jamie, I told Mr. Jake about the bears."

"That's good." She glanced my way. "She's not kidding. We have bears in the woods, a mother and her cubs have been around for a couple of months."

"I'd like to see them sometime."

Iris paused as she was about to take a bite from her sandwich. She looked curiously at me. "I think you will."

"So what else did you talk about besides bears?" Jamie asked.

"About her friends, the invisibles. Good sandwich, by the way."

"I can see that by the way it's disappearing. What did you learn about them?"

"That they're protecting Iris."

"That's right. And Iris knows that her friends protect her wherever she goes, not just here."

I could see by Iris's momentary scowl that Jamie had hit on a sore point. "Did your friends say anything about the person who painted on the barn?" I looked from Iris to Jamie, hoping I hadn't said the wrong thing.

Jamie shook her head. "We haven't talked about that yet."

But Iris piped up. "It's a trick by a mean person. That's what they say."

"Thank you, Iris," Jamie said. "You ate that sandwich very quickly. What about the potato salad?"

"I do-do-don't like it. It has eggs in it. Can I be excused now?"

"Yes, please put your dish in the dishwasher for me."

She stood up and headed for the door, plate in hand. Jamie opened the door for her. "Do you have anything to say to Mr. Jake?"

Iris's head lolled to one side, then the other. "Nice meeting you. I sa-saw your truck. Nice that you brought your stuff." With that, she walked inside and Jamie closed the door.

Jamie laughed and shook her head. "Sometimes Iris says things that are somewhat inscrutable. So that was Danny who called. He told me briefly about your adventure with him last night. What the hell were you two doing out of body at a bar in Charlotte?" She shook her head and laughed.

"Truthfully, it wasn't planned. But when I got out, I decided to see if I could find Andrea, who was supposed to be at a conference of lawyers in Atlanta."

"Andrea is your live-in love interest, I assume."

"That's right, but the interest part has waned. She was hanging out with her boss. They stopped in Charlotte on their way to Atlanta apparently for some fun and games."

"Ouch! Sorry to hear that. What was Danny doing?"

"Apparently watching me yell at Andrea with no effect. He showed me that he could knock over a beer bottle and a glass of wine, and we were joined by his brother, the CIA shrink, who's the project chief."

"Wow, what did he want?"

"I guess he was checking up on Danny. He also assaulted a server to show me what he could do." I told her the story.

"What a crude bastard. Danny told me his brother is power hungry and has lost his soul, that he's not the same person he remembers from when they were young. Did he threaten you in any way?"

"No, he just dissed me as a wannabe."

"I think we should do what we can to help Danny."

"Like what? He doesn't want to be interviewed and frankly, Jamie, I thinking this story is a bad idea. If we expose the Fliers, it would open an enormous can of worms. I'm all for government in the sunshine and exposing bad players, but not in this case. Think about what could happen if this ability became widespread and used by terrorist groups and governments. No democracy, no rules of law would be safe."

To my surprise, she nodded. "I know. No one would be safe. I share your concern. And I have a confession to make, Jake. I wasn't totally truthful with you. The reason Danny approached me was that he knew from something I'd written that I could get out of body, and he asked me to join him in stopping the Fliers."

I started to reply, but she pushed on. "I told him I wanted to know more and that I wanted you involved. If you would agree, of course."

I was confused. What was I getting into? "Wait. You mean, there's no TV series?"

"Yes, of course, my lawyer is negotiating a contract, but as I said, there's nothing firm yet. I love the ideas you've already come up with. They're great. I had you in mind for this project before Danny came along.

"Good to know, I guess. The question right now is how the hell can you, me, and Danny do anything to stop the Fliers, especially if we can't expose them?"

"That's what I asked Danny. He says they lost one of their Fliers recently and that his brother wanted him to look for a replacement. So he was going to tell his brother Bill Waters that you and I are good candidates. We just need practice."

"I don't know if I qualify. I'm an amateur compared to Danny and his brother."

"He said you have great potential, and I'd already sensed that. Otherwise, I wouldn't have approached you. You can do it. We both can. He wants to meet us out of body tomorrow night."

"How's that going to work?"

"I told him I wasn't sure we would be able to get out on demand like that, but he said it was no problem, that he would simply pull us out."

"I think he helped me out last night. But wait. Do you really want to be a Flier?"

"We're just candidates. It's a good cover."

I rubbed the back of my neck, feeling wary. Yet, I told myself I was launching an exploration of the cutting edge of psychic abilities, right where I wanted to be, in spite of the dangers. But practical matters intruded on those thoughts. "I should get going. I need to get to my storage unit and unload the truck."

I also needed a place to live. My phone dinged; a call from a Boca Raton, Florida, number that I recognized as a repeat spam call that I thought I'd blocked. I was about to stuff my phone in my back pocket when I noticed an email message that instantly caught my attention. The subject line read: *Your Lunch at Yucas.*

I quickly read it. "You are not going to believe this, Jamie. I just got an email from one of my former students Tracy, the girlfriend of our server at Yucas."

"And?"

"Well, Darren, that's her boyfriend, says that a man at a table inside the restaurant said he would give him twenty dollars if he found out my name. Here's what she says:

"Darren just blurted out your name and that you were a professor. That's all. Then the guy only gave him ten because Darren already knew who you were. What a jerk! I know Darren probably shouldn't have said anything, but it happened so fast he didn't have a chance to think about it. Anyhow, he wrote down the man's name when he paid with his credit card. Max Owens. You should Google him. He debunks psychics."

I looked up at Jamie. "I think we've found the barn painter."

"My guess is that he hired someone else to do it. Owens is a grossly overweight pediatrician as well as president of the North Carolina Paranormal Debunkers, or something. He's not likely to dirty his own hands, but I wouldn't put it past him to pull a trick like this one on me."

"I think it's North Carolina Skeptics Society. But I like your version better."

"Whatever, he's a nasty fellow. Total non-believer in the paranormal. Very hostile. I was on a panel discussion with him last year for some club and also on a talk radio show with him a few weeks ago. I won't do it again. He was really condescending."

"I don't blame you. Some people will never accept the reality of any psychic abilities."

She nodded. "I finally had enough of his B.S. and lectured him on the scientific process and open-minded inquiry. He's probably still fuming about that."

I laughed. "I can see how that might enrage him."

"And now he's trying to trick me into thinking Reverend Aimes painted the barn. I'm glad I didn't notice him. It would've ruined my lunch."

I stood up and picked up my plate. "I believe it. Hey, this was great. Thank you for the lunch, Jamie."

We walked through the house and out the front door. I could tell she had something more to say. "Thanks for spending time with Iris. I appreciate it. I'm trying to get her to be more social, but she fights me on it. Sarah just babies her, let's her do what she wants. I'm the bad aunt."

"How long is she here for?"

"Another couple of weeks."

"She's a nice kid, very attuned. These friends of hers are interesting, whatever they are."

She pointed at the bed of the truck. "So, Jake, what's going on? Are you moving somewhere?"

"Yeah, *somewhere*. Andrea and I have been heading in different directions for months. I just accelerated the inevitable."

"Enough said. Sorry to hear that. Where are you going?"

"A friend's couch until I find an apartment."

She crossed her arms, tilted her head to the side the same way Iris had done, and studied me a moment. "Would you like to look at an apartment that's available nearby?"

"Sure. Where is it?"

She pointed at the barn. "Up on the second floor. It's partially furnished. It's been empty for more than a year. My two current grooms both live with their families."

I was so stunned by the offer and the sudden turn of events that I didn't respond immediately.

"Don't worry. It doesn't stink. The manure is cleaned up every morning and stored well away from the barn."

"I hadn't even thought about that. Hey, climb in. I'll drive over and you can show it to me."

I just knew I was going to like it and hoped the rent was reasonable. Iris's last comment to me, that it was nice that I brought my stuff along, suddenly made sense.

6

Bill Waters arrived at the southwest gate of the White House promptly at 8:30 as requested. He presented his identification to a guard, who found him on the appointment list and gave him a clip-on pass to wear. The guard alerted someone through a device on his wrist and a couple of minutes later, a young woman appeared. Slender, dark eyes, possibly of East Indian descent. "Good morning, Dr. Waters. I'm Lucy, an intern with the NSA. First time to the White House?"

First time in my body, he thought, nodding.

She smiled. "Please come with me."

She guided him along West Executive Avenue to a pathway leading to the White House, chatting every step of the way, acting as a tour guide as well as escort. "In earlier times, it was called the President's Palace, the President's House, and the Executive Mansion. Theodore Roosevelt named it the White House in 1901."

"Ironic, in a way," Waters responded, "since the White House was built by slaves." Lucy hesitated before answering. "That's something I usually don't mention, unless I'm asked. It is true, though there were also non-slave laborers."

They turned into the West Basement entrance, where another guard checked his pass and told them to wait. Less than a minute later, a suit arrived and handed Waters a sealed envelope with a presidential stamp on it. A Secret Service agent, Waters guessed. He sensed that whatever was in the envelope was important, not just some formal welcome to the White House letter.

They descended a few stairs on the right and came to the White House Mess. The door was open, and several people sat at a table with coffee cups in front of them. Lucy pointed at a door across from it. "That's the Situation Room where you're scheduled to meet President Novak. But he wants you to wait in a quieter environment." They continued down the hall until Lucy stopped and opened a door. "Here you go. I'll be back when the president is ready for you."

He entered a small room with a leather couch, a low table, and a couple of matching leather chairs. On the table was a bucket of ice cooling several bottles of water. He settled onto the couch and opened one of the bottles, took a sip, then turned his attention to the envelope.

He broke the seal and found hand-written instructions.

Please take a 'personal' tour of the John F. Kennedy Conference Room while you're waiting and report to me later.

The message was obscure and innocuous and probably written by someone other than President Novak. But Waters knew what the message meant. He made no effort to get up and find Lucy so she could give him the tour. This was a different kind of tour and didn't require him to leave the couch. Instead, if all went well, he would leave his body behind and search for that conference room. He'd never heard of it but knew he could find it. He had confidence in his out-of-body GPS.

He took one more sip of water, settled back into the couch, and closed his eyes. He pushed away his annoyance that he still had to prove himself, even after the four successful prison missions. He suspected the exhibition was for someone other than the president, who he'd heard was quite convinced.

He'd gotten only a few hours of sleep after a late-night outing, prowling a bar in pursuit of Danny, who was out cruising on his own in an effort to find a new Flier. He knew his brother wasn't one hundred percent behind his itinerary for the Fliers, and Waters recognized the potential problems of abuse and misuse of their advanced abilities. He pushed aside those thoughts and began to focus. He easily entered a relaxed state and silently repeated the name of his target—John F. Kennedy Conference Room.

Usually, he would take at least five minutes preparing for his journey. But he knew if he allowed himself to relax too deeply, he would fall asleep. After just a couple of minutes, he rolled out of his body and floated up near the ceiling. He drifted out of the room and down the hall. He felt pulled toward the door that Lucy had called the Situation Room. When he attempted to move on in search of the Kennedy Room, he was immediately pulled back. Usually, that meant he'd reached his target. Reluctantly, he moved toward the door and drifted right through it.

Moments later, Waters jolted into full consciousness back in the waiting room, his head jerking up and down like a bobble doll. The door opened and Lucy asked, "Do you want the lights dimmed, Mr. Waters?"

He'd barely had time to scan the Situation Room, where a meeting around a long table was breaking up. He gathered himself together and mumbled, "Leave it," and Lucy retreated. *Shit.* Even if he'd entered the right room, he hadn't had time to obtain any significant information or see anything distinctive or unusual that he could report. He needed to take a second journey, but getting out twice within an hour was a difficult task. The few times he'd tried it, he'd simply fallen asleep. He needed to make an effort. He didn't want to disappoint or embarrass Novak. Or embarrass himself, for that matter. However, now he feared his shortage of sleep might work against him, and that was exactly what happened. He dozed off, and ten minutes passed before he bolted awake.

Stay awake. Stay awake.

He relaxed and focused, and within a minute felt the familiar vibrations whipping up and down his spine. He imagined himself climbing a rope that hung above him, pulling himself out of his body. But nothing happened, and he began to drift off again. *Don't give up.*

He initiated the vibrations again, letting them course up and down his spine over and over again. This time he simply rolled over and found himself hovering next to his body slumped on the couch. He directed himself to the Situation Room and found himself there. The room was a blur of activity, and he had a hard time focusing on any one person or object.

The best thing to do, he decided, was to find the president, even if he wasn't in this room. If he could locate him and remember something about what he was doing or saying, that should be enough.

Where's Novak?

He felt himself pulled across the room to one of several doors on the far walls. He moved through it and found his target.

Lucy stepped inside the small waiting room and touched his shoulder. "Mr. Waters," she whispered. "Sorry for the wait, sir. I'll take you to the Sit Room now. The president is ready to see you."

He nodded and glanced at his watch, amazed that sixty-eight minutes had passed since he'd sat down. He rubbed his face, coming fully awake. He'd fallen into a light sleep after returning from his target. "Of course."

"Don't forget your letter, sir." Lucy pointed at the envelope and note that rested on the table. He scooped it up and thanked her. He wondered how much she knew about what he was doing here. Probably nothing. But someone had asked her to see if he wanted the lights turned down. He followed her down the hall.

"Sorry for interrupting you earlier," she said. "I was told you wanted to meditate deeply before you met the president and you might like dimmer lighting."

He smiled. "No problem."

Even though he'd met Novak late last year at CIA headquarters, this was his first time in the White House, and he felt honored to be here. But he also felt the weight of what the president might want from him. He was certain there was more to this meeting than a mere test of his skills. He was fairly certain that Novak considered him a secret weapon, one that he might be ready to trigger. But how far would Novak want him to go?

Lucy stopped short of the Situation Room where a guard was stationed. "Unless there's something else that I can do for you, I'll hand you off here."

"Thank you. There is one thing. Where is the John F. Kennedy Conference Room?"

Lucy laughed. "Right here. It's the formal name of the Situation or Sit Room."

"I thought so."

"It was set up by President Kennedy after the Bay of Pigs disaster in 1961 to address the need for rapid and secure communications so the White House could coordinate national security information."

It was interesting that Novak had requested him to penetrate a secured surveillance-free meeting room; his ability to penetrate the SCIF at Langley while out of body had launched the new turn in his career at the CIA. He had impressed Director Sutter by successfully describing three men and two women in the room and summarized their conversation. After that, Sutter put him and Danny to work on investigations. He'd targeted subjects for several months, resulting in breakthroughs in a couple of difficult cases. That convinced Sutter of the worthiness of the project, and he then directed Waters to find others who could join him and Danny on a team of Fliers, as the group eventually was called.

He realized Lucy was continuing her spiel about the

room—more than five thousand square feet, staffed with about thirty personnel, organized around five Watch Teams for 24-7 monitoring of international events. A generic Watch Team included…blah, blah, blah.

"That's good to know."

A guard examined his pass and alerted someone inside, then opened the door. Waters stepped into a frenzy of activity and was quickly met by another uniform, who introduced himself simply as the duty officer. People moved about purposefully, some entering or leaving offices on three sides of the room, just as he'd seen during his brief OBE. No one was sitting at the long conference table now where he'd first glimpsed the president. When he'd returned for a second peek, Novak was in a smaller room within the SCIF with a man Waters recognized as Novak's national security advisor.

The duty officer led him to a conference room with a table and four chairs on either side. "Make yourself comfortable. The president will be here in a few minutes."

Just like going to his doctor, he thought. Wait in the outer room, wait in the examining room. He settled in and reminded himself how fortunate he was to be waiting for a meeting with the most powerful person in the world. After all, he was a mid-level administrator in resource management at the CIA. He tested and evaluated the cognitive and emotional state of potential employees as well as agents whose mental faculties had come under question. But the testing that interested the president was something else altogether.

For the past eighteen months, Waters's regular duties had served as a cover as he pursued his secret endeavor, a mission that was literally beyond the frontier of what was considered real and possible. Now here he was seated in a SCIF, waiting for his second meeting with the President of the United States.

After several minutes of idling, Waters glanced at his watch. When you're in the midst of an adventure—and that's what he considered this experience—you weren't supposed to sit around and wait. Indiana Jones never waited, not even when he was tied up. Unfortunately, he was very familiar with being iced. The 'hurry up and wait' scenario reminded him of his time in

Iraq when the commander would order him into the interrogation room but then leave him waiting an hour for his subject. He always figured the tactic was intended to annoy him so he would push harder on the prisoner. But he'd also heard that it was politics, that the commander didn't like the CIA in charge of interrogations instead of his own soldiers.

The duty officer opened the door. "The president."

Waters quickly stood. Novak walked in, followed by CIA Director Dale Sutter and National Security Advisor Richard Croft. The president extended a hand and offered a warm smile. "Good to see you again, Mr. Waters." Novak introduced him to Croft, who had been Pennsylvania's Attorney General until Novak tapped him for his administration shortly after the election. Croft and Sutter, his boss, were allies of the president, and Waters knew that anything that transpired in the meeting would be protected from loose tongues.

At forty-one, Waters was a decade younger than the other three, and his shaved head, goatee, and muscular build set him apart in appearance. Novak had the best hair, steel grey and perfectly quaffed, a strong jaw, a handsome retired Army general elevated to the presidency to repair the damage created by his predecessor. He had an appealing smile but was known by insiders as a ruthless politician.

Sutter had risen through the ranks and achieved the directorship of the CIA a year ago after twenty-six years of service. His most notable feature? Those narrow beady eyes that skewered whoever fell under his gaze. His thinning hair was combed straight back, and his appearance gave off the not-so subtle message: *Don't fuck with me.*

Richard Croft was a heavy-set dude with a crew cut and round face. He looked soft, as if his body had not found its way into a gym in a decade. He was known for straight talk that was sometimes mistaken for arrogance.

Sutter and Croft sat on either side of Waters, while Novak sat directly across from him, facing all three. No question who was in charge here. Waters threaded his fingers together and rested his hands on the table as if he were about to say grace.

He was puzzled by the absence of the FBI director James

Merrill, who had attended his first meeting with Novak, as had Sutter. He was about to ask if the director would be joining them when Novak told him that Merrill was unavailable. "He knows about the meeting and will be briefed." Waters wondered if Novak actually had blocked the FBI director from attending. Merrill, known to have an independent streak, had clearly irritated Novak at their first meeting. Initially, Merrill had been impressed by the potential for obtaining hard-to-get information on criminal targets, and he'd been convinced by the documented work of the Fliers. But he'd sharply questioned the new turn of the project ordered by Novak that would result in the execution-by-Fliers of several death row inmates. And that escapade was just the beginning, Waters suspected.

"Let me start by telling you that Richard, who wasn't at our first meeting, knows everything that I know about the Fliers. Except I'm not sure he really believes it. So tell us what you saw going on in this impervious situation room. Were you able to penetrate the walls?"

"Yes, twice actually. The first time there was a meeting around the big table that was just breaking up. I was interrupted, but I tried again awhile later and found you and Advisor Croft seated in this same room, Advisor Croft on this side of the table. You two were playing chess, and I tipped over the president's king."

Novak laughed and slapped the table. "Exactly. I knew I didn't knock over the king. I never touched it. I told you that, Richard."

Croft met Waters' gaze. "That was impressive. But the president is correct. I am somewhat skeptical." He reached under the edge of the table and jiggled something.

"The drawer is locked, Richard."

Waters realized that the game must've been put away in a drawer. He couldn't help wondering how often Novak came here to play.

Croft smiled. "Well, it's a stretch to think that someone who is sleeping can strangle another person a thousand miles away. What's the trick?"

"Truthfully, I don't know how it works. It just does. But I do know that I'm not asleep or dreaming. I'm awake and out of my physical body and in a second energy body. I've had these experiences since I was a kid. So has my younger brother, who is also a Flier. It was only as an adult in the military, under constant threat in war zones, that I began to take control of the ability. Then back in the states I found that I could meet my brother, Danny, while we were both out of body."

"Runs in the family, does it?" Croft commented.

"Only me and Danny in our family. My sisters can't get out. But I approached Director Sutter about this ability and told him that I believed Danny and I could work as a team."

"After they provided me some fascinating results, I told Bill to expand his team," Sutter said.

"I was very interested in seeing if I could partner with others with the ability. The big surprise was that we discovered we could manipulate matter."

"I know it's unbelievable, Richard, and that's why we didn't tell Bill and his team to take out just one inmate on death row," Sutter explained. "All four were selected in advance, and believe me, they were particularly nasty characters or had been on the row for decades. They each went down, death by compression to the throat."

Novak nodded. "You can't call that a coincidence. It's an amazing tool we have on our hands."

Croft rubbed his jaw. "I read your reports, Dale. If it was just about information gathering, it would be a wonderful asset. A way of getting around privacy rights in cases where we can't prove that someone has committed a crime without some kind of inside information. The Fliers in such cases are essentially invisible informants. But truthfully, I agree with Director Merrill. I find this ability to kill quite disturbing. Imagine a serial killer on the loose with this ability. How would you stop that person? How would you even identify him or her? There would be no fingerprints, footprints, no evidence."

Croft gestured toward Novak. "If you're good with it, Phil, I'm one hundred percent behind you, of course. But frankly, it's frightening, and I wish I never heard about it."

Sutter cleared his throat. "Don't worry, Richard. Bill reports to me daily. The Fliers are being closely monitored. They aren't allowed to go out on their own. And, if they do, the others are aware of it. They're linked together, so to speak."

"That's true," Waters assured Croft. "Once we started working as a team and going out together, we inadvertently created a mind-link. Now when one goes out, the others know it."

Novak pointed at Croft. "The important thing, Richard, is this project, this ability, has to be kept secret. That way our enemies remain unaware of it."

"Also, if somehow rumors get out about this project," Sutter said, "I will immediately initiate a disinformation program to make anyone claiming this ability exists to look like a fool."

Novak nodded. "Good. I want to see weekly reports with details of what actions are being planned or pursued. Billy, you know that we can't afford any mistakes or any leaks, or anyone going rogue." As an afterthought, he added: "Oh, I almost forgot to mention that it was very unfortunate what happened to one of your Fliers."

"Yes, it was." Lance Wallen, a former sheriff's deputy, and one of the Fliers, drowned a few weeks ago. Supposedly, an accident. But Wallen was the only Flier who had refused to participate in the death-row killings. Waters had dismissed him as being unfit. Now Novak, in his alleged sorrow for Wallen's death, had just laid out a threat.

After a few awkward moments, Sutter cleared his throat. "The beauty of this project is that no one, not even people who have had out-of-body experiences or those who believe in it, accept the idea that physical objects, including people, can be manipulated from the OBE state. There's no research out there that even suggests such a thing is possible."

Waters realized he needed to proceed with utter caution. He certainly wasn't about to tell Novak that he had initiated missions that weren't reported to Sutter, or that all seven remaining Fliers occasionally went out on their own for personal flights. They needed to do it to recharge themselves after difficult assignments. That was how they came to realize that they were able to manipulate people and objects on their own.

"That's good to know," Novak said. "Now I have another mission for you, another test."

Here it comes, he thought, a mission with a political motivation. Novak couldn't stay away from it. Merrill had told Sutter that he needed to order the Fliers to refuse any such blatant request. That was probably why he wasn't here now. Distasteful and regrettable as the assignment might be, Waters knew that rejecting it might be dangerous, even suicidal. Lance Wallen, case in point.

Suddenly, horns blared, drums pounded, and Novak grimaced. He reached into his coat pocket, pulled out his phone, and tapped a button, ending the refrain of *Hail to the Chief*. He frowned at whatever he read and stuffed the phone away.

"Avery Metcalf, CEO of NetHubster, the fastest growing internet corporation."

For a moment, Waters thought Novak was telling him that was who called. But he quickly realized that wasn't the case. "Just last month the bastard told me he was a big supporter of my presidency. But now he's a big contributor to the Lisa Jenkins campaign and has been mentioned as her probable VP candidate. That really pisses me off."

Waters knew that Metcalf became a billionaire in the company's first three years by creating a series of popular privacy apps. He was also an outspoken critic of cell phone tracking devices, favored by Novak, that allowed law enforcement agencies to invade anyone's text messages and phone logs, and everything else on a target's cell phone. If he only knew what was going on beyond the tech world, Waters thought.

"He's very successful, but he's got a big mouth and he's backing the wrong person. Jenkins will make her VP pick this Saturday, and all the bets are on Metcalf. That's the day I want you to deal with him. Push him down a staircase or off the stage, something that looks like an accident. It'll be a terrible sign for the Jenkins campaign."

"Are you certain about that?" Waters asked. "She could get a wave of sympathy support."

Novak studied him for a few moments. "You're a shrink, Bill. Don't you think Senator Jenkins will see the writing on the wall?"

Waters hesitated. "She's very determined and probably will just move on to picking someone else to run with her. Accidents happen."

"We'll see. If that's the case, well, as you say, accidents happen. What do you think, Richard?"

Croft looked disturbed and attempted to temper Novak's eagerness. "I think Senator Jenkins just might take the hint when she sees what happens to her running mate."

Novak smiled. "Dale, how about you? Are you in?"

"What about Merrill?"

"This mission goes no farther than the four of us. No one else should be involved."

Director Sutter looked to Waters, who nodded, then answered the president. "We're in."

It was like Danny had warned, Waters thought, the Fliers were now political tools of the president. He'd known that, but he'd figured that Novak would employ them for spying, not killing other Americans. He should've known better when they were given the death row assignment. Besides, Novak's background wasn't exactly that of a pacifist.

He was the first general to become president since Dwight Eisenhower and, like Ike, he had been a NATO Supreme Allied Commander. He'd campaigned on "honesty and order, knowledge and reason," a sharp contrast to the previous president on all counts. Everyone had expected a more stable government headed by an honorable president. Instead, since Novak assumed office, journalists had exposed multiple sexual affairs and a deceptive nature that had been largely overlooked during the campaign. Novak, it was clear, craved the same power as his predecessor to rule without opposition. Jenkins, for her part, compared Novak's campaign and presidency to a South American "junta," a military take over.

Novak turned his gaze fully on Waters. "With the Fliers on our side, politics will never be the same again."

7

Astonishingly, I began moving into my new apartment within half an hour of looking at it for the first time. After all, I was packed and ready. I just didn't know I would find a place this soon, and certainly not in such an unexpected manner. My only request to Jamie was that I wanted my own bed. I'd stretched out on the one in the apartment, and the mattress felt like it was stuffed with rocks. She gladly obliged and got her two grooms to remove the bed and put it into a shed. After I'd unloaded my truck, I made a trip to my storage unit for the bed and television, a couple of lamps and a matching pair of small tables with drawers—one for the TV, the other for my bedside reading lamp. On my way back, I picked up some take-out Chinese and ate my first meal in my apartment.

It was after ten o'clock when I finally headed back to Andrea's house to complete my evacuation. Maybe I should've confronted Andrea in person rather than on the phone. She'd chided me for not doing so. Certainly, if I'd been the one indulging in a new relationship, she would've waited until she got right in my face, and she wouldn't have held back, not for a moment, even if a fire alarm had sounded.

But I just wanted to move on with my life. To that end, I'd found an ample supply of boxes behind an A&P. One of them even contained a fresh-looking head of cauliflower, a treat for Sam. He loved chopped cauliflower as well as carrots. Go figure, a dog who likes vegetables.

My plan was to pack the remainder of my stuff, spend the night, then leave the key under the mat. But when I pulled up to the house, Andrea's Porsche was parked in the driveway. *Shit.* She'd come home early.

I sat in the truck composing myself. My preference was to remain civil and avoid a shouting match. But she'd already put the blame on me during our second conversation, and I expected more of the same. She was fiery, and though I could hold my own in an argument, her debating skills were supreme. If she could get a murderer freed, which she'd done once as a public defender, she could certainly defend herself.

The front door was locked. That was different. Andrea had chided me for locking the door while we were home. The neighborhood was quiet and safe, everyone had at least an acre of wooded property, and from her place you couldn't even see another house in any direction. All reasons that some people would keep their houses locked at all hours, I'd told her. I'd finally convinced her to install a home security system that monitored the property, even though she thought it was a waste of money. I'd noticed that it was turned on as I'd approached the house. She knew I was here.

I unlocked the door, stepped inside, and immediately sensed something wasn't right. Then I realized what it was. Sam always greeted me at the door. In fact, Andrea had told me that he somehow sensed my imminent arrival and stationed himself at the front door a few minutes before I arrived. I heard a whimpering and walked over to the guest bedroom. I opened the door. He barked once and wagged his whole body as he sauntered over to me.

I knelt down and petted him. "What were you doing in here, big guy?"

"He was in the way, Jake."

I turned at the sound of Andrea's voice and slowly stood up, stunned by what I saw. Andrea was back, and so was Chad. They both stood there, staring at me. "Oh, this is nice. How sweet of you both to show up."

Chad was dressed in his tailored lawyer suit—but tieless— and Andrea wore slacks and a blouse. I had a sudden urge to punch the smirk off lover-boy's mug, and maybe he sensed it. He took a step back. "I'm here, Jake, because I insisted on it. Not because Andrea asked me to come. I just want to make sure that nothing bad happens."

"Did you consider the possibility that you might have that backwards?" The two exchanged a quick glance, and I guessed that was Andrea's take.

"Look, Jake. If you had married Andrea, instead of just moving into her house, it would be a different matter. I wouldn't be here."

"I'm not sure what that means, and frankly, I don't care. What I do know is that I would like to finish packing and be on my way. I don't want to interfere with lawyers in love."

Andrea turned to Chad. "Would you mind waiting in the kitchen while I talk to Jake?"

He turned up his palms, as if surrendering. "Of course."

"Thanks. You could make some decaf," she called after him as he retreated.

"You think he knows how?"

"He can manage. Jake, let's not get emotional. We're adults. It's best that we part ways. I was getting ready to tell you, but you beat me to it."

"Save your breath. It's been obvious for months that things were headed south. I've got some boxes I need to bring in so I can get the rest of my stuff."

She touched my arm. "Look, Chad's a fair person, and he understands your position. He would like to give you a check to help you through the transition."

"A *check*? He wants to buy me off?" I started laughing. I couldn't help it. But hey, how much was it worth to ole Chad? "How much is he willing to pay me?"

"Ten thousand."

"Well, now you know what you're worth to him. He can keep it. I'm not going to give you or him any trouble. Like he said, we're not married."

"I'm glad you're taking it so well, but there's no need to insult me. I know exactly what I'm doing. I've enjoyed our time together, but it's over."

"Go drink your decaf with Chad. I'll be out of here in an hour."

"Is that all you can say after three years together?"

I was going to miss her, I already did. It was over, and I felt a stab of loneliness. But she shouldn't have brought him here, even if he had insisted. It was tacky. "Well, I could tell you how I know that you were the one who wanted to get out of the bar in Charlotte and up to the room before the band started playing again. But that might be too upsetting. So I'll leave it at that."

She stared at me, her features frozen in a look of astonishment.

"Amazing. You actually hired someone to follow me?"

"No, I was there."

"You? So you were playing private eye? Good one, Jake. Too bad nobody was paying..." Her voice trailed off as she realized that someone inadvertently was willing to pay me—her new love interest. She walked away to join him.

A few moments later, I heard nervous laughter from the kitchen and wondered what was so funny. I continued packing, then went out to the truck for more boxes. When I returned, Andrea was casually inspecting my boxes, making sure I wasn't taking any of her stuff, and Chad watched quietly from a distance.

He was her witness if anything should go wrong, if I took anything of hers, if I damaged anything, if I even touched her. In his mind, I posed a threat and he was ready to act. His presence had already made it clear that I was now an intruder and could be dealt with as one if I acted in any way that threatened either of them.

I couldn't wait to get out of here. I probably had overlooked some things that were mine, but I didn't care. I didn't belong here or want to be here any longer. Andrea was on another path, and Chad was her protector, her fellow traveler.

"Jake, if you were in Charlotte watching me, why didn't you say something then?"

"I did. You didn't hear me or see me."

"You're lying. You weren't there."

I was holding back as best I could. Clearly, I had reason to be angry, to rage about how terrible she was for getting involved with someone while living with me, and how it really sucked that she'd brought the guy here with her. But Chad was clever, and by accompanying her he was guarding against any backsliding on her part. His mere presence both enraged me and kept me from acting out.

I stepped closer to Andrea as she pawed the stuff in one of the boxes. She picked up an oblong case for glasses, opened it, and pulled out a plastic bag with half an ounce of weed. She held it up with her thumb and index finger as if displaying evidence in a courtroom.

"I told you not to bring pot into this house, Jake. You did it anyhow."

I laughed. "No one was ever going to raid this house in search of that."

"How do you know?"

I rolled my eyes, snatched the bag from her hand, stuffed it in my pocket, and barreled out the door without taking any boxes. I clasped onto the door handle of my truck and realized I was overreacting. *Fuck it,* I thought, and climbed into the cab. I would get Sam and the boxes in the morning after she'd gone to work.

I sat up and looked around at my new surroundings as the murky dawn light filtered through the bare windows. I'd slept on the floor on my mattress, which had a comfort level only slightly better than the bed that had been here. My belongings were strewn about the loft apartment. It was one large room with a kitchen at one end and a bedroom at the other, separated partially by a partition. Small, but adequate. The porch and the view of the valley beyond it made up for the apartment's shortcomings.

I leaned over, picked up my cell phone, and saw that I had a string of text messages from Andrea. They'd begun shortly after I left the house. My phone was muted, and I hadn't noticed them last night. I'd gone right to bed as soon as I got here. I read them in order.

Where the hell did you go? Are you coming back? (11:42 PM)

You forgot Sam and all your boxes. (11:48 PM)

You're not dumping this dog off on me. Come and get him and your stuff. (12:03 AM)

Would you please answer me? I left you a voice mail. (12:08)

I clicked over to voice mail.

"Jake, I'm sorry about how things turned out. You're a good guy, but we're moving in different directions, and I completely understand how you must feel about me. It's late now, but please come by in the morning and get Sam and your things. Thanks."

I glanced at the time. Another hour and she would be on her way to the office. I certainly wasn't going to show up now for coffee with her and Chad. But I needed to text her.

I'll be by after you and Chad are gone. I'll clear out my stuff. Thanks for taking care of Sam.

She didn't waste any time in responding, and it sounded like she hadn't gotten her coffee yet.

FYI, Chad did not stay here last night. Don't forget to leave the key and please take Sam.

With a sigh, I climbed to my feet and headed to the bathroom. The sooner I got over there, the better. If Andrea had just stayed out of my stuff, I would've been finished there last night. But her prissy attitude about weed had annoyed me all along, and bringing it up last night, on top of everything else, pushed me over the edge and I bolted. I didn't want to spend another minute with her looming over me. But it was just about over now.

I opened the double doors, stepped out onto the balcony, and immediately forgot about my concerns. I drew in a deep breath of fresh morning air and gazed out over a scene that resembled a landscape painting. I could see clearly down the valley, but it was a bed of fog that caught my attention. It hovered over a low-lying area a couple hundred yards away. Three grazing horses were in the midst of it, the fog reaching their withers, only their heads and manes visible.

Definitely a surreal scene, but no more so than my own situation. I found myself ensconced in an apartment above a stable owned by the woman who had hired me for what originally sounded like an incredible opportunity, but was turning into something else altogether that was beyond strange. Namely, playing undercover initiate of a secret government project involving out-of-body travel. But so far that wasn't happening either.

I was more preoccupied with reckoning the end of my long-time relationship. I had to get past the annoying thought that the breakup with Andrea was just a spat and everything would work out fine. In spite of everything, I already missed her. But, bottom line, we weren't compatible. There would be no going back. It was over. Fin.

Just then, I saw movement out of the corner of my eye. I

glanced toward the house and spotted a black bear standing up on her hind legs, peering at me on the balcony. Nearby three cubs frolicked, tumbling over each other.

At that moment, Jamie stepped out of her front door and walked over to her golf cart. She waved to me and pointed at the bears as they ambled back toward the forest. I'd gone directly to the apartment last night and hadn't let her know I was here. I didn't think it mattered. As I waited for her to drive to the barn, I noticed the fog had vanished and the horses were now fully visible.

"Hey, I didn't want to bother you last night when I came in," I called out after she stopped just below me. She wore a red jumpsuit and high-topped white sneakers.

"It's your apartment now. You don't need permission to come and go. Are you getting settled in?"

"I'm working at it. I need to go back to the house for one more load and my dog."

"You should've brought Sam last night. I'm sure he'll fit in with the other dogs on the ranch. They're all pretty mellow."

"That's great. He'll be here soon."

"We'll talk later," she said and put her golf cart into gear.

I made coffee, cereal, and toast, unpacked a couple of boxes, and put clothes in my old dresser that I'd brought from the storage unit. I started to assemble the bed frame but realized my tools were in the truck. I walked downstairs, and that was when I saw Jamie watching Juan, one of the grooms, who was painting the barn wall to cover the scrawled diatribe. Her arms were crossed, and she was frowning.

When I opened the front door, Sam was lying on his side on the living room floor. He raised his head, let out a single faint woof, then put his chin down and stared at me, his sad bloodhound eyes looking even sadder than normal. "Sorry, boy. I'm back. I'm moving to a new home, and you're coming with me. So grab your dog bowl."

He perked up at that, sat up, and yawned. I never knew how much he understood, but he often acted appropriately with what I said. Sometimes, it might be the tone of my voice, but he definitely maintained a substantial vocabulary of commands, praises, and admonishments. Not too many of the latter, however. He was a good dog. The best.

I let him outside, and he conducted his usual sniffing procedures, an olfactory chemical analysis of everything in his immediate environment. He never wandered far, so I left him outside as I went back to packing and loading the truck. I was almost done when I went into the kitchen to snatch a couple of plates and bowls from an older set that Andrea had asked me to take to Goodwill. I picked out some silverware, and a few glasses and set it all on the table. That's when I saw her note to me.

Take the dog dish, but don't even think about taking any of my good dishes, glasses or flatware.

P.S. I know you didn't want to take Chad's money and I can understand that. But please take mine. Consider it moving expenses. You can go anywhere you want.

I lifted the note and saw the check that was under it. *Twenty grand*? Should I tear it up to show her my belligerence, my superior position? I hung onto that possibility for no more than a couple of seconds. Hell, no. *I'll take it.* The fact was, I could use the money, and she knew it. And if it made Andrea feel better, why not? I slipped the check into my pocket. I had no guarantee that the TV series would come about, in spite of expectations. But now I had a cushion and could take off to anywhere in the country, if I felt like it. Meanwhile, I was even starting to like the idea that I was being recruited for an out-of-body battle.

8

Jamie brushed the grit off her hands after she finished reorganizing the tack room. She'd repeatedly tried to gently persuade the boarders to put away their gear—saddles, helmets, chaps, bridles, bits, halters, and leads—in their respective places. But it seemed she was the only one who paid attention to orderliness in the tack room. Her trainer, who came once a week to give her a lesson, was appalled by the disorder, and told her to loudly admonish the horse owners for their slovenly behavior. But that wasn't Jamie's style, and she didn't want to lose her paying clientele. So she told the grooms to pick up after them or she did it herself.

She stepped out of the barn and gazed over the valley now encased in long shadows in the hour or two before dusk, the mysterious minutes between light and dark. A single crow flew over the barn, cawing, and soared toward the darkening forest behind the house. She could smell food cooking from Jake's apartment and was pleased not only that he was seemingly on board with her and Danny, but that he was living on her ranch. In the past, a groom had resided in the apartment. She'd never imagined that a college prof would be living here, much less one who was also working with her. To say nothing of his earthy good looks.

He was right that exposing the Fliers might be futile and dangerous. Futile because who would believe it and where was the proof? Dangerous because of the threat to democracy and rule of law that the Fliers represented. He also worried that hostile countries might quickly train their own out-of-body assault teams.

For her part, Jamie's primary concerns were closer to home. Even if word got out, it was unlikely that a horde of invisible foreign attackers would suddenly surface. The more immediate threat was a personal one. If the Fliers could kill inmates, they could just as easily kill anyone threatening to expose or stop them.

So why was she putting herself in this position? Did she really want to get involved? A part of her was infuriated with Danny for approaching her and urging her to help him stop the Fliers. She had a good life here on the ranch. She loved writing her books, making media appearances, and now potentially her own TV series. There were people, like Reverend Aimes and the debunker Max Owens, who criticized and complained about her emergence as an iconic media star. But the Fliers were something totally different.

Ironically, their abilities actually bolstered the good reverend's position that dabbling in the psychic world was dangerous, while denigrating Owens's conviction that there was nothing to it: smoke but no fire. It looked like there was plenty of fire, even though it was invisible. What was worse than being attacked by someone you couldn't see? Maybe it was time to back out and let Danny work with Jake. After all, Iris would be here for two more weeks, and she had to consider her niece's safety.

She headed back to the house to make dinner. She would talk to Jake afterward and decide whether or not she would stay onboard. Cooking for Iris was easy but frustrating. She tried not to be judgmental and repeatedly reminded herself that Iris was not her kid. Iris's repertoire of acceptable foods was limited, and Sarah told her not to force Iris to eat anything new, just stick to chicken nuggets, Mac and cheese, hot dogs, and mashed potatoes with a lot of butter. "Do not put anything green, especially broccoli, on her plate or she'll call me and complain," her sister had told her. In spite of that, Jamie had gotten Iris to try chicken breast, salmon, and sweet potatoes. She'd taken a couple of bites of each, then said she was full, only to snack on corn chips or popcorn later on.

She found Iris in her room, where she spent most of her time, playing a game on her computer. "I'm making turkey burgers and French fries. How does that sound?"

"Not good. Fr-Fr-French fries, yes, and Mac and cheese. Aunt Jamie, will you pl-play Scrabble with me af-after dinner?"

"Tell you what, I want to work for a little while after dinner, but if you take one bite of turkey burger, just a taste, then yes, we'll play a game before you go to bed. Deal?

She made an angry face and stewed on the matter for a few moments. "Okay! But only one bite, and I'm gonna hold my nose."

Jamie laughed. "Maybe your friends would like to taste it."

"They do not eat food and they are happy."

"Well, I eat food and now I'm going to go cook for both of us."

After dinner, Jamie managed to work for nearly two hours uninterrupted on her new book project before Iris reminded her about her promise to play Scrabble. She had to make an effort to clear her mind from the book that she was calling *The Secret History of Out-of-Body Travel*. She'd started it several weeks ago and from the first day had felt driven to pursue the subject with an intensity that surprised her. She spent every free hour of her day working on it, staying up for hours after Iris went to bed. The subject so dominated her thoughts that it remained on her mind when she was handling her daily chores on the ranch and all the mundane aspects of everyday life. She was convinced that the intense energy that she'd poured into the book was what had attracted Danny to her.

"Okay, we've got time for one game, then I've got to do night check." Jamie opened the Scrabble box on the kitchen table.

"I'm going to win because I asked my fri-friends to help," Iris said, and went to work turning up the letters.

"Wait. Iris, the letters go face down. You know that."

"I know, but they want to see the letters. They want to spell something for you."

"Oh, that would be cheating if your friends can see the letters."

Iris frowned. "It's not the game, Aunt Jamie. It's a message."

"Why don't they just tell you and you can tell me?"

"They have their reasons."

She continued turning up the letters and Jamie watched, intrigued but clueless about what was going on. When Iris finished, she tilted her head as if she were listening to something. "Okay. They want you to pick the letters and put them on the board.

Jamie shrugged. "I'm ready. I'll start from the left side."

"S...A...V...E. Space. Leave a space they say."

"Hold on, I'm still looking for the V. Got it. What next?"

"L...I...S...A. Space."

"That's it?"

"There's more." Slowly now, she spelled out the rest of the message. "A...N...D. Space. H...E...R. Space. C...A...L...F. That's all."

"Save Lisa and her calf." Jamie looked up from the board. "What does that mean?"

"They say you know."

"We don't have any cows here, but if we did I might name one Lisa."

Iris scowled. "They say it is not a joke."

Jamie puzzled over the obscure message. Who did she know named Lisa? "Oh my God. Could it be Lisa Jenkins and Avery Metcalf?"

Iris shrugged. "Who are they?"

"Two people, um, Lisa wants to be president. She wants Avery to be her running mate." Iris had no interest and little knowledge about politics beyond knowing the name of the president. Did her invisible friends know something? "Can I ask them a question?"

"No. They say we should ju-just play the game." Iris began turning over the pieces. "What's a running mate?"

"Oh, it's someone who wants to be vice president."

"Avery doesn't want to be president?"

"I don't think so, but if they win he has to be ready to take over if something happens to the president."

"Okay. Pick seven letters."

It was nearly ten when Jamie headed to the barn for night check. She stepped outside and saw that Jake's pickup remained next to the barn, and lights were on in the apartment. She pulled out her phone and texted him. *Can I come up to see you in 15 minutes?* She realized he might think she was requesting a late night social visit and quickly added, *We need to talk about tonight.* Better, she thought, and sent it.

She cruised through the barn making sure that the seven horses—five boarders and her two, Isabelle and Debutante—were settled in for the night with hay and clean water. Horses were grazers; they ate and drank water all night. Most people didn't realize that horses only sleep two to three hours a day and usually not more than twenty minutes at a time. She kept her phone on vibrate when she was in the barn at night, and felt it alerting her to a text.

To her surprise, it was from Danny. She read it over twice, frowning. Just then a text arrived from Jake.

Hey, sorry. Just saw your text. C'mon up.

She mounted the stairs to his apartment, and he was standing at the door in a t-shirt and drawstring pants. "I hope I didn't wake you, Jake."

"No way. I was just laying in bed reading. I had a feeling I should get up and look at my phone. It was on the kitchen table."

The apartment looked surprisingly organized considering the short time that Jake had lived here. There were boxes, some empty, some still filled or partially so, piled along one wall. Otherwise, the place was orderly, with the bed set up and all the furniture in place, including a desk with a computer on it. She smiled as a droopy-eyed bloodhound waddled over to her. She crouched and petted his head. "You must be Sam. What a good boy." He gazed up at her, then slumped to the floor and let out a satisfied snort.

"I'm amazed. You're all set up," she remarked, looking around.

"Sort of. I need a bookcase. But it's coming together. The best part is the view from my porch. So what's up? Are we still on for tonight? I almost forgot."

"Truthfully, I almost did, too. In fact, I was thinking of backing out altogether. But I just got a text from Danny, and he really wants our help. Something big is coming up, and he's got a plan. He wants to know if we can be ready to get out by one o'clock."

"I'm usually drifting off by midnight. I could make us a pot of coffee."

She laughed. "No way. I'd be awake all night."

"I guess you're right. So how are we going to do this?"

"He's coming to my place first to help me out, if I need it. Then we'll both come here to get you. He'll spin you out if you have trouble. Actually, I'd kind of like to see him do that."

"Can he do that to anyone, even if the person's asleep?"

"I doubt it. It's hard enough, I understand, even if you're a willing participant."

"Not to pry, but have you been out already with Danny?"

She laughed. "A couple of times. He's very good."

"Yeah, I bet."

She punched Jake lightly on the shoulder. "Shut up. You

know what I'm talking about. No matter what it sounds like."

"Just kidding."

"I had no idea how far they've taken this ability or how easy it is to train someone who can stay out. He says you have the talent."

"Hey, I'm willing to try. But what are we going to do once we're out?"

"That's up to Danny. We'll find out about his plan. I gotta go."

"See you later."

I stretched out on my bed and relaxed. I'd made sure that I was wearing clean bedclothes, maybe a silly concern, but nevertheless I'd picked out a recently laundered pair of drawstring pants and a matching t-shirt. I took a few deep breaths and let my thoughts drift to my day of unpacking and organizing.

I'd recovered my 19-inch television from three years of storage, dusted it off, and texted Jamie for the WiFi number. I'd taken another trip to my storage unit to get my desk and somehow managed to wrangle it into the back of the truck on my own. Upon returning, Juan helped me carry it up to the apartment. If the groom wondered why my name was on the barn wall with Jamie's, he hadn't asked.

When I hadn't heard from Jamie well into the evening, I'd begun to wonder if she might be backing out of the plan to work with Danny. I certainly wouldn't blame her. But apparently she'd made up her mind after Danny texted her. I would play along, but I really doubted that I could be seriously considered a recruit for the Fliers.

Andrea came to mind again. She and Chad together in the Charlotte bar and again at the house as I packed. I still hadn't fully adjusted to the idea that she'd paid me off, sent me on my way. Had she done it out of generosity or guilt? Maybe both. She was well off financially, but I suspected that she'd taken Chad's ten grand and added her own. For Chad, it was simply a payoff so I would go away quietly.

Relax. Let it go. Let it go.

Life with Andrea was over. I was moving onto something

new. I made up my mind. I would make an effort to get out. If nothing happened, I would just roll over and go to sleep.

I checked the time. Ten to one. I was feeling drowsy and began to drift off. I sucked in my breath, caught myself, and wondered how much time had passed. I began creating the vibrations, moving them up and down my spine and around my body. I increased their speed. Halfway through, I heard a loud buzzing sound, and suddenly I rotated to the right and literally spun out, rolling over and over and rising at the same time.

Nothing like this had ever happened. After a few moments, I got control of my movements and stopped spinning. I stared at the ceiling just a couple of inches from my nose. I rolled over, looked down, and there was Jamie next to my bed looking up at me, a smile on her face.

"C'mon down, Jake."

I sank to the floor and stood next to her, amazed. "Wow, I literally spun out of my body that time."

She laughed. "Danny showed me how to do it."

"You mean you..."

"Yeah, I spun you out. You would've gotten out on your own, but I gave you a spin and you popped right out."

"Thanks, I guess. Now what?"

Danny suddenly appeared next to me. "Good job, Jamie. You catch on fast."

I looked at my sleeping body, a meat package that wasn't really me. At least, not now. I felt comfortable with Jamie and Danny and eager to explore.

"Let's move away from your carcass, Jake, so you don't slip back."

Carcass. I didn't like that word. It implied death.

"Jamie, give me a target, just the name of someone you know," Danny rushed on. "You don't have to be friends. We'll go visit."

"I don't know," Jamie said, then added: "Okay, Max Owens. He lives somewhere near Asheville, but I don't know where."

"Not a problem. Take my hands."

My fingers curled around Danny's hand and seemed to

penetrate, but his hand took on substance and I felt resistance, almost like a real handshake. Then we were moving, up and out, through the ceiling, the roof, and into the night. The landscape blurred into streaking beams of light against the darkness, and again I felt the odd sensation of air brushing against my face as if someone was lightly patting my cheeks. The sense of movement was accompanied by a loud hissing, and suddenly I was hurtled through a wall.

I found myself floating slowly to the floor inside of a dimly lit bedroom. A king-sized bed filled half of the room and a large lump covered most of one side, a quilt covering the form, except for the head.

"That's him," Jamie said. "I don't think we should do anything to him. He's so overweight he might have a heart attack."

She and Danny stood on either side of me as if they were guarding me from soaring back to my body. "Especially since he doesn't believe in spooks," I added.

"Oh, he believes, but he's afraid," Jamie replied. "That's why he's so against anything paranormal."

"It doesn't matter," Danny said. "We're here for us, not him. Let him sleep."

"Isn't it dangerous for you to be here?" I asked. "Don't the other Fliers know you're out?"

"Yes, but they know that I'm working with you two as potential recruits."

"Wonderful," I muttered. "How much do they know about me?"

"Very little. Officially, Jake, I'm just testing you. You don't know anything about the Fliers, only that I'm working for a secret government project studying psychic abilities. Got that?"

"Yeah, so what're we really doing?"

"Getting ready. We're on a deadline. Tomorrow evening the Fliers are taking out Avery Metcalf at a rally in Philadelphia. That's where Lisa Jenkins will announce that Metcalf is her running mate."

"*Taking out*? As in...killing?" I asked.

"That's the plan. Novak is enraged that Metcalf has turned on him."

"How long have you known about this plan?" Jamie asked.

"I didn't know the specifics until two hours ago. But I've suspected something like this would be coming up ever since Novak ordered the killings on death row."

Jamie's unease was obvious. "Can't we just warn Metcalf?"

"And say what...that invisible attackers are coming after him? That would go over well. Jenkins's Secret Service detail would investigate you as a potential threat." Danny shook his head. "Don't do it."

"Then what's our plan?" I asked.

"To be there, out of body, of course, and to protect Metcalf without getting identified by the Fliers."

"That's not a plan, that's a goal," I countered. "How do we do it?"

"Hang on, I'm getting there, Jake. We have the advantage that there will be a crowd, and you two will be among them. Even if one of the Fliers sees you, he won't know that you're out of body unless you approach him and say something. I walked right past you in the bar in Charlotte, Jake, and you didn't know I was out, not until I started talking to you. Rule No. 1, don't confront any of the Fliers. Don't reveal yourselves."

"Good points," Jamie said. "But what can we do besides watch?"

"You want to get as close to the stage as you can. No one will stop you, of course. They're going to look for an opportunity to push Metcalf head-first into the orchestra pit. You want to position yourselves to break his fall."

That made no sense to me. "How can we do that? He'll fall right through us. We came here right through a wall."

"That's your lesson today, how to manipulate matter." Danny stepped forward and reached for the quilt that hung over the corner of the bed. His fingers went through the material as if it wasn't there. "See, I can't pick it up. But now watch."

Danny rubbed his hands together, turned his palms toward the quilt, and wriggled his fingers. He reminded me of a magician about to perform a trick. He patted the quilt lightly, and after several taps it started to move. "It's a mind thing. You put your mind to it and believe strongly that you can manipulate physical objects. Try it. First, try to feel the texture."

I duplicated his hand gestures and imagined that I was touching and moving the quilt. It didn't move. My fingers slipped through the material as if it wasn't there.

"Focus, Jake. Jamie can do it. So can you."

I patted again and it felt like cotton balls. If I could feel it, I could move it, I told myself. "There, it moved. I saw it. I'm doing it! It's moving."

"Good. Now pinch the materials between your fingers and tug on it."

I tried to grasp it, but the quilt slipped through my hand like water. "I can't hold it. It's not working."

"You're not using your intention, Jake," Jamie said. "Make it happen. Don't doubt it. Look." She tapped the quilt a few times, then clasped onto it and shook it." She made it look easy.

"Good one, Jamie," Danny said. "You do it now, Jake."

Annoyed now, I didn't think about it. I just reached down, grasped it, lifted it. "There, I did it. It works."

Danny stepped next to me. "Of course it works." He snagged the quilt, tugged, and backed away, dragging it off the bed, and off of Owens. He was curled in a semi-fetal position and wore baggy shorts and a voluminous t-shirt partially covering his more than ample belly fat. He gasped for breath, patted the bed in search of the quilt now puddled at the base of the bed. Then he sat up and looked around in confusion. "What the hell?"

He threw his blubbery legs over the side of the bed and hobbled to the end of it. He slowly bent over, mumbling something about slippery covers, and picked up the quilt. Danny, standing next to him, abruptly reached out, pinched his right cheek and gave his left cheek a firm pat. Owen cried out, dropped the quilt, and hurriedly waddled to the bathroom, slamming the door behind him.

"You scared the shit out of him, Danny," I said.

"That was just a little pat to wake him up to a bigger reality."

"I don't think it will work," Jamie chimed in. "Not with him."

"Do you think you could catch him if he stumbled and fell?" I asked Danny.

"Not his bulk, but I could catch his head, and that's what you two need to do if Metcalf falls off the stage. Go for his head." He looked around the bedroom. "Ah, our friend is a football fan." He walked over and snatched a football from a shelf. He played catch with himself, tossing it up and catching it a few times. He looked at me. "Get ready, Jake." He spiraled the ball underhand at my chest. I raised my hands to catch it, but it literally shot through my hand and then through my chest.

"Not good, Jake. You've got to focus your intention, know that you can do it. Push the ball over here with your foot."

I peered down at the ball and saw that it was inscribed with player autographs, probably the Carolina Panthers. I gave it a kick, but my foot sliced through it, and I felt like Charlie Brown after Lucy pulled the ball away. Remembering what I did with the quilt, I tapped the ball lightly with the inside of my foot, like a soccer player preparing to make a penalty shot. After several repetitions, I felt the ball against my foot, and the next kick sent it rolling over to Danny.

He picked up the ball. "Ready. Focus. Catch."

He tossed it gently over to me. This time I caught it. Excited by my success, I slammed it onto the floor and it rolled over to the bathroom door. It was slightly open and Owens was peering out. As the ball rolled toward him, he slammed the door shut again. What could he be thinking after watching his football seemingly moving around the room by itself?

"I think you two are as ready as you'll ever be. The event starts at four, but Fliers aren't arriving until five o'clock."

"Wait a minute. How am I supposed to get out at that time?"

Danny laughed. "I figured you'd ask that question. The answer is don't sleep very long tonight and take antihistamines a couple of hours before launch time to make you drowsy. Nap time is flying time."

"I hope I can get out and find the rally."

"Big events with crowds and energy are easy to find. But if you think it'll help, you can look up the location on Jenkins's website."

I started to feel as if I might be pulled back to my body at any moment. But Danny wasn't done with us yet. "One more thing. See if you two can put the quilt back on the bed."

Jamie and I moved to opposite sides of the bed. I was more confident this time and after brushing my hand over the surface a few times, I lifted my side of the quilt. Jamie did the same with her side, and we slowly pulled the quilt over the bed. I looked back at Danny, who nodded in the direction of the bathroom. Owens was standing by the door, staring at the bed. He suddenly made a loud keening sound of a man who had bolted awake in his worst nightmare. He swayed from side to side a couple of times, then crumpled to the floor.

"Jesus, Danny. I hope we didn't kill him," Jamie exclaimed.

Danny stepped forward, leaned over and touched the side of Owens' throat, moving his fingers around for half a minute. "I can't find a pulse in that thick neck, but that doesn't mean anything. If he is dead, he died of fright."

The room started to fade, and the last thing I saw was Owen starting to sit up and calling out, "Dear God."

9

From his position on the edge of the stage, Bill Waters gazed out over the crowd that nearly filled the 10,000-seat auditorium. Avery Metcalf was about to make his first public appearance since Waters had received his orders, and the Fliers were here to prevent him from becoming Lisa Jenkins's running mate. But there was a problem. He had studied the stage design and had been concerned that the podium might be placed too far from the edge of the stage to make it feasible to trip Metcalf and hurl him head-first, like a dive-bombing osprey, into the orchestra pit.

As it turned out, that wasn't the issue. The floor of the pit apparently was on a lift of some sort, and it had been raised to the stage level. Now the edge of the stage was near the first row, which was only three feet below the stage. Metcalf would probably land in someone's lap, like a basketball player falling off the court into the first rows of seats. He might be hurt and embarrassed, but chances were he would survive. That wasn't the plan.

Waters had very little time to cook up something new. The mayor of Philadelphia was at the podium and about to introduce Jenkins, who would no doubt talk up her campaign and Metcalf for a few minutes before bringing him on stage.

Damn, it would be so much easier to eliminate him away from a crowd. Like at home in his bedroom. But Novak wanted the impact of a public death, preferably in the presence of Lisa Jenkins, rather than the report of a so-called terrible accident.

That might be a fine strategy, but from a tactical point of view, killing Metcalf in public had some shortfalls. Pulling it off was a challenge, one that Waters found both thrilling and dangerous. Thrilling because of the goddamned audacity of it, and the sense of power that came with the ability to make physical contact, to maneuver and constrict. Dangerous, though, because the president was a player. If Novak was willing to knock off his opponent's proposed running mate, he might also be ready to dissemble the Fliers if things went bad…or turned too weird for the public to comprehend. Would he let them walk away as if none of their undercover dealings had ever happened? Waters had his doubts about that, especially after Novak's none-too-subtle reference to Lance Wallen's death.

Waters had selected three Fliers to join him, Harris, Wilhelm, and Danny. All the Fliers had expressed their willingness to be on the strike team, which pleased him. But he couldn't help wondering if their support reflected suspicions about Wallen's demise after he rebelled against killing inmates.

The Philadelphia mayor wrapped up her introduction for Jenkins, and the senator came out on stage to thunderous applause and cheers, shouts and whistles and waving banners. Waters motioned to Harris and Wilhelm, who were standing a few feet away. "Let's go backstage and get him."

He looked for Danny and spotted him on the opposite side of the stage. He was peering down toward the front rows at something or someone. What the hell was he doing? Was he talking to someone? He took a few steps toward Danny, and now he could see a man and a woman standing in the aisle. What the hell! If he was talking to them, they were travelers. Danny abruptly turned and met his gaze across the stage. Waters motioned for him, and Danny took two steps and launched into a long acrobatic leap, landing next to him.

Waters shook his head. "Too bad nobody out there saw that impressive move. Unless you think some freelance travelers have shown up for the event."

Danny shrugged. "It's too early for typical night fliers. But I invited my apprentices. They're here to try out for Lance's spot. I figured I'd let them play with the big boys."

"Christ, Danny. That's wasn't very smart. You're exposing us to outsiders. That could be trouble."

"What're they going to do, report us to the cops? I don't think so. Besides, they both know what we're up to, and they agreed to come."

Waters looked past Danny. The two were now on stage and headed their way.

Our plan to save Metcalf by catching his head as he tumbled off stage never sounded like a winner to me. But I didn't have any other suggestions. So I wasn't greatly displeased to discover that the orchestra pit was no longer a pit, but part of the stage. But what was the new plan? Jamie and I were at a loss. Four Fliers, including Danny, were on stage and from our perspective looked like bodyguards. But of course Jamie and I were the only ones who could see them.

Danny spotted us standing at the base of an aisle and walked over to the corner of the stage. He motioned us to join him. Neither one of us moved. "Danny, I thought you didn't want us to be seen by the others," I called up to him. I was still amazed that we could hold this conversation and nobody around us could see or hear us. Not even the Secret Service agent who stood five feet away, continually scanning the crowd.

"New plan, now you're on a tryout with me. No need to hide from the others. They'll get it."

"Yeah, but how are we going to prevent Metcalf from getting killed? Isn't that our purpose?" Jamie said.

"I know. I know. Let's see what happens. Do your best to screw things up without making it obvious."

Great, I thought. How the hell were we going to do that, and what would be the consequences? At that moment, Danny turned and vaulted across the stage as if he were attached to wires and performing a ballet. "What do you think?" I asked Jamie.

"I guess we can try jumping up on stage, if he can do that!"

I was tempted to make a much bigger leap right back to my bed where I'd laid down for a nap, but I wasn't about to abandon Jamie. "Then let's go."

With that, we both moon-walked onto the stage. The audience applauded and for a moment I imagined they admired our dual leap. But the mayor had just completed her talk and Lisa Jenkins was waving from the podium. I felt the energy and excitement in the crowd behind us, and I couldn't imagine how that would change if the Fliers had their way. We had to stop them, but how?

Waters led the Fliers backstage, easily brushing past the Secret Service and other security players stationed near the rear corners of the stage. The guards might've felt a momentary breeze or chill, nothing more. Waters looked around in confusion. The backstage area was divided into several sections by curtains attached to frames. They reminded him of privacy curtains in hospitals. He heard voices from one of the sectioned areas, took two long steps over to it, and peered through an opening.

Metcalf was a slightly-built middle-aged man with thinning hair. Seated at a table, he was engrossed in a conversation with a kid in his twenties who sported short pink hair shaved at the sides with tats covering his neck. Numerous piercings dotted both ears and his lower lip. Pink Head was showing something to Metcalf on a handheld device and explaining what it meant. The technical jargon was meaningless to Waters.

He looked back and saw Danny, Harris, and Wilhelm awaiting instructions. The latter two, out of body as well as in, looked menacing, both standing at least six and half feet, burly and muscular like linemen in the NFL. Where were the other two—Danny's so-called apprentices? Had they bailed already? What a mistake on Danny's part to break them into the Fliers' world on this mission. Unbelievable. If they were even still around, they'd better just stay out of the way.

The kid was an unexpected complication, and it didn't

look like he was going to leave before Metcalf went on stage. Metcalf, for his part, seemed unconcerned about the address he was expected to give, but was clearly focused on whatever he and Pink Head were babbling about. Waters knew they could take out both of them, two on one. They literally would never know what hit them. Maybe they could drag Metcalf out onto the stage and finish the job there. But they would have to stand him up and avoid making it look like he was being dragged across the stage.

Waters motioned for the other Fliers to encircle the table. Not only did they have the advantage in numbers as well as the element of surprise on their side, but they could speak among themselves without being heard. "Okay, as soon as I lunge for Metcalf, Danny, you pull out the chair from under the kid and hold him down. Harris, you back up Danny, and make sure the kid doesn't get away. Wilhelm, grab Metcalf by the throat, and I'll help you walk him to the podium. That's where you finish the job. Got that?"

Wilhelm nodded. Waters had chosen the big guy, a former Marine, because he'd seen Wilhelm, while out of body, lift a man off his feet at a park where the guy was badgering a woman.

Metcalf would die by the same means as the death-row inmates, but this time it would get a lot of attention. Waters couldn't wait to see the video. His death would be puzzling, to say the least. It didn't matter how many investigators were put on the case, no one was going to catch them. Even if one of the Danny's new recruits turned on them, where was the evidence? There wouldn't be any. Who would believe such a crazy story, especially if he had the chance to doctor the medical records of the complainant and show that the person had mental issues.

Just as Waters took a step toward Metcalf, Pink Head stood up. "Okay, Avery, I got it under control. Good luck with your talk, Mr. Future Vice-President."

"Let him go, Danny." It was better that way, easier with only Metcalf to deal with. Pink Hair patted Metcalf on the shoulder and walked away. Metcalf didn't move, his eyes were closed now. He looked as if he were meditating, awaiting the moment. Now, perfect timing, Waters thought.

A loud thud from the stage distracted him. Shouts, commotion, gasps, screams. What the hell was going on? Metcalf slipped away and raced toward the stage. Waters and the others pursued him.

It was a rude thing to do and would cause chaos, but I didn't see any other option. Whether or not we could act in time to save Metcalf's life was debatable. But an idea came to mind as we trailed after the Fliers, who were headed backstage. I grasped Jaimie's arm and she felt surprisingly physical to me. I told her my plan.

We cautiously approached the podium where Jenkins was speaking. I felt like an invader, an invisible one. In fact, that was exactly what we were. We stood next to the podium less than three feet away from Jenkins, five feet from a Secret Service agent. Jenkins had an open iPad and a piece of paper with some scrawled notes on the podium. I leaned closer and was able to read the capitalized words at the top: INTEGRITY, HONESTY, CAPABLE OF LEADING.

Jamie began tapping the side of the podium. I did the same. At first, it felt squishy, but as I focused and continued tapping, it hardened. I could tell that Jenkins was getting close to introducing Metcalf. I glanced at Jamie. She nodded. We raised our hands and pushed the podium. All it did was rock, and Jenkins' note fluttered to the floor.

"We've got to push harder," I said.

"Wait. I've got an idea. You push on your side on three." Jamie stepped back three feet from the podium. "One...two... three." As I pushed, Jamie leaped forward and applied a powerful sidekick to the podium. Of course, she was a blackbelt!

The podium tilted and crashed, and the top of it broke apart from the base. A microphone screeched as if in pain. Two seconds passed as everyone froze and stared. Not good enough, I thought, and lunged for Jenkins and jerked her down to the floor.

She shrieked and started scrambling away. Her political allies behind her scattered. I rolled away as Secret Service agents rushed forward amid shouts and cries from the audience.

Everyone must've thought it was a terrorist attack. The crowd stampeded toward the door, the aisles jammed. Two agents pulled Jenkins to her feet and rushed toward a side door. Right behind them two more agents guided Metcalf to the exit.

A surprisingly calm, but firm voice boomed over the public address system. "Please leave the auditorium in an orderly manner, folks. We are simply taking precautions."

There was nothing more for us to do. Jamie and I had ruined Lisa Jenkins's introduction of her vice-presidential candidate, but we also probably saved his life. I spotted Danny amid a dozen or more security people who had flooded the stage. He met my gaze with a worried look, waved me away, and that was all I needed. I glanced around and saw that Jamie was already gone.

I focused on my apartment and my bed, and suddenly I was soaring right through the roof of the auditorium and out into the dusk, picking up speed, and again felt that odd sensation of air blasting against my cheeks. I blinked a couple of times and covered six hundred miles. I caught my breath and sat up in bed.

Damn, we did it. We stopped the Fliers. Now what?

I flopped back onto the bed for a couple of minutes and went over everything that had happened. In spite of my recent experiences, there remained a sense of the surreal when I recalled these OBEs. They were real and dreamlike at the same time. It felt like a dream, yet I knew for certain that I had traveled to that bar in Charlotte, to Max Owens's bedroom, and the auditorium in Philadelphia. I had not only witnessed real events but also but participated in them.

I sat up, threw my legs over the side, and hurried to the bathroom. After relieving myself, I splashed water on my face and stared in the mirror. I still felt vaguely disjointed, like I wasn't fully back yet. The incident in Philadelphia must be on the news by now, and I was curious about how they would cover it. TV Journalists and their camera crews had huddled on an elevated platform in the back of the auditorium and surely filmed the entire scenario. I dried my face, walked over to my couch, slumped down, and aimed the remote.

CNN came on with Anderson Cooper standing outside the auditorium in Philadelphia. "Avery Metcalf was to be anointed this evening in Philadelphia as Lisa Jenkins's running mate. But Metcalf was shot just minutes ago after a bizarre incident on stage."

"What the fuck," Jake murmured.

"Both Senator Jenkins and Metcalf were quickly escorted out of the auditorium by security officials after the podium seemed to implode and crash, taking Jenkins to the floor. Secret Service agents rushed her and Metcalf outside. Metcalf had been backstage and was about to join Jenkins at the podium when the incident occurred.

"Moments after he was outside, an unidentified man fired three shots at close range. Metcalf was rushed to a hospital. One of the agents shot and killed the assailant. The yet unnamed perpetrator was described as a white male in his late twenties. There is no known link between what happened on stage and the shooting that followed.

"Okay, here it is. Avery Metcalf did not survive the attack. He apparently died en route to hospital."

Jake's phone rang. He answered when he saw it was Jamie. "Are you watching this?" she asked.

"I just turned it on less than a minute ago. I can't believe it."

"I know. So much for saving his life."

Cooper disappeared from the screen, replaced by a video of the podium crashing, Jenkins falling and crawling away. I knew the video would be played endlessly over the next few days as experts analyzed it and tried to figure out what happened on stage. I had a bad feeling about it.

Waters was stunned by the news. Metcalf was dead. *Fin.* Finished. It happened in spite of the bumbling actions of Danny's recruits, who thought they would give the Fliers cover to kill Metcalf backstage. At least that was Danny's explanation. He couldn't think about that now. He needed to come up with his own explanation for Novak.

He'd first considered the idea that the killer was his backup plan in case something went wrong. But Dale Sutter, who he contacted immediately after the shooting, thought that was a terrible idea, and he realized Sutter was right. The CIA chief, it seemed, wasn't so much concerned about lying to the president as he was about giving Novak potential leverage over both of them.

His phone chimed, an incoming text. The name of the sender read: *Frank Furter*. Nobody he knew. With a name like that, it was probably a joke. He clicked onto it, just in case it was a friend.

"Was that YOUR back-up? I'll look for your full report tomorrow."

Whoa. Novak? Would he really be that audacious? Did he think a fake name couldn't eventually be traced to him?

He turned off the television, and darkness consumed the room. He stared at the ceiling, recalling Novak's last words to him. Politics will never be the same again. The phone chimed again with another text message, illuminating the room in a momentary moon glow. He picked it up from his bedside stand. The same name. Now what?

"Hey, bro, did I catch you napping? Bet you thought it was POTUS, didn't you?"

"Shit." Instead of texting a reply, he called Danny's cell. "What the fuck is wrong with you? Are you losing your mind? Instead of playing games with me, you should be apologizing for bringing those two dimwit amateurs to the event."

"Hey, relax. I just wanted to tell you they got a label on the kid. He worked with Metcalf and got fired last week. Security guys saw him standing out by Metcalf's car and questioned him. He said he was Metcalf's driver."

"Where are you getting this from?"

"Harris recognized a guy he knew working security inside the auditorium. He texted him, asked what he knew."

"It wasn't that pink-haired kid, was it?"

"Don't you know who that was? Wayne Somebody. A weird genius. Metcalf tapped him to hold the reins on his company—at least the tech side—while he was campaigning."

"You're a smart guy, Danny-Boy. You're also damned lucky that Metcalf got taken out after your two clowns screwed things up. I never want to see either of them again. Who are they, anyhow? You were supposed to send me their profiles."

"I didn't have time. As I told you, one's a teacher, the woman is a part-time psychic and freelance writer."

"Well, she better not write about us. I'll leave it at that. They are *out*, got it? But *you* are going to keep an eye on them to make sure they don't start talking. Are we clear?"

"Of course, Billy-Bro. I'm on it. But I'm not worried. We're too unbelievable to be taken seriously, if they tried to expose us."

"Yeah, that's what we keep saying. Let's hope it's true."

"Trust me, those two are probably scared shitless right now for screwing things up."

He hung up. Fucking brother. He loved him, but he could be annoying, and someday he would tell him that he didn't like it when people said, "Trust me." Whenever Indiana Jones expressed that sentiment, it always meant just the opposite.

RIVEREÑOS

BY T. J. MACGREGOR

Eva waits on the upper deck for him, in the sweet lushness of the Peruvian night. There is enough starlight to see the black shape of the jungle on shore. She feels its weight pressing up against her, an impenetrable wall, impossibly rich and dense. Below her, the muddy Amazon rushes past, whispering in some ancient tongue, dark and seductive.

She isn't sure what she's doing here, waiting for a man who isn't her husband, a man she met, in fact, only yesterday when she boarded the boat. This isn't something she has done before. She has been happily married for more than ten of her thirty-six years. She and her husband own an import shop on Miami Beach, and she has been traveling through Colombia and Peru buying native art and crafts. A simple trip. Purposeful. But there's something about the heat and smells here in the upper Amazon that stirs a deep fever in the blood, a delirium of need, a certain eroticism that stalks the dormant self.

"One Pisco sour," says Pablo, coming up behind her.

His cool mouth brushes the back of her neck, and the bright burn of her betrayal blazes inside of her as she turns, smiling, and takes the drink. It's a local whiskey concoction as mysterious and powerful as the river, and it scorches a path down her gullet.

"Any more of these, and I won't be seeing tomorrow."

Pablo chuckles. "No problem. The doctor here has many cures for hangovers." Despite his accent, his voice is buttery and smooth and slides through her in much the same way the voice of the river does. He touches the small of her back and tilts his head toward the hammocks, an invitation that implies more than she may be willing to give. "It is more comfortable over there," he says.

She hesitates, but not for long, and moves toward the hammocks. They settle into the same one, both of them slipping toward the middle until their shoulders seam. He leans back and stretches out his legs, sandals pushing against the pole until the hammock starts swaying. His nearness, the heat of his skin, the boundless sky overhead: all of it makes her heart drum. She feels lightheaded, not quite herself, and sips quickly at her drink. Its chill paralyzes her esophagus, but her insides are as hot as the night air. Such extremes are symptomatic of something, but she isn't sure if it's physical or mental. Perhaps both.

She asks him to point out the Southern Cross. His arm lifts, and a long finger points slightly off to her left. "There. See it?"

It takes Eva a few moments to find it. But detecting the cross is a bit like recognizing a fundamental truth: once she sees it, she can't imagine how she missed it before. It glistens against the black skin of the sky, a constellation unique to the southern hemisphere, a phenomenon as strange to her as the way water here, below the equator, swirls counterclockwise down a drain.

"It is not in the same place it was when I was a boy," he says.

She thinks he's joking and laughs. But his expression is so solemn, he reminds her of her husband when he's driving himself crazy during tax season, juggling the store's books within the parameters the tax code allows. An honest man, her husband, a prince whose world is as distant from Pablo's as Neptune is from the sun.

"Really. It is not a joke, Eva. All things here transform. The sky, the jungle, the river, the animals. Everything. You know the pink dolphins we saw this morning?"

"Sure." The dolphins, pink as bubble gum, followed the ship for nearly an hour at dawn. They leaped from the muddy river in graceful, shimmering arcs, water shooting from their blowholes, then dived again. It was as if they were escorting the ship through a treacherous zone.

The pink dolphins, he explains, are the best known of the changers. Sometimes, when there are festivals in the villages, they come ashore as men. You can always tell a dolphin/man because he's wearing a white suit and a white hat that covers his blowhole. He dances with the prettiest woman, charming her, mesmerizing her, until she consents to go away with him. Then he whisks her to his underwater city and makes love to her. When her child is born, he too has the magic to transform. "This is the Amazon's way of keeping itself alive and vital, part of the web."

The dolphin did it: it sounds like a good way to explain an illegitimate birth, so a woman doesn't lose respect in her village. But Eva keeps her opinion to herself because the myth is real to Pablo. It's an intimate part of his roots, roots that bind him despite his self-education, his contemporary veneer, his Westernization. He is, after all, an Indian who was born and raised on this river. Perhaps that is the source of her attraction to him.

"What other creatures transform?" she asks.

He speaks softly, in the voice of the river. "Many. And they change in a variety of ways. We call them rivereños."

She has heard the term. It refers to Peruvians who move back and forth between life on the river and life in the city, existing in two worlds, but belonging to neither.

Music blasts from the lower deck, American music. The Rolling Stones. Pablo's foot taps to the rhythm. The music is out of place here and irritates her, reminds her of home, of the husband whose face, even now, seems less clear to her than it was yesterday or even this morning. She tries to shut it out, to focus on the music of the river instead.

As this old ship, which once hauled rubber up and down the Amazon, moves deeper and deeper into the jungle, her other life seems to be fading, becoming less real. Perhaps by the time they reach the city of Iquitos she will have no memory at all of her former self; her conscience will be as flawless as an infant's. A nice thought, but she knows it won't happen. She has an excellent memory. She will recall every detail, every nuance of tonight—the sharp, bitter taste of the Pisco sours, the heat of his arm as it slides around her shoulders, the smell of the river, even the way the shape of his mouth changes as it seeks hers. Her memory, which has often been her salvation, will become her curse. Maybe in the end, she will be like the rivereños, resident of two worlds, citizen of neither.

She stares at herself in the tarnished mirror in her cabin's bedroom, expecting to see another woman looking back at her, a woman she has never met. But her face is the same. The dark eyes remain a shade too small, too widely set. The cheekbones are still prominent, the chin rounded, the nose too straight. Her features, in fact, seem clearly defined, oddly American, obvious. Only her hair looks different, the blond so pale it's nearly white, as if she's standing in a pool of jungle light.

Eva shucks her T-shirt and turns on the shower. Not much pressure, but the water is hot. She stands under the paltry spray longer than necessary, eyes squeezed shut against last night. But memories rise unbidden, a wild current of images and colors, scents and noises, and in the heart of it is her husband's face, a sharp picture, hurtful in its clarity. Her breath hitches in her chest. She presses her hands to her face, ashamed of her betrayal and her pleasure. She wants to cry but can't. The pain isn't deep enough. It lacks power, conviction, reality, because given her druthers, she would make the same choice again. And again.

Later, as she's drawing a comb through her wet hair, she notices a mark on her neck, a bruise, where he sucked at her skin. *A hickey*, she thinks, and starts to laugh, a quick, fluted sound, false. She pulls at the skin with her fingers, trying to get a better look at it. She hasn't had one of these since high school, when they were a statement of possession, of territory, like a ring dangling from a chain at your throat. How long will it take to fade, anyway? Two days? Three? She will be back in the States the day after tomorrow. Steve, her husband, will notice it. He has always seen things that aren't meant to be seen. He will comment on it, ask what it is, how she got it. A bite, she will say. Something bit her one night when they were out on the skiffs, in one of the black water tributaries. She will lie for the first time in ten years of marriage, and he will believe her because he has no reason not to.

All day, the collar of her shirt is turned up so it hides the mark. She stays away from the other passengers, loses herself in a book in a hammock on the upper deck, her solitude a kind of penance.

2

"You avoid me," Pablo says.

It's just the two of them, sitting across from each other at the long wooden table in the dining room.

"What?" She laughs a little, as though she hasn't understood what he said. Dusk fills the windows in front of her and slides up against her back, warm, humid, beckoning. "You. Avoid. Me." His jaw is set, stubborn, and his face is hard, more Indian than she recalls. "Yes?"

"No, of course not. Why should I avoid you?"

Pablo covers her hand with his own, trapping it like a small bird, and strokes her knuckles with his thumb. Small, smooth strokes that promise more of last night, a universe of pleasure. She gently pulls her hand back.

"You will have my children, Eva." A smile shadows his mouth, and his dark eyes are so intense the back of her neck prickles with alarm. She pushes away from the table.

"I'm not having anyone's children." She hurries out of the dining room and feels his gaze against her spine, a hot, relentless pulse.

3

The skiff putts through the still waters of a tributary as black as the sky, the din of its Suzuki motor competing with the jungle noises along the bank. They are out here looking for caiman, although Eva isn't sure what's supposed to happen if they spot one. Probably nothing. The point of the trip is to experience the river at night.

Eva and six other passengers are crowded together in the

skiff, with a guide at the back who steers the boat and Pablo standing at the front like an Indian chief ferrying his tribe to a safer place. The beam of his flashlight dances across the shore. Branches close off the sky. The press of the jungle is oppressive, claustrophobic. She winces every time a branch brushes across the back. Her heart leaps when something splashes in the river several feet from the boat. The stink of insect repellent mixes with the smell of water and trees. The stuff coats her skin, her shoes and hair, her clothes, and radiates from everyone else as well, a ludicrous testimony of civilization. But all of them are immunized against yellow fever, diphtheria, typhoid. They have quinine tablets, Kaopectate, antibiotics. They drink bottled water and Pepsi without ice and don't eat salads. They follow the rules. But what immunization is there, Eva wonders, for what ails her?

"There!" Pablo hisses, and the beam of light fixes on a pair of red orbs glowing from the dark wall of trees on shore. "A caiman." Goosebumps erupt on her arms as the driver cuts the engine.

The sudden absence of sound is quickly filled by jungle noises. Frogs, screeches, rustling in the trees, fish splashing in the black waters. The red orbs vanish. Pablo's flashlight darts right, left, searching, finding nothing. He grabs onto a nearby branch, pulling the skiff closer to shore, then leaps off, bare feet sinking into the mud. The night sucks him into itself. For a few seconds, Eva hears him clicking his tongue against the roof of his mouth, as if he's calling to the caiman. Then she hears only the jungle and the excited murmurs of voices in the skiff.

Someone asks where Pablo went. The driver pats the air with his hands and whispers, "To find the caiman."

Now that the boat has stopped, mosquitos swarm around their heads. She slides the hood of her windbreaker over her hair, sprays herself with Off, then passes it on when someone asks for it. Something swoops low over the skiff and a woman on board yelps.

"Bats!" exclaims one woman.

"Ssshh," scolds the driver.

A scuffling in the brush, a shriek, then laughter. Pablo and a man emerge from the trees. *"Un amigo,"* Pablo shouts to the driver, slapping his companion on the back. *"Un buen amigo."*

"What happened to the caiman?" someone asks.

"He was too fast," Pablo replies as he and his companion climb aboard.

The stranger is tall, compact, muscular, with dark hair and the sharp features of an Indian. His eyes seem to glow in the dark.

All things here transform.

She stares at the stranger.

He's one of them.

No way.

A rivereño.

Hysteria bubbles in her throat as Pablo settles at the stern and the stranger sits across from her. She barely resists the urge to get up and move to the back of the skiff. Eva stares at her feet, hands clasped tightly in her lap, and forces herself to take long, deep breaths. She tries to conjure details from her other life—the color of her bedroom, the scents in the shop on Miami Beach, the shape of her husband's face. But the Amazon has swallowed all of it.

She hears Pablo say, "The insects they do not bother me," and looks up. He's holding the can of Off, her can, and now he tosses it toward her. "Catch, Eva."

She misses it. The damn thing rolls noisily across the floor of the skiff. She reaches for it, but the stranger plucks it up first and holds it out like an offering. She blinks and for an instant, sees a hand that is leathery, like a caiman's hide. She blinks again and sees skin. Her imagination. But if he *is* a caiman, then what is Pablo?

Stop it.

Pablo and the stranger are only men. She silently repeats this. *Men, they are men.* Her panic begins to ebb. She's tired, that's all, tired and confused and a little frightened. The jungle exhausts her. Makes her see things that aren't there.

She takes the Off from him and murmurs her thanks. For a beat or two, their eyes meet. His impale her. She looks quickly away and shoves the can in her bag. The mark at her neck burns and itches. The skiff rocks as the engine cranks up and chugs farther into the tunnel of trees. The thick richness of the river fills her, intoxicating her. She's afraid to lift her gaze, to look too closely at the stranger, but she can't resist the temptation to see if his eyes really glow or if it was only another trick of the jungle, the dark. She raises her head. The stranger already watches her, smiling as if he has been waiting for her to do exactly this, and for just an instant, his eyes burn pink.

Eva wrenches her gaze away and hugs her arms around her, air congealed in her lungs like blood.

4

Heat, so much heat. It blazes a path through the center of her being, baking her from the inside out, blackening her organs, her muscles and sinews, her skin. She's dreaming, she knows she is, but she can't break out of the dream; it has snared her, it holds her, it whispers to her in the voice of the river, the jungle. *You are mine. I have claimed you, you are mine, mine.* The voice rises and falls inside her, echoing, and becomes Pablo's voice. *You will have my children…*

Now he moves through the steaming green of the jungle, coming for her. Eva can't see him, but she senses him, feels him advance through the trees, the underbrush. She catches his scent in the humid air, a wild, musky scent, not human.

She runs, crashing through the jungle. Branches snap back in her face. Roots spring from the black soil, tangled, gnarled, blocking her path. A monkey swings in front of her, chattering, teeth bared. She cuts left. Parrots squawk and fuss, and a flock of them lift from the trees, wings beating the hot air. Her head jerks around. She still can't see him, but he's close, very close, and she hears him breathing, hears the jungle opening up for him, helping him. Vines tangle in her hair and seize her ankles.

Eva stumbles and tries to catch herself, but she pitches forward with a scream, into the dark, wet foliage. Leaves the size of cats slap wetly across her face, blinding her. They squeeze around her arms, trapping her, holding her against the ground.

Branches clamp around her ankles like vises. Her legs snap open. Her clothes are gone. Insects scurry across her belly, her breasts, her face. Something squats on her eyelid. A worm burrows into her ear.

Mine, you are mine, you will have my children, he whispers in the voice of the jungle, the river, the wildness.

"Señora? Señora?"

Eva bolts forward, frantic, a scream already rolling down her tongue, and stares into the face of a pretty flight attendant. *I'm on the plane, on my way home.* Giddy with relief, she says she's okay, really, she is, and asks for a glass of water. When the flight attendant has walked off, Eva's hands tighten against the arm rest. She smooths her palms over her slacks, touches her fingertips to the cool glass of the window. Real, all of it real.

She peers out into the endless blue sky, thinking of home, of her husband, of the life she can barely remember, but which she nonetheless is rushing home to claim. She will return to the woman she has been for the last ten years, and everything will be fine, just fine. The memories of the jungle and the mark on her neck will fade.

They will.

They have to.

5

Her husband believes her story, that she was bitten by something. Maybe you should see a doctor, he says. No need, she replies, the mark is fading.

But it doesn't fade. Within seventy-two hours of her return, it seems to be swelling. She touches it during the day when she's at the shop, feels it at night when she lies awake in the dark, examines it every morning to see if it's larger or redder. Within a week, she feels a hardness just under the skin, a cyst, a knot, something that wasn't there yesterday.

She hurries into the bathroom at the back of the shop. Shuts the door. Locks it. She's trembling. She hears Pablo whispering of transformation, rivereños, his voice slick and warm. She slaps her hands over her ears, struggling against the seduction of that voice, and when she's silent inside, she turns down her collar and scrutinizes her neck in the mirror.

Eva can see the lump. It fits perfectly within the borders of the red mark, a hard nub shaped like a bullet. It looks like a birthmark or an allergy of some kind. But of course it isn't.

Her fingers touch it gently. It moves from side to side like a glob of fat in water. She presses her palm over it and feels heat, the intense jungle heat that steams, oppresses, stalks, kills. Something is inside her, she felt something inside her, Jesus, she can feel it sinking deeper and deeper into her muscles, tendons, bones, taking root inside her.

6

"I want it cut out."

Her family doctor smiles and shakes his head. "I think that's a little drastic, Eva. It's a mosquito bite that's gotten infected. A good dose of Amoxicillin should take care of it. I'll give you a prescription."

"Okay, but I still want it cut out." She hears the quaver in her voice, the incipient hysteria. "I don't like it there."

"The cyst is the infection, hon. Trust me, okay?"

She has known him for twenty years, and of course she trusts him. He removed her tonsils, her appendix, has treated her for colds and the flu. Trust. He gives her an injection, writes a prescription, and she takes it to the pharmacy next door to be filled. Amoxicillin is a derivative of penicillin, the wonder drug. Can it battle jungle magic? Will it silence the soft whispers in her head? Will it obliterate the nightmares? The memories? The mark? Yes, yes, yes.

On her way back to the shop, the sweet beach air fills the car and the hot sun beats the hood and the drug rushes through her bloodstream, working miracles. She tells herself that the throb in her neck, the movement deep inside the cyst, is nothing but her imagination, and she almost believes it.

Almost.

7

Three days later, a Sunday. The weather is warm, the sky a clear, hot blue. She and Steve are playing softball with friends in a park near their house. She's the pitcher, and Steve is coming to bat. He flashes her a grin as he steps up to the plate, a smile that challenges, and she grins back.

Her arm swings, and she lobs the ball. It arcs into the cobalt sky, high and smooth, and floats down across the plate. Steve smacks it. The crack echoes across the field, and the ball zips toward her.

But before Eva can react, it slams into the side of her neck and the impact knocks her to the ground. Black dots swim in her eyes. Dust swirls in her nostrils. She's sprawled in the dirt. Her head aches. Her neck feels like it has been severed. People are shouting. She's trying to sit up.

Her hand jerks to her neck and she feels something warm and wet. When she brings her hand away, she screams. It's covered with them. Hundreds of them. *Spiders.* They scamper over her hand and up her arms and into her hair and down the front of her shirt and across her face. She screams and screams as she leaps up, trying to brush them away, to get them off. But there are so many of them, and they keep pouring out of her neck, some of them covered with her blood, others as clear as cellophane. Eva claws at her neck, digs her fingers into the hole where they had nested, and scoops them out, her screams still shredding the air.

The breeze lifts the smallest ones. The trails of its web as they rise into the sky look like tiny kites, and even as she shrieks, Pablo's voice is everywhere, whispering, *You will have my children.*

Forever whispering.

THE UNIT

BY T. J. MACGREGOR

I live in The Unit, where the nurses and orderlies smile all the time and speak in loud voices, as though they think we're all hard of hearing. But I'm not. My hearing is sharp, always has been. It's just my mind that is sometimes fuzzy.

Right now, I can hear Jim across the hall, whimpering in his sleep. I can hear the whisper of the cat's paws as she prowls the dimly lit, silent hallway. And more distantly, I hear the squeaking of the orderly's shoes against the floor as he makes his way from one room to another, delivering meds. I can tell from his gait that the orderly tonight is Dan, a hulking bulk of a man with rippling biceps.

Whenever a resident falls, the nurses send Dan to get the person situated in a chair or in bed. Whenever residents of The Unit wander off, Dan is the bloodhound who brings them back. I don't like him. Beneath his engaging smile, his courtesy, the way he addresses residents by their first names like he's some long lost relative, lurks something darker. He's the bogeyman in the closet, the shadow that hides beneath the bed, the monsters both great and small that my son Steve feared when he was a toddler.

Steve is now fifty. I once told him what I thought about Dan, and he rolled his eyes and told me it was my *imagination*. That's the word people use with dementia and Alzheimer's patients who report that their spouses or siblings, who are dead, dropped by for a visit. "Mom, Dan's a great guy, a terrific orderly. Everyone here loves him."

"Who's everyone?" I asked.

We were sitting in the atrium when we had this conversation. I remember how the sunlight angled through the window, spilled across the potted plants, and melted over Steve's face, revealing the new wrinkles his second divorce had carved at the corners of his eyes. The new threads of gray in his beard, his hair. Right then, he looked older than me, and I'm pushing eighty.

"Everyone on the staff, the administration, family members, they all love him," Steve said.

"But none of the residents do."

Steve just shook his head. *Mom, the hopeless case.*

The squeaking in the hallway stops, and I hear Dan greeting one of the residents up the hall. Then I hear muffled voices and giggling and suddenly, Gretchen slips into my room, Lucy right behind her. Gretchen is dressed in a suit and high heels and wears a soft blue sunhat the same color as her suit. Lucy wears a bathrobe and floppy Snoopy slippers, and her gray hair is uncombed, wild. They hurry over to where I'm sitting.

"Hey, Rachel, you coming into the city with us?" Gretchen asks, voice hushed, eyes bright with excitement. "We're going to see *Hair.*"

She never remembers that my name is Rose, not Rachel, but I don't correct her. I also don't tell her that she and Lucy live in South Florida, not in New York anymore, and that *Hair* opened on Broadway in April 1968 and ran for 1,750 performances. There's nothing wrong with my long-term memory. But I can't recall what I had for breakfast this morning or yesterday morning.

"Did you call a cab?" I ask.

"Yup," Lucy says, head bobbing. "Yup, sure did. It's on the way. We need to get outside, Rachel. C'mon, get dressed." This from the woman dressed like a cartoon character.

Before I reply, there's a soft rap at the door, and Dan the Man hurries into the room, pushing a meds cart. "Ladies, ladies." His massive hands, encased in sterile gloves, pat the air. "*What* is going on here?"

"*We* are going to the theater," Gretchen informs him.

"Ah, right." Dan nods. "To see *Hair*. I've heard it's terrific. Is the cab on the way?"

"Of course it is." Lucy sounds indignant. "We aren't walking all the way to Broadway. You want to join us?"

"Can't, ladies," Dan replies. "Have to work. But before you go, I've got something for you here." He eyes the cart, picks up a plastic bottle, shakes a med into the palm of his hand. "Here's yours, Lucy."

He hands it to her, and Lucy, who has been in The Unit longer than either Gretchen or me, pops it in her mouth and swallows it without water. She knows the drill. "C'mon, Gretchen, let's go."

Gretchen straightens the handbag that hangs from her shoulder, a beautiful black leather bag. "You coming, Rachel?"

"I think I'll pass." I hold up the book I've been trying to read. "Want to finish this."

"Before you leave, Gretchen, I've got a happy pill for you, too." Dan shakes another med into his palm.

"Thanks, but no thanks." Gretchen shakes her head. "I'm doing fine." She touches Lucy's arm and waves at me and Dan. "Catch you all later."

That darkness sweeps across Dan's face, fleeting, but real. It terrifies me. Then he moves swiftly toward the two women and grasps Gretchen's arm. She whips around so fast that her pretty blue sunhat slips off her head. I'm not sure if Dan spun her around or if she did it herself. She stumbles back, fire burning in her eyes. "You will NOT touch me that way," she snaps.

"Uh-oh, uh-oh," Lucy murmurs repeatedly, shaking her head. "Trouble, Dan is trouble, Gretchen is trouble, uh-oh," and she backs toward the door, shoulders twitching.

"Take the med, Gretchen, then go catch the goddamn taxi." Dan holds out his hand, the small red pill like a drop of blood in his gloved palm.

"Dan said bad word," Lucy says. "Bad word, goddamn, bad word. Shit, goddamn, bad word, bad word…" Lucy's hands fly to her face, and she shrieks, *"Bad man bad Dan bad man…"*

Her voice tears through the silence, and as Dan lurches toward her, I bolt to my feet and shove the med cart at him. It slams into his back, and he topples forward into Lucy, and they both crash to the floor. Lucy keeps shrieking, and Gretchen goes after Dan with her handbag, hitting it repeatedly over his head, his back, his legs, and screaming, "Get off her, you monster, get off of her!"

I lost my balance when I shoved the meds cart into him and am on my knees when wailing and squeals of terror erupt throughout The Unit. The alarm screams through the building, and the night nurse and three orderlies rush into the room. By then, Dan has rolled away from hysterical Lucy, who scoots across the floor away from him, alternately sobbing and sucking her thumb, her robe torn open, one of her Snoopy slippers in the doorway, as though it hoped to escape the chaos. Gretchen keeps swinging her bag and screaming that Dan grabbed her arm and tackled Lucy.

One of the orderlies subdues Gretchen, calms her enough to walk her out of my room, through the throng of residents now crowded around the door. The second orderly tends to Lucy and gets her to the edge of my bed. The third orderly hurries over to me.

"Rose? You okay?"

My hands clutch my aching knees. My heart throbs in my throat. I finally raise my gaze. Tony, the beautiful man from Kenya with skin the deep black of a moonless night, and dark chocolate eyes, is crouched in front of me, frowning, concerned. He usually works the day shift. I know we have talked at length about his wife and family in Kenya, but I no longer recall the specifics. My brain has become a sieve for the details of other people's lives. It barely has room to accommodate details about my own life. It's tired, my brain is tired, so the small yesterday details have evaporated first.

"I… I think so."

Tony holds out his hand. "Let me help you up, Rose."

If he were Dan, that extended hand would be a trick. I hesitate, but not for long. My white, wrinkled hand clutches his, and the stark contrast between the colors of our respective skins, melded together like this, is so hauntingly beautiful I nearly weep. "Thank you." I can barely speak.

Once I'm standing, Tony helps me back to my chair. "What happened, Rose?"

"I'll tell you what the hell happened," Dan bellows. "She shoved the meds cart into me!"

"C'mon, man," Tony exclaims. "She can't move without her walker. She was freaked out and jumped up and *fell* into the cart."

The night nurse, Marsha, is a sinewy woman in her forties who looks like she may have a black belt in karate. She insinuates herself between the two men and thrusts her arms out to either side of her. "That's enough, gentlemen." She doesn't shout. She doesn't have to. Her voice carries such authority that even Dan is silenced. "We're now going to get Lucy back to her room, bring Rose a snack and a cup of hot chocolate, and we're going to my office for a chat."

Tony glances at me. "I'll get that snack, Rose."

Then he walks past Marsha and Dan, who are now scooping up the fallen meds and putting them back on the cart, and vanishes into the hall. Dan glares after him, then turns his attention to Marsha. "Look, I…"

"Shut up." The words hiss from her. "That's the kind of stuff we can get sued for. Get the cart outta here."

Dan hurls a hateful look my way, then slips out into the hall, where other orderlies and nurses are clearing away the bystanders. The alarm has stopped screaming. The Unit struggles to return to normalcy.

Marsha comes over and sits in the windowsill. "What happened, Rose? Can you tell me?"

"Gretchen wanted to go into the city to see *Hair*, and she and Lucy invited me to go. Dan wanted them to take their meds first and Gretchen refused. He… grabbed her arm." I blurt it out before it can vanish into the same black hole where yesterday's memories go. "I was scared. I…I leaped up…and fell into the cart…" And then I start to cry and press my silly, knotted fists against my eyes.

Marsha gives my shoulder a quick squeeze and leaves my room, her footfalls quick, certain, and audible for a long time. When my fists drop away from my eyes, the resident cat is sitting on the floor in front of me, staring at me. She leaps into my lap and settles down, purring loudly. She's a black and white tuxedo cat named Maddie, and I find comfort in her company.

2

I haven't seen Dan for days. I haven't seen Gretchen or Lucy, either. I've heard nothing about them through the grapevine, but when Jim sits next to me at breakfast, I have a feeling he knows something.

He's older than I am, this man who whimpers in his sleep. His bent spine is curved like a question mark, he hobbles around with a cane, his fingers are gnarled from arthritis, he's completely bald. Once upon a time, he was a Wall Street guy but got out before the market crashed and moved to Florida where his daughter and her family live. That was years ago. Now his grandchildren are grown. I don't know why he's in The Unit; his brain has fewer holes in it than mine.

"How're the pancakes, Rose?"

"Surprisingly delicious."

"You like those blueberries on top?"

"What's there not to like?"

He chuckles, even though what I said isn't funny at all. "I bet the color of Dan's bruised ego is a deeper blue than those blueberries," he whispers.

I look over at him, but his eyes are fixed on his plate of pancakes slathered in blueberries, on his cup of coffee, his juice, and the little pile of meds next to his spoon. I understand that he doesn't want the orderly on breakfast duty to pay any attention to us. "You willing to share or are you just teasing?" I ask.

He steals a glance at me; I can't read the strange expression in his pale blue eyes. "Share. The atrium. After breakfast."

Atrium is the code word all of us understand. As a nurse confided awhile back, it's the only place in The Unit—except for our rooms—that isn't rigged with security cams. It's the private place for residents and their visitors. But I worry that the administrators have lied about the privacy. I practiced criminal law for decades and learned to never trust anyone else's version of the truth.

Jim and I meet in the atrium awhile later. We sit at the deepest point, at the edge of a noisy fountain where sunlight pours through the glass above us, feeding all these gigantic ferns and other plants that are perpetually green, happy. Maddie follows us here and plops down in a slice of sunlight.

"Do you know what happened to Lucy when they took her back to her room that night?" Jim asks.

"I haven't heard anything."

"They shipped her out for electroshock treatment in Miami."

"They don't do electroshock anymore, Jim."

"They did it to Anne Sexton, the poet. You've read her, I know you have."

"That was in the sixties." Maybe his brain is riddled with more holes than I thought.

"Well, they sent her out, and you can be sure she didn't end up in a resort."

"Where's Gretchen?"

"Her daughter sprang her and took her home to care for her."

"And Dan?"

"Suspended for a week. He'll be back tomorrow."

"Tony?"

"He got fired."

I have Tony's cell number. I'm not supposed to, this kind of interaction between staff and resident is strictly forbidden. But in my book, rules in the Unit are meant to be broken. "Let's walk in the garden," I suggest.

The garden, like the atrium, is enclosed, walled in, but the grounds are lovely, filled with trees—palms, papaya, mango, avocado—and all sorts of bright, vividly colored flowers. The sun beats down against us as I push my walker along the path and Jim hobbles along beside me with his cane. When we reach some trees, I punch out Tony's number.

"Rose?" That's how he answers the call, with a looming question mark in his voice. "Are you all right?"

"Jim and I are out in the garden, Tony, and he told me you were fired. Is that true?"

"They threatened to fire me, so I quit."

"Lemme talk to him." Jim snatches the phone from my hand.

"Tony, Jim here. If Rose and I can get off the grounds, can you pick us up and take us…"

"*What*?" I grab the phone away from him, and in my haste, the call is disconnected.

"Call him back." Jim paces in small, tight circles, his cane tapping out each step. "I know where we can meet, I've thought about this, planned it. C'mon, Rose."

"That's crazy."

I hurry away from him, pushing my walker along in front of me, pushing it fast, wondering if I can possibly walk without it. After all, there's nothing wrong with my legs, nothing wrong with the nerves in my legs or feet, no reason I shouldn't be able to walk under my own volition. I stop, push my walker to my right, and step forward without touching it. Without touching anything. I stare at my feet, talking to them, willing them to move.

Feet, you are well and whole. You can walk without assistance. You can do this. I take one step, two, half a dozen, wobbly steps to be sure, but *unassisted steps.* And then I grab onto the nearest bench and settle onto it. After a few moments, Jim hobbles toward me—pushing my walker with one hand, the cane in his other hand tapping out a word in Morse code. *Escape.*

Sure. And go where?

3

I don't immediately recognize the man who sits down with me at dinner. He's much younger than I am, yet his beard and hair are totally white, and he looks exhausted. He has the same sad eyes that my husband, Ben, did at the end of his life.

"How's it going, Mom?"

Mom? I'm your mother? If it's true, why can't I remember it? "What's my full name?"

"Rose Rutledge Matheson. RRM. That's how you used to sign your briefs."

And just like that, the memories slip into place. Steve. This is Steve, my son. "Okay, you passed."

His truncated laughter sounds nervous. "Marsha e-mailed me a report about what happened that night with Dan, Gretchen, and Lucy."

"It's ancient history." I honestly don't know how ancient it is, but it feels ancient to me right now.

"I emailed it to Will Sullivan."

My attorney. "Why?"

"I forward all the reports and medical stuff to him. We really don't need him, you know, and he's damn expensive. But only you can fire him."

Why would I? Will Sullivan visits me once a week and brings me cash so I can get my hair washed and colored and go shopping when the facility takes us on excursions. Will was my husband's star student when Ben taught criminal law at the University of Miami. "I like Will. Where've you been anyway?"

"I started a new job, teaching at FAU."

I should know what the letters stand for, but the only thing I remember is that FAU is a university around here.

"It's been time-consuming," Steve adds.

Well, guess what, Steve? You were time-consuming as a child, but I took care of you, anyway. I don't say this, of course, but my fury at such a remark must be evident on my face because he touches the back of my hand. "Mom, you can't make waves here, okay? Your pension would cover only a fraction of the more expensive facilities, and until I get back on my feet, I can't afford to supplement your care."

This is a complete, blatant lie. Not long before I was brought here by my son, I gave him access, through Will Sullivan, to my accounts, and I know there was several million in investments, properties, and other assets. Some of the money was inherited, but most of it was earned. Ben and I worked hard and invested wisely. I may have forgotten yesterday, may not have recognized my son when he sat down beside me. But my memory for facts and figures is impeccable. When Ben died, we were wealthy. Now Steve is talking poverty. Right.

I stab a piece of chicken on my plate, but when I try to bring the bite to my mouth, I miss my mouth completely and stab my fork into the back of Steve's hand.

4

My shrink is a woman who asks me about my dreams. I burst out laughing. "What dreams? I'm too medicated to dream."

"You're on donepezil and memantine. They shouldn't affect your dreams."

Easy for her to say. She's about forty, in the prime of her life, and doesn't have a clue what it means to be where I am. Also, Dan is in the room with me, providing her with info about my erratic behavior these past weeks. My demands to meet with Gretchen and Lucy, to talk to them, my refusal to eat certain foods, to follow certain rules. Yes, I've been difficult. But why should this woman or anyone else have such power and control over my life? *Leave me alone, all of you, please.*

5

Will Sullivan and I sit in the atrium. He's a tall, slender man in his late fifties, a runner, happily married for decades, with two college-aged daughters. Today he has a briefcase with him and looks quite lawyerly in his suit and shiny shoes.

"Steve emailed me the report about the incident that happened several weeks ago, Rose, and about some other events that have occurred recently."

"Like my stabbing a fork through Steve's hand?"

He frowns. "There was nothing in the emails about it. When did that happen?"

"The...last time he visited."

"I just saw him two days ago, Rose. His hands looked fine to me."

That isn't possible. I stabbed that fork so far into the back of his hand that it bled all over the table. But the more I think about it, the less sure I am that it actually happened. "Maybe I...imagined it. I know I...I really *wanted* to stab the fork in his hand. I was furious at him. He…he said I couldn't afford any other facility, like I…I'm poor…and I shouldn't make waves here. He…he wanted me to fire you."

Will's expression darkens. "Interesting that he suggested it. The reason I saw him two days ago, Rose, was because he was indicted for grand theft. He wiped out your stock investments. If you recall, you allowed him to oversee that part of your finances. It came to my attention because he started withdrawing money from your other accounts. We've been building a case against him since last summer."

I wish I could say I'm surprised. "What's the bottom line? How poor am I?"

He leans toward me, his kind eyes wrinkling with amusement. "Fortunately, when Ben was in hospice, he asked me to move money into a brokerage account and hold it in trust for you. Steve doesn't even know about the money, Rose, so you're in good shape. And I have an idea I'd like to run past you. I didn't want to bring it up until Steve was indicted. Do you think you could live on your own if you had an in-home aide?"

"I don't have a home anymore, Will. Steve sold it."

"You still own that small condo over on the beach, and the renters left last month. The community provides free transportation to doctors, the grocery store, and so on, and there are a lot of seniors living there. It has a pool and dozens of activities. "

"It sounds wonderful. Can my friend Jim come, too? Can you talk to his granddaughter?"

Will frowns again. "Jim Ritter, right? I met him and his granddaughter last month when you and I were talking about moving you to another facility. She later called me and said to keep her in the loop because she felt he would be heartbroken if you were moved. She agreed to move him to wherever you were going."

I don't remember any of that. "If we were talking about this last month, why didn't you mention the possibility of a move to the condo?"

"Because it wasn't feasible until the indictment came down, Rose."

Such complexities exhaust me. "How soon can I move?"

"How's two weeks sound?"

Not soon enough. "Why so long?"

"I need to interview some home-health aides and have a cleaning service go through the condo."

"I know a great health aide," I say, and tell him about Tony and give Will his number.

"I'll call him."

Ecstatic and overwhelmed, I throw my arms around Will and begin to cry.

6

Dan is the orderly of the night and breezes into my room with his phony cheer, his phony compassion. Doesn't he ever go home? Take a day off? He holds out a pile of pills that are large and small and cover the spectrum of the rainbow. "Your meds, Rose."

I'm sitting in my favorite chair near the window, struggling to get through Anne's book of poetry *To Bedlam and Party Way Back*. Maddie is curled in my lap, purring loudly.

Dan can see the cover of the book. "She was nuts, you know. I read her stuff in college. She eventually killed herself."

"So did Hemingway."

"That was different."

"Why?"

"Take your pills, Rose."

"You didn't answer my question." I scoop the pills from his hand, stuff them into my mouth, hide them under my tongue, and pretend to sip from the glass of water he hands me. They start to melt, but my hope is that he will turn away before they melt completely so I can spit them out.

"The women in Hemingway's life made him crazy," Dan remarks.

Just like the women in my son's life, his two ex-wives, forced Steve into circumstances that left him no choice but to steal from me and put me into The Unit. Sure. I get this. Blame the mother, the sister, the wife, the mistress, *the seductress who made me do it.* I don't say anything. I just want him to leave.

"Marsha thinks it would be a good idea for you to go on the community outing tomorrow," Dan says as he's pushing the cart out toward the door.

"To where?" My words sound garbled because of the pills under my tongue.

"That small shopping center where the frozen yogurt shop and bookstore are. But I told her you've been so hostile and violent lately that you shouldn't be permitted to go." He glances back at me as he says this, his eyes glinting with revenge.

"I don't like shopping centers."

He laughs, a small ugly sound, and clicks his tongue against his teeth. "You once told me how much you love that chocolate frozen yogurt and how you can wander around for hours in that bookstore."

Did I? "Your point?"

"You got me suspended from this job for a *week*, Rose. And I'm going to make your life miserable. That's a promise. Hell, maybe I'll mix up your meds and make it so you don't even know who you are." He laughs again and pushes the cart out into the hall.

7

I spit out what's left of the meds, gulp from the glass of water on the table, and swirl it around in my mouth. I spit it back into the glass, but the taste of the meds lingers. *Mix up your meds.* Maybe that's what he just did.

Panic explodes in the center of my chest. I move without my walker to the closet, pull out my suitcase, and start packing. I can't wait two weeks. I could be dead in two weeks. Dan the Man might slip in here some night while I'm sleeping and press a pillow over my face, and who would ever know?

I'm going to make your life miserable. That's a promise.

When my suitcase is bulging, I change out of my night clothes, pull on slacks and a t-shirt and my comfortable walking shoes. I slip across the hall to Jim's room.

He's standing in front of his closet, jerking clothes off the hangers and tossing them into a suitcase. He's startled when he sees me. "Shut the door," he whispers, gesturing urgently.

I do so. "You're leaving, Jim?"

"Damn straight."

"Tonight?"

"As soon as the night shift ends and the morning shift people are arriving. That's when it's most chaotic around here."

"Where're you going?"

"I'll live under a bridge if I have to. I just can't take it anymore. You know what Dan said when he was in here a while ago? That I'm going to be admitted to a psyche unit, that my granddaughter wants me evaluated."

"But *why?*"

"Because if I'm declared incompetent, then she can take over the handling of my finances." He moves over to the bureau, scoops out clothing, drops everything into the suitcase. "Dan didn't say that was the reason, but I know it is. My granddaughter is the nutcase, not me."

My son, his granddaughter. Greed is a contagious disease. "We won't make it out of the building dragging our suitcases around in broad daylight."

"We?"

I quickly tell him what Will told me the other day, about my condo and hope I didn't imagine that entire conversation. "I just texted Tony. He'll be outside the service entrance in thirty minutes. We need to leave now, while it's dark. And forget living under a bridge. My condo has two bedrooms."

Tears course down his wrinkled cheeks.

Then everything happens quickly, strangely, like we're in one of those old Charlie Chaplin movies where everything is speeded up. Jim is peering out into the hall. "Coast is clear," he whispers. "Head toward the fire exit. That's how we'll get downstairs."

"Won't the alarm go off?"

"It's been broken for weeks. There were some guys out here a few days ago, fiddling with it, and I heard one of them say the whole system has to be replaced."

Jim opens the door wide and we move out into the twilit hallway. My heart hammers, my breath catches in my throat. It all feels unreal, dreamlike.

The wheels on our suitcases clack across the tiled floor, and I hope the racket can't be heard in the nursing station. The two security cams in the hallway are capturing our images, but at this hour of the night, it's unlikely that anyone is monitoring them. The night nurse and orderlies are probably in the employee room, drinking coffee and talking about all the horror they have to put up with from the residents.

When we reach the fire exit, Jim turns and leans back into the door. No alarms shriek. He holds it open with his cane until I'm in the dimly lit stairwell, then slips in behind me. The door whispers shut behind us, and we both eye the steep stairs in front of us. "Let's just lay our bags flat and give them a good shove," he suggests.

I push mine first and its descent is so noisy we decide to carry his suitcase down the steps to the landing. It's tricky. He has to hook his cane over his shoulder, take hold of the suitcase with one hand, and grip the railing with the other. I'm at the opposite railing, the suitcase like a third person between us. Even though I can move now without my walker, my gait isn't steady, and before we reach the landing I miscalculate, stumble, and my end of his suitcase hits the stair, and Jim is thrown off balance and nearly pitches forward.

His suitcase clatters on down the stairs.

We look at each other. I know that the terror I see in his face is reflected in my own. But behind that terror rises an exhilaration that neither of us has experienced in years. We're doing it, we're escaping this terrible place where other people monitor and control every facet of our lives, from blood pressure to bowel movements, to the food we eat to where we can go and what we can do and the meds we take. We are liberating ourselves.

Jim and I reach the landing, grab the handles of our suitcases, and move toward the door that opens into the garden. When it whispers outward, the night air rushes over us, the sweet scent of freedom.

"How're we going to get outside the wall?" Jim asks.

I have no idea. I haven't thought that far ahead. We move along the narrow sidewalk, beneath a trellis loaded with bougainvillea and night-blooming jasmine. My cell phone buzzes, a text from Tony. *Am at service entrance. I still have a key to the gate and unlocked it. Flashing my headlights now.*

I glance up quickly, but Jim has already seen the lights. "There," he whispers, touching my shoulder. "Is that Tony?"

"Yes. And he unlocked the gate."

"Let's move."

I'm in the lead, and the wheels of my suitcase clatter across the cracks in the sidewalk and behind me, I hear the steady *tap tap* of his cane. Suddenly, a door flies open, a security light overhead winks on, and Dan the Man steps out, massive hands fixed to his hips. "Seriously?" he laughs. "You two really thought you could just walk outta here?"

"That's exactly what we're doing," I snap, but Dan moves directly in front of me, blocking the way.

"Nope. Sorry, Rose. And what happened to your walker? Was that just a prop?"

As he grabs the handle of my suitcase, Jim's cane whistles through the air and slams down against Dan's nose. He shrieks in pain and stumbles back, hands flying to his face, blood pouring from his nostrils, and then the cane comes down again and again, against his shoulder, his knees, *whack, whack, whack.* Dan the Man crumples to the sidewalk and doesn't move.

A pool of blood seeps around him.

For a moment, Jim just stands there, breathing hard, his cane raised in the air. It's as if the horror has paralyzed him, frozen him.

"Move!" I yell and grab his arm and pull him forward.

We move shockingly fast, dragging our suitcases across grass, pebbles, toward the now open gate, toward freedom. Behind us, lights blaze, exposing us like bones on an X-ray. Then we burst through the gate and reach Tony's dark truck. "Get in, fast," he says. "I'll get your bags."

Jim and I pile into the front seat, Tony tosses our bags into the rear bed, and in front of us, the facility is now lit up like high noon and the night staff, all four of them, rush outside. Tony leaps into the truck, slams it into reverse, does a one-eighty, and we take off at the speed of light.

I sit there in a kind of shock, my hands gripping my thighs.
"Did I…I k-kill the bastard?" Jim stutters.

"If you did, it was in self-defense," Tony says. "I already called Mr. Sullivan, Rose. He's going to take care of everything. He'll come by the condo tomorrow to take your statements."

My head drops back against the seat, the tension rushes from my body. Jim squeezes my hand, and I touch Tony's arm so the three of us are connected. As the unit fades away behind us, I suddenly bolt forward in my bed, fully clothed, my bulging suitcase on the floor nearby.

I'm nearly crushed by the reality that I'm still here. Did I imagine everything? How has the border between the real and the imagined become so blurred for me? But I'm fully dressed, still wearing my walking shoes. My suitcase is packed, so that part of it was real. Did I actually talk to Jim?

Panic flutters through me again, and I force myself to take deep breaths, to calm down. *Think, Rose, think.* I pick up my cell phone. Did I text Tony? I go through my text messages. There are plenty of messages to him, but nothing about picking me up.

I find Will Sullivan's number and text him. *Do I own a condo on the beach?*

Yes.

Relief floods through me. *Was Steve indicted?*

And goes to trial in two months. He's sitting in the county jail.

When can I get out of here?

I'm picking you and Jim up tomorrow morning.

Sobbing with joy, I stumble across the hall to tell Jim the news, that we are headed into the next chapter of our lives, and he doesn't have to kill Dan the Man for it to all happen.

A VERY THIN, THIN LINE

BY T. J. MACGREGOR & ROB MACGREGOR

Cal noticed her the moment she entered the club. A knockout brunette, a Latina beauty with flowing black hair so shiny it reflected the light. Dressed in blue, like the woman in the Springsteen song that was playing, she didn't look old enough to be here. Then again, neither did he.

She maneuvered her way through the crowd of South Beach locals, some of whom he recognized, the wannabes who hungered for contact with the *Miami Vice* stars, Don Johnson and Philip Michael Thomas, and the others.

Her slender hips swung slightly to the music, and she looked around as if she were expecting someone. But he already knew there was no one else in the club like them. Cal made his way toward her, eager to meet her, talk to her, dance with her, find out how she had ended up here.

She turned before she reached the bar, their eyes connected, and she smiled hesitantly. "You can see me?" she asked.

"*Uh, si. Quieres bailar?*"

His Spanish accent sucked, but she didn't seem to mind. "*Depende.*"

"On?"

She switched to English that was much better than his Spanish. "Are you like this song that's playing now?""

"*Tougher Than the Rest?*" Once upon a time he was. Now, not so much. But he really wanted to dance with her. "Tough enough, I guess. Besides, you're the woman dressed in blue. Just like the song that was playing before."

She threw her head back, laughing. "And we're walking a very thin, thin line."

Another Springsteen song, he thought, and took her in his arms.

Graceful, exquisite, her feet moved in rhythm to her hips. "I'm Cal."

"Anna."

They moved among the other dancers, unseen, like phantoms. "Why'd you say we're walking a thin line?" he asked.

"It's a *very*, thin, thin line. And isn't it obvious?" She threw her right arm out to her side. "There's no one else here like us. I'd say that's a pretty damn thin line." Her hand tightened on his shoulder. "If you're like me, how come you feel so solid and real?"

"I don't know. I was about to ask you the same thing. I've never come across anyone else like me, and I've been coming to Mango's for months."

"I've been other places, but this is my first time here," she said. "Where do you live?"

In a cramped apartment in the Edison, the premiere Art Deco hotel on South Beach where his mother managed the cleaning crew. But it sounded so pathetic he couldn't bring himself to say it. He just shrugged. "Here on South Beach. You?"

"Little Havana. We came over on the Mariel."

His arm tightened around her slender waist. He now felt ashamed for being so evasive. The Mariel boatlift started in the spring of 1980–seven years ago—when thousands of Cubans, hoping to gain asylum, took refuge on the grounds of the Peruvian embassy in Havana. The Castro government finally relented and announced that anyone who wanted to leave could, and refugees fled in droves. By the time the boatlift ended, some 125,000 Cubans had reached Florida any way they could—boats, rafts, even on windsurfing boards.

Cal had heard some of the harrowing stories from friends at school. One kid and his dad had windsurfed from Mariel harbor to the Florida Keys, where they'd been rescued by the U.S. Coast Guard. Another guy and his family had been smuggled in on a fishing boat that had capsized, and after drifting for two days, clinging to pieces of the boat, they'd been rescued by fishermen in Key West. Stories like that. Experiences that become such an intimate part of who you were that it colored everything that came afterward.

"How did you...get out?" Cal finally asked. "Was it difficult?"

"Difficult?" She looked incredulous, then rested her head against his shoulder. "I was just ten, my youngest brother was four, my older brother was twelve. I remember our parents woke us in the middle of the night, told us to grab our escape bags, that we were fleeing to the Peruvian embassy. But..." She raised her head and looked at him, her beautiful eyes haunted. "Our car was chased by soldiers, and just outside the embassy wall, we leaped out, and as my dad herded us toward the entrance, he... he was shot."

Shot. Killed. End of the line. Cal had a vivid image of her dad pitching forward, slamming into the ground, and Anna shrieking, trying to get to him, and her mother and brothers shoving her forward toward the embassy gate. "My God, I'm so sorry."

She dropped her head back, looking at him as if searching for something in his face. "You don't have a dad either?"

How did she know that? he wondered. "He left us a long time ago."

"Us? You and your mom?"

"And sister."

Tougher Than Me had ended and was seamlessly followed by *In the Air Tonight*, the old Phil Collins song revived by *Miami Vice.*

"I love this show," Anna said.

"Me too." The music soared and pounded through the club, and he felt his connection to Mango's growing more tenuous. It frightened him. He needed more information about her—her full name, home address, where she went to school, her phone number. But he wanted to impress her, too. "Hey, you want to see something?"

He reached out toward an empty beer bottle on the bar, tapped it, and it tipped over. A guy nearby grabbed it before it rolled off the bar, and stood it up again.

"Wow, Cal!" She reached out toward the bottle, flicked her hand, and her fingers went right through it. "How'd you do that?"

"Practice, and focus, I guess." He shrugged. "Listen, Anna, can we meet in the real world? In the physical? What's your address? How can I find you?"

She smiled but took a step back. " My last name is Cardenas." Her laugh sounded choked. "My last name sucks. It means chains in English. What about you?"

"Smith. Cal Smith. There're hundreds of Smiths in Miami, but only one here on Ocean Drive."

"You may not like me much as a physical person," she said.

"I was just about to say the same thing."

She poked him gently in the chest. "No way, Cal. My situation is far worse than whatever yours is."

"I don't know about that." He wanted to ask her to explain, but her fingers were becoming transparent. "Don't go! Not yet!"

"I can't…control it. It's a thin, thin line."

Cal heard the panic in her voice and slung his arm around her shoulders and drew her to him, but as their lips were about to meet she faded to nothingness. "I'll find you," he called out to her.

2

A nna bolted awake, the pounding of the music in Mango's still echoing in her ears, her body burning with life, desire, and then disappointment. A dream, a vivid dream, nothing more. *Nada.*

She threw back the sheet that covered her, swung her legs over the side of the bed, and reached for her cane, resting against the chair where she left it every night. The crushing weight of her reality was so great she couldn't pull herself to her feet yet. She could still see his face, a handsome guy with dark hair and wide chestnut colored eyes. She still felt his hand against hers, his arms tight at her waist as they danced to Springsteen's *Tougher Than Me.* She could still feel the moment of that near-kiss.

Impossible. A dream, nothing more.

She got to her feet and tapped her way into the bathroom. Shower on. Hot water. Once, she had been able to see the spray of this water. She had been able to see the color of the walls, the rooms where she lived with her mom and two brothers. Now, the color lived on in memory, but her reality was defined by boundaries her hands discovered.

"Epa, Anna!" shouted Enrique, and pounded at the door. *"Vamanos, chica!* We overslept! Diego is already out in the car!"

Enrique's booming, impatient voice was like that of an over-bearing parent, but he was just eleven. The night their dad had been shot, he'd been carrying Enrique, and when he'd fallen forward, her little brother had leaped out of their father's arms and hit the ground running. It had saved his life. The older he got, the more that memory haunted him and the bossier he became, as if that bravado would safeguard him somehow.

"Hold on," she shouted. *"Ya vengo!"*

Their mother had left for work an hour ago and her older brother Diego usually drove Anna and Enrique to school. Two different schools. Enrique attended the public middle school on Calle Ocho in the heart of Little Havana, and Anna attended a special program for kids with handicaps. She was the only blind student in the school.

Fifteen minutes later, she and Enrique were in Diego's old truck. He barreled through Little Havana, and she recognized every rut and pothole in the road, every streetlight, every irregularity. Year after year, her blindness had led her to rely on her other senses, and the more developed those senses were, the greater her ease in moving through her life.

"Diego, do you know where Mango's is? On South Beach? Could you take me there some afternoon?"

"You're too young to get in, chica."

"Then just drive me over to South Beach. Take me around to the old Deco hotels." Cal had said something about those places on Ocean Drive.

"Why? So you can see Crockett?" he joked.

"Are they filming there this week?"

"That's what I hear."

"Then yeah, let's do it!" she said.

"Me, too!" Enrique bellowed.

"Okay, I'll ask my boss about getting off early on Friday," Diego said.

Friday was a lifetime from now.

3

School that morning was awful. Her Braille teacher was out sick, and the substitute didn't read Braille and asked Anna if she'd like to listen to a book on tape. Sure. Anything to pass the time.

The book was Stephen King's *Misery*, a story not much different than her own—the protagonist trapped by circumstances rather than blindness, a crazed fan instead of an optic nerve that had gone haywire when she'd seen her father shot outside the Peruvian embassy seven years go. Trauma, the physicians had said. It might reverse itself someday. But now she wondered if that was really true. Surgery was given a 50-50 chance of restoring her sight, but if it failed she would be blind for life.

At least she, unlike the protagonist in *Misery*, didn't have to kill anyone to be free. All she had to do was remain patient and bide her time until the school got her into a special government program that would cover the cost of her surgery. Bureaucracy was slow, that was what the school said. But she was nearly eighteen and had been waiting more than six years. At this point, she was no longer hesitant about surgery. If the money came, she was willing to take the chance even if the odds were only 50/50. Her blindness already felt permanent.

During lunch, she went to the pay phone in the hallway, dropped in a quarter, and her fingers moved across the buttons, punching out 411. "Operator. How can I help you?"

"South Beach. Cal Smith."

"Just a minute, please." Moments ticked by, then: "I don't have any Cal Smith listed on South Beach."

"Is there a Cal Smith anywhere in Miami?"

"Hold on."

The bell rang, signaling the end of lunch hour. *Hurry, please hurry.*

"There are plenty of Smiths, ma'am, but no Cals."

"Thank you." She barely contained a sob.

4

Every night since she'd met Cal, Anna had tried to get out of body as she started to fall asleep. But nothing happened. She'd never had control over the ability and knew she might go six months without getting out. Tonight was different. She lay in bed, struggling to start the vibrations that would ripple up and down her body and allow her to roll out of her physical self. But, again, nothing happened. She finally sat up, picked up the receiver of the phone next to her bed, punched out 411.

"Operator, how may I help you?"

She was about to ask for Cal Smith's number again, but instead said, "What's the number for one of the oldest Art Deco hotels on South Beach?"

The operator chuckled. "Which one, honey? All those Deco places are old. Park Central, The Marlin, The Raleigh, The Edison, The Tides, The Carlyle…"

"Yeah, I see your point. Thank you."

She quickly disconnected, feeling stupid and naïve. Anna slipped back under the covers and struggled against a growing despair that Cal Smith and all the rest of it had been just a vivid dream. That was when the vibrations finally began.

5

Five nights after Cal had met Anna, five nights of failure in attempting to return to Mango's, he found himself outside the place. His heart soared in anticipation at seeing her again. He slipped past the bouncer checking IDs, and moved into the sound of a Latin beat, Gloria Estefan and the Miami Sound Machine singing *Rhythm is Going to Get You.*

Women in tight, colorful dresses and wearing loads of makeup tore up the dance floor with men in tight jeans and flashy shirts. Smoke filled the air. People jammed the area around the bar. Lights flashed in blues and reds and golds, disorienting him. Cal moved across the dance floor, looking for her, but it was so crowded he couldn't avoid walking through some of the men and women. It felt strange, as though he were no more substantial than a breath of air, a cool breeze that caused them a ripple of discomfort.

Then he glimpsed a woman in a blue dress, her dark hair falling over her shoulders, the same slender build. She moved through the crowd toward the bar and Cal followed, getting closer and closer. He shouted: "Anna!"

She didn't turn. Maybe she couldn't hear him over the music. Then she glanced back. The woman was in her thirties. His heart sank. His imagination had turned the woman into Anna. Maybe Anna only existed in his imagination. A very thin, thin line, he thought, recalling her words, between the real and the imagined.

His head pounded from the music, his search continued and grew more frantic, his concern that he'd imagined her escalated with each passing moment. By the time he reached the other side of the dance floor, he still hadn't seen her. *Go home, you idiot. She's not here. She doesn't even exist.* He hated that niggling inner voice, the same voice that repeatedly told him he would never be normal again. He refused to believe it and refused to believe she wasn't real. He could still feel her body close to his as he leaned in to kiss her—the kiss that didn't quite happen—and that thick softness of her hair that fell over his arms as they hugged.

Maybe she wasn't able to find her way back here.

Day after day, he'd called information to find a phone number for Anna Cardenas. The answer was always the same: no listing. And there were dozens of listings for Cardenas, the operator had informed him. Was the number listed under another name? Probably. But he didn't know her mother's name, her address, or anything other than what she'd told him.

After school today, he'd spent hours in the library, poring over a map of Little Havana. The area was huge, but Calle Ocho was the heart of it, with tons of cafes, restaurants, and parks where old Cuban men sat around playing dominoes. If his older sister would drive him over there, he could ask around. Surely someone would know of her or her family. *During the Mariel, her father was shot outside the Peruvian embassy...*

The idea had smacked of such stupidity that he immediately abandoned it. Now, though, it seemed more feasible and probably more productive than wandering around in Mango's.

Cal made his way toward the door, through the rhythmic beat of drums, the thickening smoke, the peals of laughter, all of it a reminder of a life now denied him. As he stepped outside, passing a line of people waiting to get inside, he suddenly saw her, a solitary figure wearing jeans, a t-shirt, sandals, standing at the curb like she was waiting for a cab. It had to be her.

"Anna!" he shouted.

She spun around, her face lit up. "Cal!"

They ran into each other's arms, Anna whispering "You're real, I knew you were real."

He cupped her face in his hands, kissing her, filling his senses with everything about her, certain he would recognize her anywhere. "I need your address, Anna. A phone number."

"I called information. You weren't listed." She swiped at her damp eyes.

"I did the same thing." He took her hand, and they started walking, fast, away from Mango's. "It's the Edison Hotel. That's where I live. Will you be able to remember that?"

"Yes. Yes, definitely. My brother is trying to get off work early on Friday so he can drive me to South Beach after school. I can meet you somewhere."

Panic. Did he really want this to happen? What would she think when she saw his situation? Maybe it would be better if he met her at a restaurant, and he could be seated at a table when she arrived. That way he could size up the situation. "How about if I come to you, maybe a café near your place?"

"That'd be easier. I don't know yet if my brother can get off early from work. My mom works on Calle Ocho at Cafe Cortadito. I can meet you there. What time?"

He didn't know. His sister was in her second year of nursing school, and Cal didn't know her schedule. But she didn't have classes on Saturday. "Let's try Saturday. It'll be easier to get a ride."

"Saturday will work. It…"

He didn't give her time to finish. He wrapped his arms around her, just like last time. Their noses touched, her eyes widened, and he kissed her again. Her mouth tasted sweet and mysterious, an undiscovered country. She eased her head back, touched his lips with her index finger. "I'll find you," she whispered.

And just like that, she faded away and Cal stood there, feeling like a coward, hating himself for hesitating, for wanting to size up the situation, whatever the hell that even meant. Was he afraid of what *she* would think when she saw him or what *he* would think when he saw her? Suppose she was disfigured in some way? Maybe she'd been in a fire or was crippled or… He choked back a sob and covered his face with his hands.

Then he was back inside his body.

6

Cal grabbed onto the metal bar above his bed, hauled himself to a seated position, slipped his muscular arms under his useless legs, and moved them over the edge of the mattress. His bare feet touched the floor, but he couldn't feel anything. Dead from the waist down. "Fuck." He punched his dead thigh.

He reminded himself that the car accident that had rendered him a paraplegic could have been worse. In rehab, he'd met a hit and run victim who was paralyzed from the neck down and unable to breathe on his own. Cal clung to a small hope that the tests his neurologist had run on him a week ago would indicate he was a candidate for a new and still experimental surgery that would restore the use of his legs.

He made sure the brake on his wheelchair was engaged, clutched the armrest, and maneuvered his body into the chair. Two years, two months, and two days. But who was counting?

His bedroom door flew open and Isabella rushed in. "Hey, I've got to be at school early to study for an exam. Can you, uh, be ready to leave in ten minutes or so?"

"Yeah, if you help me with my jeans."

Usually, when he had the time, he managed to dress himself. He disliked asking his sister for help, but Isabella was so good-natured about it that modesty was no longer an issue. "You're making me a better nurse," she remarked and whipped his jeans off the chair and went to work.

The van she drove was equipped for a wheelchair, and getting on and off was as simple as steering the motorized wheelchair up or down the ramp. "Hey, Bella," he said when they were on the road, headed for his high school. "Have you ever left your body?"

"I'd be dead, wouldn't I?"

She looked over at him, her pretty face skewed with amusement—or concern, he couldn't tell which. "You just drift out of your body in a second body that's not physical. You might hover above your bed for a while, see yourself sleeping." *Or you might zip on over to Mango's.* "Or you might find yourself soaring through the ceiling and out into the world."

"Sounds like something out of Castaneda, Cal."

"What's Castaneda?"

"Never mind. What you're describing has been reported by people who have near-death experiences. We had this woman in ICU who suffered a massive heart attack and when we revived her, she told us how she'd watched the team resuscitate her. She even related some of our conversations. Verbatim."

"You never told me about that."

"I figured it wouldn't interest you."

"Ha. It's been happening to me pretty frequently for the last year."

Now she looked alarmed. "Have you told your doctor?"

"Oh, yeah. Sure. So I can get a referral to a goddamn shrink? You're the only person I've told." He nervously rubbed his palms over his jeans, determined to phrase this right so that she didn't think he'd lost his mind. "The reason I'm telling you is because I met this girl when I was out. At Mango's. She was out, too. She lives in Little Havana and we've agreed to meet. In the physical."

Isabella braked for a light. "You realize how this sounds,

right?" She gathered her blond hair behind her head, snapped an elastic tie around it.

"Nuts."

"Yeah."

"Except it happened."

"Look, Cal, it could've been a lucid dream."

"I know the difference between a dream and being out."

"Hallucination?"

"Nope."

"How do you know it happened?"

"Her name is Anna Cardenas. She's handicapped in some way and her mother works on Calle Ocho at Cafe Cortadito. She has two brothers. When she and her family escaped during the Mariel, her dad was shot and killed."

"Shit, Cal. Maybe you should be writing fiction."

"Very funny. Could you drive me over to Calle Ocho Saturday morning?"

"Aw, c'mon, Cal. This is all really fascinating, but the…"

"Anna and I agreed to meet there on Saturday."

The light had changed and Isabella now drove way too fast, a sure sign she was worried about him, that she thought he had cracked. It ticked him off. "Look, Bella. I know what the hell I experienced. You believed that woman who had a massive heart attack and died, but you don't believe me? That's fucked up. If you won't do it, I'll ask one of my friends."

"I didn't say no, Cal. Of course I'll do it. Did you two, uh, agree on a time?"

"She faded before we got that far."

"*Faded?*"

"That's what I see when she returns to her body."

"Uh-huh."

"Forget it. I'll ask someone else."

She raised a hand from the wheel, patting the air. "No, no, I'll drive you over there. What time? Early?"

"Yeah. Around nine. I'll just hang out and wait for her to show up."

"And you'll call me afterward so I can pick you up? And meet her?"

"Yes."

"Maybe I'm the one here who's nuts." She shook her head. "Promise me something, Cal."

"Anything."

"We don't mention this to Mom. It's our secret." She held out her palm. "Deal?"

He slapped her palm. "Deal."

7

Anna's mother didn't work on Saturdays. She raced around, running errands, visiting friends. So at breakfast that morning, Anna asked Diego to drive her over to the café to meet up with friends.

"Since when do you and your friends meet there, chica?"

She nibbled at the omelet Diego had made for her, sipped at the coffee she'd made, and tried to ignore her annoyance that he often treated her like a kid even though she would be old enough to vote in just a few months. "When it's convenient, *bobo.*"

"Hey, you know something I don't about where Don Johnson hangs out when he's not on South Beach?"

"Ha. I wish." Even though she'd never seen *Miami Vice,* she'd listened to the show, and Diego always gave her a play-by-play. And she was well aware of the wild popularity of the show not only in Miami where it was filmed, but everywhere.

"How're you going to get home?"

"One of my friends."

"Then why isn't one of them picking up you?"

She felt like flinging her omelet at him. "Never mind!" Anna snapped. "I'll take the bus."

"*Ay, caramba!* We're a bit testy this morning. Relax, okay? I'll drive you over after we finish eating and clean up this place."

8

Isabella pulled up in front of the café at 8:45 Saturday morning. Cal hardly had slept and now he was so stoked he spun the chair around and faced the top of the ramp as it slid to the ground. "Hey, Cal," his sister called. "Your Spanish is better than mine. What's *cerrado* mean?"

"Closed."

"That's what the sign on the door says."

No, fuck, no. "It just hasn't opened yet." He started down the ramp, and when he reached the bottom, Isabella was standing there.

"I'll wait with you. Just in case it doesn't open on Saturdays."

Angry, he threw his arms out. "Look around at all the people out here. Of course it opens on Saturdays. Don't worry about it, okay? And thanks for the lift."

With that, he pushed the chair's gear forward and sped away from her before she could say anything else. And he immediately worried that maybe the cafe *didn't* open on Saturdays. And suppose he waited here all day and she never showed up? Suppose she wasn't real and he really *was* losing his mind?

Then you'll end up in a padded cell, the inner voice snickered.

He shut out the voice. Cal hoped he recognized her. He knew there would be something different about her. Same with him. When he was out, his legs worked. He was *normal* again.

As he neared the door with the red *cerrado* sign on the front, he noticed a small sign that listed the café's hours: 7 a.m. to 7 p.m. Monday through Fridays, and 9 a.m. to 8 p.m. Saturdays and Sundays. His mood soared. He parked his chair to the left of the door, against the wall and waited. It felt like the longest fifteen minutes in his life.

The morning heat beat down, cars whizzed past him, pedestrians hurried by, a group of Hispanic kids with a boom box rounded the corner from a side street. Fifteen minutes stretched well beyond that. Finally, at 9:20, a short woman with salt and pepper hair, wearing jeans and a black t-shirt, emerged from the alley between the café and the next building. Was she Anna's mother?

She walked briskly toward the front door, her keys rattling, and glanced at Cal. *"Lo siento."* She tapped her watch.

She was apologizing for being late. *"No problema,"* he replied.

The door swung open, and she gestured at the ramp. *"Entra, por favor."*

"Gracias."

He steered the chair up the ramp and into the air-conditioned restaurant that looked as if it had come straight out of Havana. Colorful walls, wooden tables covered in cotton tablecloths decorated with red bougainvillea vines and CUBA emblazoned across them. Pictures of saints hung here and there, interspersed with black and white photos of a younger version of this woman standing outside the Café Cortadito in Havana.

He ordered a cortadito, a shot of Cuban coffee in a small cup with milk and sugar, parked his chair at one of the tables, and waited. He considered sliding over to a chair and asking the woman to put his wheelchair somewhere out of sight. But that was stupid. Anna would find out soon enough.

Every time the door opened, his breath caught in his throat. By 10, locals crowded the place, a cook and a waitress had arrived, and platters of fried eggs, bacon, and arepas and glasses of juice appeared nearly as quickly as the orders were taken. The air smelled so good that Cal's stomach rumbled, reminding him he hadn't eaten anything before he and Isabella had left the Edison. He'd been too excited to eat. When the short woman approached his table and asked if he wanted another cortadito, he nodded.

"Y uno de esos." Cal pointed at the breakfast a man was eating at the next table.

"Bueno."

As she scribbled down his order, he asked, *"Eres Señora Cardenas?"*

The woman looked surprised, then smiled and shook her head. *"Marisol no trabaja hoy."*

"Holy shit," he murmured. Had she said what he thought she had? That Mrs. Cardenas, Anna's mother, wasn't working here today? "She *exists*?" he blurted out.

The woman frowned, then laughed and walked off.

Desperately in need of clarification, Cal slammed his hand against the gear, turning his chair away from the table so that he could speed after her. The tables in here were pushed so closely together he wouldn't be able to reach her without barreling into at least two tables. But his sanity depended on it. *"Señora,"* he shouted, waving his arms like a mad man, drawing looks from everyone in the café. *"Lo siento, pero ella existe?"*

Does she exist?

The woman glanced back, regarding him with suspicion, like he might be a crazed gringo, then gestured toward the door. *"Aqui viene la hija.* Ask her."

He turned his chair again and there, coming through the door, was the woman he'd seen at Mango's. The woman with whom he'd danced, whom he'd kissed. Anna Cardenas.

Her black hair was pulled back from her face in a single braid that rode over her left shoulder. She was taller than he'd thought, and not just pretty but drop dead gorgeous. Flawless skin, a seductive mouth quick to smile as people in the café greeted her. Dark glasses hid her eyes. The people in the café called out greetings.

Hola, Anna.

Buenos dias, Anna.

Come andas, chica?

Then he noticed the cane that tapped along in front of her, sometimes moving from one side to the other, making sure the space was clear. *You may not like me much as a physical person,* she'd told him that first time in Mango's.

A blind woman.

A paralyzed man.Sweet Christ.

His hand froze on the chair's lever, he couldn't take his eyes off of her. He wasn't crazy. He hadn't been hallucinating or dreaming. She was as real as he was. But everything inside him screamed, *Get outta here fast.* Not because she was blind, but because he—regardless of whether he could walk or not—would never be her equal.

Before he regained control of his hand, the short woman shouted, *"Anna, hay un joven preguntado acera de tu mama. A tu derecha."*

"Gracias, Elena." Anna waved and tapped her way to the right, where he sat frozen in place. Her cane touched the edge of his

wheelchair. "You were asking about my mom?"

Cal cleared his throat. "Anna."

"Cal?"

Something happened to her face. It seemed to collapse, as if beneath the weight of excessive gravity, and she leaned forward, a hand reaching for him. He grasped it and pulled it gently to his face. She dropped her cane and placed both hands over his face, reading his features with her fingers, exploring every bone, fold, crease, curve, every pore.

"*Dios… mio.*"

Her choked, whispered voice filled him with the most agonizing pain he'd ever felt. His hand fell away from the chair's gear, his arms came around her back, and she sank down on his lap. Her hands slipped onto his broad shoulders, her fingers ran over his muscular biceps.

Cal slid his fingers over her braid and then into the knots, freeing them, freeing her lustrous hair. It tumbled to her shoulders, and she pressed her forehead to his. "Real."

"Real."

"Are we…sure?"

"Absolutely," he replied. "We're not nuts." He tilted her sunglasses back onto the top of her head, and his thumbs traveled across her lower lip, the tracks of tears on her cheeks, the corners of her beautiful dark, unseeing eyes.

He was vaguely aware that the café had gone as silent as a cathedral. She brought her mouth close to his ear. "I think we, uh, have an audience, Cal."

"You're not going to disappear or fade away, are you?" he asked.

"Not a chance." She rested her cool hand against the right side of his face. You?"

He drew her head toward him and kissed her, and the café erupted in applause. It struck him as so corny that he told her to hold on and sit tight, then pressed the lever forward and aimed the chair at the front door. The short woman ran ahead of them and opened it.

Down the ramp they went into the hot South Florida morning, both of them laughing.

A GAMBLER'S SUPERSTITION

BY T. J. MACGREGOR

"I'm feeling it," Dad says.

"Feeling what?"

We're having lunch on the front deck at Bart's, where we come at least once a week. It's a lovely spot in Key Largo, tucked away in palm trees on a prayer rug of a beach. The Gulf of Mexico spreads out before us, the water as blue and breathtaking as the cloudless sky. Gulls sweep through the cool February air, their cries echoing.

"The lottery burn. I need to buy a ticket when we leave here."

"What's the jackpot for the next drawing?"

"Big." He slips his phone from his shirt pocket, his hands trembling badly today from the Parkinson's. He uses a stylus to navigate to the lottery site. "It's estimated at five fifty."

"Five hundred and fifty thousand?"

He laughs so hard he nearly chokes. "Spoken like a non-lottery player, Jo. Five hundred and fifty *million*. After taxes, it would be about half that."

Max Baker, lottery expert. "Maybe I'll buy a ticket too."

"I might actually buy several. The last time I felt the lottery burn was the year your mom died. I won fifty grand. That enabled me to pay off the mortgage and take her to Hawaii."

My mother died a decade ago, when I was thirty, of a sudden heart attack. She was only sixty-four. Dad couldn't stand living alone in the house that held so many memories of her. So he retired from the high school where he'd been a guidance counselor for more than half his marriage, sold the house, and moved to Key Largo.

In 2012, shortly before he was diagnosed with Parkinson's, he married Anne. At sixty-two, she's twelve years younger than Dad, manages one of the bars on the beach, smokes and drinks too much, and parties like she's eighteen. As we say in my profession, she has issues. A lot of them.

I'm not sure what he sees in her other than companionship. She's the complete antithesis of my mother, but maybe that's the point. Maybe when you're married to your soul mate for forty years, the second time around demands someone at the opposite end of the spectrum. I wasn't invited to the wedding, probably a good thing.

We finish our lunch, I pay the bill, and we make our way to the parking lot and my car. He uses a cane when we're out, but at home he resorts to his walker or an electric wheelchair. Anne complains about the wheelchair, says he's always bumping into walls, nicking the paint and the door frames. When I was at their place a couple of weeks ago, I touched up the nicks and scrapes and cleaned the place from top to bottom. Anne doesn't lift a finger to keep the house clean, and the rooms stink of smoke. I opened all the windows, turned on the ceiling fans, and went through the house with Febreze. She complained about that, too, said the smell made her sneeze.

None of this is new. But it's getting worse.

Once we're in the car, his cane propped alongside him in the seat, I tell him that the cleaning woman I hired will be at his house two days from now, on Friday at nine. "Jo, I appreciate it, but Anne doesn't want some stranger coming into the house to clean."

"What do *you* want, Dad?"

"Just to keep the peace and win the Lotto."

"What will you do if you win?" I pull out of the lot and onto a dirt road that eventually takes us to U.S. 1. "What would you do with that many millions?"

"Give half of it to you, that's first. So you don't have to work so hard."

"I love working. But a long sabbatical would be great! What else?"

"Get a stem cell transplant, and if it worked, I'd buy us a

house in Tuscany. And I'd divorce Anne."

"You can divorce her now, Dad, and move in with me. I've got an extra bedroom." It isn't the first time I've suggested this, but I've never before heard him say he wants to divorce her.

"You've got your own life, honey. I don't want to intrude."

My work is my life. I'm an outsourced school psychologist. I travel to schools throughout the Keys and tend to students with issues both simpler and more complex than my father's or Anne's. I'm divorced, no kids, have a friend with benefits, love to read and garden and travel to exotic places when I have the time. That about sums it up.

"You wouldn't be intruding. Since I'm on the road so much, I could hire someone to cook for you and watch after you when I'm gone."

"Anne does that." He points at an old fishing shop coming up on the right. "Hey, let's try that Mom and Pop place for our Lotto tickets. Those places are sometimes luckier."

I pull into a parking space in front. The windows are plastered with signs: *We sell Lotto tickets! Live bait! Fishing poles! Spare engine parts! And even a few groceries!* "Okay, what numbers should I play for you, Dad?"

"Jo, you never let anyone else buy your Lotto tickets. That's the first rule."

Oh, of course. I should have known this. Dad has been buying $1 Lotto tickets twice a week for years. "What's the second rule?"

"*Believe* that you're going to win. *See* it in your head. *Feel* that you've already won. *Imagine* what it's like to live with those winnings." He opens the car door, grasps his cane, swings his legs over the edge of the seat, and gets out.

"Any other rules?" I ask as we start up the steps to the front porch. He has trouble with steps sometimes. He grips the railing with his free hand, leans on the cane with the other.

"Third rule. Never allow yourself to get into a situation where you're so dependent on others that winning the lottery becomes your salvation."

I really dislike what that implies. But before I can ask him about it, the front door of the shop opens and Dad greets the old guy who hurries out, a fishing pole in one hand, a bag of bait in another. "Hey, Charlie."

"Max! Good to see you." Charlie shakes Dad's hand like a man pumping water. "Looks like you're getting around fine. We miss you on our fishing excursions."

"I may try them again. Give me a call when you're planning another one."

"You bet. Anne won't like it one damn bit, though," he says with a laugh.

Dad dismisses the remark with a wave of his hand. "Don't know why she'd care."

"She thinks you might fall overboard."

Dad laughs. "Yeah, right. Have you met my daughter, Charlie?"

He introduces us and we chat for a few minutes about their last fishing trip together and what a hissy fit Anne had about it. "She carried on like your dad was non-functional." Charlie remarks.

Issues, like I said. Anne has issues. "She obviously exaggerates," I say.

"I'm feeling the lottery burn, Charlie," Dad says, changing the subject. He's apparently uncomfortable talking about Anne.

"Just bought mine." Charlie pulls a ticket out of his shirt pocket and wags it in the air. "Someone's got to win, right? Gotta get moving, Max. Nice meeting you, Jo."

"You too, Charlie."

I open the door for Dad. "Why does Anne throw a hissy fit when you go fishing?"

He shrugs. "She seems to have the idea that I should be housebound."

"That sucks, Dad. You should get out fishing as often as you can, be with other people."

"So I can listen to her bitch and gripe about it for days? No, thanks."

His cane taps along the floor as he makes his way to the counter, his shoulders hunched, his gait a shuffle. He moves through narrow aisles of fishing hooks, poles, weights, buckets, all the paraphernalia of what he loves to do. It infuriates me that Anne puts up a stink when he goes fishing with his friends. I immediately entertain the idea of moving him into my place today.

But why should *he* move? The house belongs to him. Anne should move out. He can divorce her, and I'll use his place as my home base until I can find a job that doesn't require as much travel. And until that happens, I'll hire someone to come in, just like I told him earlier.

A plan. I'm one of those people who needs a plan.

2

"Afternoon, Max," says the cheerful young woman behind the counter. "Fishing supplies or the lottery?"

"Lottery, Barb."

"Random or do you have numbers?"

"Both."

"Okay, random first." She taps at a machine, a ticket slides out, she hands it to Dad. "Numbers."

"Five, six, seven, eight, sixteen, thirty-one."

"Aren't those the ones you usually play?"

"Yup."

It takes me a moment to realize these are birthdates—his, Mom's, and mine.

"Here you go, Max. Two bucks for two tickets for February tenth. And good luck! You'll know by eleven tonight if you've won five hundred and fifty million! Just remember me when, huh?"

He laughs. "Absolutely." He drops a pair of ones on the counter, checks both tickets, slips them into his shirt pocket, and steps aside so I can buy a ticket. "Honey, I'll be over in the fishing pole area."

I buy my ticket, and when I turn to look for Dad, Anne is coming through the door in her bar management attire. She has the body of a much younger woman, slender with curves in the right places, and dresses like she's half her age—skin-tight jeans, a pale blue shirt with the name of the bar written across the pocket. She's a blonde, one that comes from a bottle, and wears her curly hair chin-length. At one time, she was undoubtedly attractive, but now she looks weathered and used in spite of the plastic surgery she had before she met Dad. Traces of that surgery are evident around her mouth and eyes, where the skin looks as tight as her jeans.

She's with one of her employees, a younger woman I recognize who works the bar but whose name always eludes me. They're laughing about something on her phone. When Anne glances up, she sees me and struts over.

"Jo."

"Hey, Anne."

"I thought you and Max were having lunch."

"We did. Now we're buying Lotto tickets."

She rolls her dark eyes and leans toward me, touching my arm. "Between you and me? It's not just the Lotto tickets anymore. It's scratch-offs, Powerballs, Megas, Fantasy Fives. He's got a problem, Jo."

I touch her arm in the same spirit with which she touched mine, that woman-to-woman stuff that teenage girls sometimes use when I'm evaluating them. "Between us, Anne? *You've* got a problem. Why do you put up a fuss about him going fishing with his buddies? Why don't you ever take him out for lunch or dinner or just out for a drive? You can't even drive him to a doctor's appointment. He has to take a cab. And why do you bitch at him for a few nicks in the paint? And since you don't clean the house and he can't exactly do it hobbling around with his cane or a in a wheelchair, why the hell should you care if I pay for a cleaning woman to come in once a week?"

Her dark eyes widen and she rocks back, away from me. "Wow, where did all *that* come from?"

"Right from the heart," I snap. "In fact, I think it's time for Dad to move in with me or, even better, for you to move out. It's his house. Your name isn't even on the deed."

Her nostrils flare, blood rushes up her neck and into her face, turning that leathery brown skin even darker, and her hand flies toward my face to slap me. But my reflexes are fast and I grab her wrist and jerk her toward me, our faces so close I can smell the booze on her breath. "Don't screw around with me, Anne."

She wrenches free of my grasp. "Let's see what Max has to say about all this."

She marches away from me, swinging her tanned skinny arms, and I follow her into the aisle where Dad is examining a box of fishing weights. "Max," she snaps. "Your daughter is way outta line, and you need to set her straight fast."

Dad glances up, surprised to see Anne here, now, and fear shadows his eyes. It shocks me to see it, to realize that Dad is actually afraid of his wife. "What're…you doing here?"

"Didn't you hear what I just said?" Anne demanded.

"My God, Anne, lower your voice," Dad says.

"We're going outside," I tell her, touching Dad's arm. "Where the three of us can talk without disturbing anyone else."

Dad and I start up the aisle, but Anne rushes up behind us, grabs the back of his shirt and spins him around so fast that he loses his grip on the cane and it clatters to the floor. He stumbles, I steady him, then scoop the cane off the floor and point it at her. "Back off, Anne. Your stuff will be in the driveway by this evening."

"Jo… c'mon… please," Dad stutters.

"See?" Anne says. "See that? You're meddling, Jo. You've always meddled, you've never liked me, you've always tried to come between Max and me."

I hook my arm through Dad's, and we head for the front door. I pass him the cane and he clutches it as though it's his last best hope, and my heart bleeds for him, for the tangled mess of his life. He has always been my biggest supporter, has always been there for me. Now he needs me the way I needed him when I was learning to ride a bike and lost control of it, when I was bullied in middle school, when I got stood up for my high school prom, when my marriage fell apart, when Mom died, when he threw himself between me and a car that nearly hit me. Always, the look on his face was, *I'm here*. Now I'm throwing myself between him and Anne. Our roles are reversed.

Customers stare at us. I hear Anne's sandals slapping the floor as she hurries after us, and Barb at the counter shouts, "Don't you dare come back in here, Anne!"

Witnesses. There are witnesses to what Anne did, grabbing

the back of Dad's shirt, spinning him around so fast that he lost hold of his cane and would have pitched forward if I hadn't caught him. Elder abuse. The courts in Florida take it seriously, even here in the laid-back Keys.

Once we're outside, I walk Dad over to a bench on the porch, and he sits down, rubs his hands over his face, looks at me with haunted eyes. "Not good," he murmurs.

"Dad, do you want her gone or not?" I ask.

"Yes," he whispers. "Yes."

Anne barrels through the door, rage radiating from her in waves. I can smell it, a scorched earth stink, and I taste its burn inside my mouth and hear its bellowing voice in my head. I turn to face her, this woman with more issues than I could ever treat, and she stops dead. She slowly raises her arm, a Shakespearean gesture, and stabs her red-painted nail at me.

"You're to blame for all of this, Jo."

"You're just an observer?"

"I'm a victim of...of your hatred...for me." Then she moves tentatively toward Dad. "Do you want me gone, Max?" Her voice is soft, sensuous, perhaps even a little seductive. The idea of the two of them making love sort of grosses me out, my being the daughter and all. But that's what I hear in her voice.

Dad doesn't raise his head. He rubs his hands over his thighs, *fast,* as if to tame his trembling fingers. The scraping sound of skin against fabric is so irritating I want to punch Anne for causing his hands to move like that. Her soft question triggered it.

"Dad? Anne asked you an honest question."

Honest is the operative word here.

Now he raises his eyes and meets Anne's glare. If he says *no,* I will try to honor that. If he says yes, I'll hire an attorney to handle the divorce, shuffle around nearly every facet of my life, and her stuff will be in the driveway by nightfall.

"Do you really want me gone, Max?" Anne asks again

He starts shaking, his tongue darts along his lower lip, his glazed eyes drift to me, back to her. His shoulders stoop with exhaustion. "You hate me. I want you gone."

Then he presses his hands over his face and begins to weep.

3

The lawyer is on the divorce angle. I've called my boss, told him I have a family emergency, and he said I should take all the time I need. I feel like I'm letting my kids down, the ones I see week after week, the ones from dysfunctional families or families so poor the kids can't afford lunch in the cafeteria. But I can't allow Dad's situation with Anne to continue.

I'm now hauling some of Anne's stuff into the driveway, as promised. The problem is the furniture. I'm strong, but I'm not strong enough to carry a dresser down two flights of stairs and across the front yard to the curb. I can drag a queen mattress, but not the frame. I can't handle the mahogany nightstand even with the drawers out, the couch in the living room is a sectional, and each separate piece is way too big for me. I call my neighbor on Islamorada and offer to pay her twin sons to help me out.

The strapping sixteen-year-olds are dropped off by a friend a while later, and the three of us start moving the rest of Anne's stuff to the curb. An hour into it, I take a break to check on Dad. He's nodding off at the kitchen table, the salmon dinner I cooked half-eaten. His Lotto tickets are on the fridge, held in place by magnets, and I know he'll want to be up at eleven for the drawing, so I help him into his room. He yawns and flops back on his bed. I lift his legs onto the mattress, remove his shoes and socks, and cover him with the sheet. "Dad, I'll be back in awhile. I have to give these kids a ride home."

"Remind me to check for the winning numbers at eleven."

"I will. I'll be back in time for the drawing."

He grasps my hands and pulls himself up against the pillow. "I'm sorry you saw that. I'm sorry you saw how weak I am against her. I just want to read and fish and be left alone."

"I know." I urge him back against the bed, rearrange and fluff up his pillows. "This is going to work out. I love you, Dad."

I want to strangle the bitch.

4

Iwait in a heavily wooded lot across the street from Max's house, seething as I watch Jo and two young men hauling my stuff to the curb. As soon as they're gone, I intend to go through it all and take what I can fit in the back of my truck. What a meddling bitch. She doesn't have any idea what it's like living with him.

He twitches and shakes and drools constantly, drives his wheelchair into the walls and door frames, needs help to get to the bathroom, falls frequently, forgets to take his meds, and can't even boil an egg without making a mess. All I do when I get home from work is tend to his needs. So, yes, I've borrowed liberally from his financial accounts. I'm entitled. I'm going to miss that additional income, but I'm glad to be rid of him. Jo will discover soon enough what she's signing up for, the endless annoying details involved with caring for a seventy-four-year old man with Parkinson's.

There goes my sectional couch, my bed—mattress, frame, springs and all—and now my dresser. How am I going to get that into my truck by myself? Any decent person would give me the option of moving my stuff. But Jo isn't a decent person. She has disliked me from the day she met me, always thought I was after Max's money or something. I've got news for her about Max's money. Except for social security, he'll be broke soon, and then on top of caring for him, she'll have to support him. Karma, baby.

It looks as if they have finished cleaning out my belongings. The three suitcases at the curb probably contain my clothes. I can get those into the truck easily enough, but I may have to write off most of the furniture. Some of that stuff was expensive, from Pier 1 in Key West, and the bitch should be reimbursing me for it. But I think I've still got one of the checks from our joint checking account, so first thing tomorrow I'll be writing a check for about five grand and will deposit it into my own account. Good riddance, Max.

My phone vibrates, a text from Sam, the guy I sleep with from time to time. *You free tonite?*

No.

Isn't the old dude in bed by now?

Undoubtedly. *I'll call you tomorrow.*

Now Jo and her two helpers stroll down the driveway, chattering, and get into her car. Really? Am I about to become this lucky? She's going to drive them home? Perfect. I can get inside the house and take a good look around for stuff of mine that she just dumped in the garbage.

Her bone white Prius hums off into the dark. I hope those young men live in Marathon or somewhere else in the middle Keys; that will give me plenty of time to look around the house. Once her car turns out of the neighborhood, I quickly drive my truck into the driveway, load the suitcases in the rear, and hurry up the stairs to the front door.

Locked.

No problem. I still have a key. Jo, for all her efficiency, has overlooked a number of details—the key, the joint account Max and I have, and the fact that I know where his cash stash is hidden. It's not much, maybe a thousand, but that will help cover the cost of my furniture.

As I step into the house, the silence tells me Max is asleep. I move to the framed photo on the kitchen wall, the two of us on the day we were married in my son's backyard in Tallahassee. I remove it from the wall, set it face down on the counter, and slide the glass out. There. The envelope with his stash. I take it, drop it in my handbag.

My cell vibrates. It's probably Sam, who can't take no for an answer. But when I slip the phone from my back pocket, the night's winning Lotto numbers scroll across the screen. My heart hammers, I can't wrench my eyes away. The numbers are the ones Max always plays—5 6 7 8 16 31. My hands are shaking so badly that I jam my phone back into my pocket for fear of dropping it.

You want me outta your life, Max? Fine, no problem. I'll just take this beautiful Lotto ticket off the fridge door and be on my way. I snatch the ticket off the fridge and race for the door.

$550 million.

5

With two pit stops for gas, a bite to eat, and coffee, it takes me eight hours to drive to Tallahassee, where the Lotto's main office is located. It's the only place where winnings in excess of $250,000 can be claimed. Once you make your claim, it becomes public knowledge.

With a jackpot this large, experts advise you take the full six months to make your claim so you have ample time to move, change your phone number, consult with tax attorneys and financial planners and anyone else who can help you to invest your newfound wealth. They warn you that friends and relatives you haven't seen in years will start coming out of the woodwork and that every charity and scam artist in the country will be after you. Probably all true. But I don't care.

If my credit cards weren't maxed out, I would have flown and rented a car. But after today, maxed out credit cards aren't going to be an issue. After today, nothing in my life will be an issue. I'm going to buy this house I saw on Sugarloaf Key one day when Sam and I were out fishing, a gorgeous place made of cedar that sits on a corner lot and has a view of the bay. The yard is white sand landscaped with tropical plants, palm trees, banyans. And then I'm going to buy a new car, and maybe I'll buy Bart's. That would be a great investment. Sure, put my money to work for me.

The lottery office in downtown Tallahassee opens at eight a.m. I hit the drive-through at Starbucks first for coffee and a turkey, bacon, and cheese breakfast sandwich. Even though I'm famished, I can barely eat. My stomach churns with excitement. I'm so tired my eyes feel like they've been scrubbed with Brillo. Once I pick up the check I'll head straight to a branch office for my bank here in town and get it deposited. Then I'll use some of Max's cash for a motel room and will sleep for twelve hours.

Promptly at 8:41, I pull into a parking spot in front of the lottery office. When I get out of the car, my legs feel like hot blown glass. Even though the morning is chilly, in the thirties, my hands are damp with sweat. *Oh, Max, thank you, thank you.*

Inside the building, the air is toasty warm. Three of the five claim windows are open, and lines of people stand in front of each of them. Men and women, white and black, Hispanic and Asian, young and old and everything in between. They are holding various types of tickets, from Mega5s to Powerballs to scratch-offs. Only a few people are holding Lotto tickets. I pick up one of the forms—for the IRS, obviously—and fill it out as I wait in line.

Cold air rushes into the room as other people enter. I glance around and nearly panic. It's *them*, Max and Jo. He's using his walker and doesn't see me yet, but she does. Our eyes meet briefly, then she laughs and leans close to him, whispers something. He looks up, smiles as if at a private joke, and shakes his head. Jo is already filling out the form.

I ask the woman behind me to save my spot in line and go over to them. "It's my ticket. Your name isn't anywhere on it, Max. And I don't intend to split it with you."

"No problem," Jo says with a soft laugh. "We don't intend to split with you, either."

I don't have any idea what she's talking about.

"Better keep your spot in line," Max says.

I move quickly back to my line, certain they can't do anything to me. There's no proof that I stole the ticket. But their presence here rattles me.

6

Finally, at 9:22, I reach the window. I glance over at Max and Jo, who are second in their line. "I've got a winner," I tell the clerk, a bored-looking, middle-aged woman sipping at coffee. Her nametag reads Trudy.

"I.D, please, form, and the ticket," she tells me.

I set my license, the form, and the beautiful winning ticket in a slot. She spends the next five or ten minutes checking information, jotting my license number on the form, and asking me questions. Is the address on my license current? As of last night, no. But since Max's address is on my driver's license, I tell her yes, that address is current.

I look over at Max and Jo. They have reached the window. "Do you issue a check for the winnings or what?" I ask.

"A check, yes," Trudy replies.

I lean closer to her and whisper, "Even for a sum as large as five hundred and fifty million?"

"Wow! Lucky you. Then she reads off the numbers on the ticket. "Five, six, seven, eight, sixteen, and thirty-one. These are the numbers, honey. And what are you going to do first with all this?"

"I don't know."

"Hey, Sue, we've got a biggie here," Trudy calls out, and Sue hurries over, excited.

"My God, those are the numbers," Sue gushes. "We've got two winners here!" she says loudly.

Two?

I quickly check my phone to find out how many winners there were in last night's jackpot drawing. Just one. Me. Max usually buys two tickets, so maybe his second ticket won something.

"Just one more step," Sue says. "Every ticket has to be checked by our trusty little machine." She taps a metal box to Trudy's left and slips the ticket inside.

The machine beeps.

"Uh-oh," Trudy says. "This isn't a winner."

What? "Of course it's a winner. Five, six, seven, eight, sixteen, thirty-one. Those are last night's winning numbers. "

"That's true. But the date on this ticket is for last week."

"That's ridiculous." Anger riddles my voice. "Let me see the ticket."

"Please keep your voice down, ma'am."

She drops my license, the form, and my ticket back into the slot. I turn the ticket so I can see it. 5 6 7 8 16 31. The numbers are right, but the date beneath them is all wrong: *February 3, 2016.*

"This is rigged!" I scream. "Those are the winning numbers, and so what if I bought the ticket last week? I should get something!"

Suddenly, a beefy security guard is at my side. "Ma'am, you'll have to leave."

"Excuse me," says Sue, stepping out from behind the

window. "See that gentleman and woman at the last window?" She points at Max and Jo. "I would love to know how come you both have the winnings numbers, but only their ticket has the correct date. Coincidence?"

"No coincidence," Jo calls from the other side of the room. "She stole it off his fridge. All she saw was dollar signs. She didn't bother looking at the date."

Everyone in the room looks at me, people murmur, whisper. I'm shaking with rage. Now Max comes toward me, pushing his stupid walker along. "If you had paid attention to anything in the years you've known me, you'd realize that last week's ticket is always the one on the fridge. I don't toss it until the current drawing is over. Just one more gambler's superstition."

With that, he turns away from me. Sue hands me my license, the outdated ticket, my form, then looks at the guard. "Escort her out, please."

Around me, the crowd breaks into applause.

The guard touches my arm and urges me toward the door. *"You bastard!"* I yell, and lunge toward Max and slam into him from behind.

His walker slides away from him and he pitches forward, crashes into a woman in line, and bedlam erupts. The security guard rushes up behind me, throws me to the floor, pins me there with his knee. He handcuffs me, yanks me to my feet, and shoves me into a chair.

"The police are on the way!" Sue shouts. "Please calm down, folks. We'll get to your claims as quickly as possible."

A siren wails somewhere nearby.

7

We pressed assault charges against Anne, and the Tallahassee cops took her away. That was two weeks ago. I don't know how long they'll keep her, but the check has been deposited in my account, Dad closed out his accounts, and we've listed the house for sale.

It's unlikely Anne will find us. Tomorrow we fly to Tuscany to look for Dad's special place.

THE WORKS

BY T. J. MACGREGOR

Iknow how it is down here on the beach for the old ones now, what with rising prices and traffic and crime. They're afraid to go out at night. Their Social Security checks barely cover a month of meals at what used to be Wolfie's Cafeteria. They feel like Miami Beach's postscript.

The Art Deco craze started it, you know. Ever since the days of *Miami Vice* when folks decided Deco was in again, those little hotels over on Ocean Drive have been booming with business, charging prices like I can't believe, and yeah, people pay them. I mean, a hundred and fifty bucks for a room no larger than a closet, fifteen or twenty bucks for a hardboiled egg and a slice of bread that's badly toasted, the plate garnished with bits of pineapple or radishes, and then five bucks or more for coffee.

There's a haughty look to the hotels that really gets me, too. They stand so prim and proper at the edge of the sea, all spiffed up in pastels, windows so clean they gleam like jewels. The old ones feel like they can't even afford to walk there, and when they do, shuffling in their tired bones and worn shoes, under the weight of eighty or ninety years of memories, they're nearly trampled by the hip, youthful crowds rushing to this hotel or that bar, cell phones mashed to their ears.

So I keep my prices low and do what I can. When an old one is troubled or sad, sick or too drunk to stand, I take him or her in. Word has gotten around that Millie's Place is where you go when things have gotten bad.

Like tonight, for instance.

Toby wandered in off Washington Avenue a few minutes ago, out of the thick night heat, looking about as bad as a man can look and still be alive. He's ninety-four years old, with a spine so bent he can hardly lift his head, glasses thicker than his arm, a heart that just won't quit.

He's counting one-dollar bills from a tattered envelope with SOCIAL SECURITY ADMINISTRATION written in bold black letters across the top. If I remember correctly, he worked nearly half a century for an auto-parts plant that merged with another plant, and most of his pension got lost in the transition. His Social Security check amounts to about $600 a month, and we all know what that buys you here on South Beach.

"The room's only ten bucks, Toby," I tell him when he keeps counting out the bills.

"Want a meal, too," he mumbles, moving his dentures around in his mouth because they hurt his gums.

"Twelve bucks, then."

"And the Works. I think I want the Works, Millie."

"You'd better be sure. It's a bit more expensive."

His head bobs slowly. It reminds me of a beach ball, rising, falling, riding a wave, and I want to stroke it, embrace it, kiss his old, beautiful head. It's as hairless as a chihuahua, with a mass of wrinkles that seem to quiver and dance to the back of the skull. Not so long ago, on a rainy afternoon, some of the old ones and I gathered around Toby's head to see if we could read our fortunes in the wrinkles, like they were creases in a palm.

"I'm sure," he says softly, depositing an old canvas bag on the counter, straining to look up. "How much?"

His eyes behind those thick glasses are alarmingly small, almost transparent. I feel like they might disappear at any second. "Forty-five. I guess you know what all the fee includes."

His smile creases his mouth and, like a widening ripple in a pond, touches all the other wrinkles in his face. For a moment or two, his features shift and slide, rearranging themselves. "Sure, I came with Mink, remember?"

Mink: right. She was close to a hundred, small as a toy doll with white hair that had fallen out in spots, exposing soft, pink patches of skull. She had cancer, and the radiation or the chemo or whatever it was they'd used on her had rotted her from the inside out, but her heart ticked on. She took baby steps, I remember, like a toddler learning to walk, and drooled a little when she talked.

It's true that decades stretch between infancy and old age, but children and the old ones aren't all that different. Both are afraid. Both have special needs. Both require love. I understand that, and they know it.

"There. Forty-five." He taps the stack of bills against the counter, straightening them, then slides the pile toward me.

"Sure?"

"Positive."

"Okay, let's go take a look at the menu."

I text Sammy to run the desk, and after a few moments, he shuffles in, big as a truck and all muscle. He's not an old one, but he was living on the streets until I took him in, and now I don't know how I'd run this place without him. I've never heard him speak. I don't know if it's because he can't or just that he chooses not to. We communicate most frequently by text messages.

I come out from behind the counter, and Toby hooks his old, tired arm in mine. The kitchen is in the back, and while it's not as grand as the ones in the fancy hotels on Ocean Drive, it feels like home to me. The fridge is always filled with everyone's favorites—home-baked pies, drumsticks, potato salad, coleslaw, cookies by the dozens, turkey breasts and cutlets.

When I was doing private-duty nursing a long time ago, I made a point of cooking for my patients. They appreciated it. A lot of them were old ones, too, and I learned to prepare the food to accommodate dentures, taste buds that had gone as dull and smooth as river stones, noses that no longer worked right. It taught me the importance of spices, sauces, and garnishes that dressed the food good enough to make your mouth water.

Toby's mouth is watering now as we peer into the fridge together. I can tell. He points at what he wants. One of those, one of these, this, that. His finger is curved into a permanent claw from arthritis; just looking at it hurts me. That's how it is with me and them. That's how it always is when someone I care for is in pain. It becomes my pain. It's why I quit private-duty nursing.

"And cookies," he finishes. "Chocolate-chip cookies."

"They've got nuts in them."

"Soft nuts?"

"Not really."

"Aw, so what. Nuts are fine."

Together, we remove the items from the fridge and set them out on the counter. Before I begin preparing the meal, though, I show him to the best room in the house. It's on the top floor, in back. There's a skylight over the huge bed, a color TV that offers a wide choice from cable to Netflix, Hulu, Starz and just about any other streaming service you could want. He can even tap Pandora and Spotify for music. The adjoining bathroom has a sunken tub that swirls and bubbles like a Jacuzzi, where fluffy towels, a silk robe, and matching pajamas are laid out. He sighs as his feet sink into the thick carpeting on the floor and sighs again as he eases his tired bones onto the bed and peers up, up into a sky strewn with stars.

"You'll tell me when dinner's ready?" he asks, frowning as though he doesn't quite trust me now.

"I'll bring it up here. Feathers is going to smell that chicken. You mind if she comes up too?"

"No, no, of course not." He hooks his hands under his head, lost in the stars. He doesn't hear me leave, but Feathers hears me enter the kitchen.

She's a white Persian who has a definite fondness for chicken and the old ones. She likes to curl up on their chests and knead their old bones with her gentle paws. I toss her tidbits as I prepare the meal and explain the situation to her. She blinks those sweet amber eyes as if to say she understands perfectly—and I really think she does—and follows me upstairs when I take Toby his meal.

He's perched on the wicker couch in the black silk pajamas and robe, squinting at the TV, watching *Cocoon* on Netflix. It's a favorite with all the old ones. I set his tray down on the table and pull up the other chair.

Feather flops across Toby's feet, covering them like a rug, and he looks down at her and laughs. I can't remember the last time I heard him laugh, and I've known Toby for ten or twelve

years, since he moved down here after his wife died. I don't
know if he has kids. He has never spoken of them if he does.
But that's how it is with a lot of the old ones. When they get too
old for their kids to deal with them, when there's talk of nursing
homes, dementia units, of confinement, they get scared and run
away. Who can blame them?

"Watch this, Millie," he says excitedly, stabbing a gnarled
finger at the screen. "This is where they swim in the rejuvena-
tion pool."

I divide my attention between the screen and the turkey,
which I cut up into small, manageable bites for him. I pass him
a napkin, which he tucks under his throat like a bib, and pass
him his plate. He sets it carefully on his lap, impales a chunk of
meat, and dips it in a scoop of dressing. His hand trembles as it
raises to his mouth. A dab of dressing rests on his chin, but he
doesn't seem to notice it. He chews slowly, thoughtfully, eyes
glued to the screen.

"You believe in heaven and hell, Millie?"

Nope." A lot of the old ones ask me this question, like they
think I have insight into these things. "Heaven and hell are fiction, Toby." Sort of like *Cocoon*.

"What do you think happens when we die?"

"That depends on the day of the week."

"What?" He laughs, coughs, sips from a glass of iced tea.

"If it's Monday, I figure when we die, we're dead." That possibility doesn't appeal to me anymore than it does to Toby. I
quickly rush on to Tuesday.

"On Tuesdays, especially during the winter months when
the sun is shining and there's zero humidity and the Atlantic is
a vivid blue, I'm blissfully happy. I figure if I died right then, I'd
be just as happy wherever I ended up."

"I like that one."

"Wednesday is even better, Toby." Today is Wednesday.
"Maybe the day doesn't start off so well, but it gets better and
better with every breath I take, every step I move, and by nightfall, I'm feeling so high about life that when I go to sleep, I'm
smiling. And when I wake up, I discover I can think myself into
any body, any place, that I can create a beach or a sunset with

just my thoughts. I realize it's all thought." I throw my arms out at my side. "Everything, everyone."

"Wow." The word slides out with his breath. Then, his innermost thought: "Does it hurt?"

"No. Of course not."

"You're sure?"

"You were here with Mink," I remind him. "Did she look like she hurt?"

His mouth puckered from a cranberry. "She always hurt. From the cancer. Or the radiation. From something."

Physical pain or psychic pain: the difference isn't that great. Shift your focus, and one becomes the other. Mink knew that. "She's okay now, though."

"Yeah, she died on a Wednesday." He smiles as he says this, then quickly adds: "But I think in the beginning, she experienced a Monday."

We both laugh at his stab at humor. "You talk to her?" I ask.

"Sure. Pretty often."

"And she's better?"

"Much."

"How come she doesn't come around anymore?"

"She's finished with the beach, Millie. I think she's headed to the mountains next." He pauses. "Can you do me a favor?"

"Sure, anything."

He reaches into the pocket of his robe and brings out a sheet of notebook paper. The words printed on it are almost illegible. I can imagine Toby hunched over at the Ace Club, where some of the old ones hang out, moving a pen up and down against the paper, putting his thoughts in order. I get the point. "Okay," I tell him, and slip the sheet inside the old canvas bag. It slumps against the floor next to his bed like an aged and loyal pet.

"Can I watch another movie after this one?" he asks.

"Whatever you want. When you get tired, just tap the screen of this phone here..." An iPhone that never fails us. "...and tell Siri to buzz me. Then I'll be up to tuck you in."

"Mink didn't have a Siri."

"She had you." I start to turn away, but he grabs my hand. "Don't go. Stay here with me, Millie."

I pat his hand. "Let me get a pitcher of iced tea and your slice of pie, and I'll be right back. Was it apple or pumpkin that you wanted, Toby?"

"Both." He grins mischievously, dark spaces in his mouth where there should be teeth. He's removed part of his dentures.

"Both it is."

Feather doesn't move as I get up. She knows the routine.

From the kitchen, I fetch iced tea for myself and two slices of pie for Toby and some treats for Feathers. In my bedroom, I bring out the Works, running my hands over the smooth, cool leather, remembering. New York. My old life. The business with the nursing board. Such unpleasantness, really. Like the old ones, I have secrets I would rather forget.

I change into more comfortable clothes, cotton that breathes, that's the color of pearls. Makeup next. A touch of eye shadow, mascara, blush, lipstick. The way I look is part of the Works. Sometimes the old ones ask me to hold them, stroke them, caress them, make love to them. Other times they just want to listen to Frank Sinatra and dance or they ask me to walk on the beach with them, in the moonlight. Their requests are as different as they are, and I always comply. But with all of them, there's a need for a special memory, an event that perhaps reminds them of something else. It's as if that memory will accompany them, comfort them somehow, like a friend.

When I return, Toby is still watching the movie. His supper plate is clean. His eyes widen when he sees the pieces of pie, and he attacks the apple first, devouring it with childlike exuberance, then polishes off the pumpkin as well. We watch the rest of the movie together, Feathers purring between us on the couch. Now and then, his chin drops to his chest as he nods off, but he comes quickly awake, blinking hard and fast as if to make sure he hasn't missed anything.

When the movie is finished, I fold back the sheets on the bed. They're sea blue, decorated with shells and sea horses, the same ones Mink slept in. "Can we listen to music?" he asks.

"Sure."

I bring out my cell, connect it to the portable speaker next to the TV, and bring up my iTunes downloads. I know he likes

Harry Belafonte, so that's what I play. Toby gets up from the chair and holds out his arms, and I move into them. I'm taller than he is, but it doesn't matter. We sway, his silk robe rustling. I rest my chin on the top of his bald head and feel all those wrinkles quivering, shifting, warm as sand against my skin. He presses his cheek to my chest, eyes shut. The lemon scent of his skin haunts me a little, reminds me of all the old ones who have come here for the Works. I've loved each of them and love them still.

When the song ends, Toby and I stretch out on the king-size bed, holding each other, talking softly, the moon smack in the heart of the skylight now. He falls asleep with his head on my shoulder, and for a long time I lay there just listening to him breathe, watching stars against the black dome of the sky above us.

The window is partially open, admitting a taste of wind, the scent of stars, the whispering sea. I imagine that death is like this window, opening onto a pastel world where everything is what you will it to be. Yellow skies, if that's what you want. Silver seas. A youthful body. A sound mind. A family that cares. A state of grace.

And that's my gift to the old ones.

I untangle my arms and rise, drawing the covers over Toby. His wrinkled head sinks into the pillow. I bring the syringe from my leather case. It's already filled. I have trouble finding a vein in his arm. They're lost in the folds of skin, collapsed beneath tissue, and I have to inject the morphine into his neck, just below the ear.

And then I wait.

Always, in the final moment, there's something that seems to escape from the old shell of bones and flesh, an almost visible thing, a puff of air, a kind of fragrance, the soul released. It leaves Toby when he sighs, fluttering from his mouth like a bird, and sweeps through the crack in the window, free at last.

Funny, but the wrinkles on top of his skull don't seem quite as deep now. His spine doesn't look as hunched. If I tried, I know I could straighten out his fingers. But the most I do is kiss him good-bye.

I get rid of the syringe. Sammy will take care of getting Toby's body to the pauper cemetery after the cremation. There won't be a headstone, of course. I do have to make some concessions. But the burial will be proper, with a pine box and all.

I unzip his canvas bag for the sheet of paper I slipped in here earlier and read it over. The list of who gets what is simple; all the names are old ones who hang out at the Ace Club. His belongings are in the bag. I sling it over my shoulder and walk downstairs, where Sammy is still at the desk. He looks up and I nod. He reaches under the desk and switches on the VACANCY sign outside. I take his place at the desk, and he leaves to tend to Toby.

Many of the old ones will know about Toby before they hear it from me. They'll know because the only time the VACANCY sign goes on is when the Works are finished.

Tomorrow when I go down to the Ace, I'll also pass out my card to newcomers. After all, I've got to drum up business just like anyone else.

MILLIE'S PLACE. CHEAPEST RENT ON THE BEACH. GOOD FOOD, SPACIOUS ROOMS. THE WORKS.

THE DEVIL'S CHAIR

BY ROB MACGREGOR

Ieased into the parking lot behind the old brick building that housed the *Deland Star-Journal,* my first job out of college, my third day on the job. So far, I'd spent two days writing obituaries for town folks who hadn't died yet. They'd been well known community leaders and were in failing health. Thanks to my diligent work, we were now ready to put them on page one before their bodies cooled down.

Today, hopefully, I would get a real assignment. I wanted to see my byline, Thomas J. Reed, on an article. Then I would really feel I was a reporter here.

I'd hoped to get hired by the *Orlando Sentinel* and had an interview the week after I graduated. The personnel director was impressed that I'd been editor of my college paper, but after he looked over my resume and clips, he said, "Tom, my advice for you is to go out and work for a year on a small town paper. Then give me a call. But I can't promise anything. You know how it is these days with tight budgets."

I was disappointed, but a couple of days later I saw that the *Star-Journal* was looking for a reporter. The editor hired me twenty minutes after I walked into the newsroom. Three others had already applied, but I was a local boy and knew the town. It was an entry-level job in journalism, and the pay wasn't great. I'd already vowed I would start looking for a new job in six months. Meanwhile, I would do my best to make an impression here and get some good clips.

My roommates at Redman, the private college in this central

Florida town, had a good laugh when they heard that I wasn't leaving "Deadland" yet for a big city newspaper job. Chas and Dane could be real assholes, but I could tell they were glad I was sticking around and paying rent on our three-bedroom apartment a few blocks from campus. They both had another year at Redman and were several weeks into the fall term.

I walked into the office by the rear door and ambled over to my desk. The *Star-Journal* was published twice a week and had an editorial staff of four, including James (Flash) Gordon, the editor, the only one in the newsroom at the moment. Gordon was in his fifties, with bushy salt and pepper hair and a droopy mustache. He had a middle-age paunch gained from twenty-some years on the copy desk of the *Philadelphia Enquirer*. For the past decade, he'd moved from paper to paper, city to city, and had landed in Deland a year ago. It didn't take long for me to realize that he had a somewhat jaded sense of humor, which I appreciated.

I waved to him. "Morning, Flash."

"Tom, love your obits, but you gotta tone down the dark humor. These folks in Deland won't appreciate your Mark Twain-esque writing style."

"I was just trying to be creative with a…deadly dull topic."

"I get it. So I got an assignment for you that will allow you to go full bore into your darkest graveyard sensibilities."

"Oh, yeah? Tell me."

"First, you need to do one more obit this morning about someone who actually died last night and was well known in town. After that, I want you to take a drive over to Cassadaga. You know about it?"

"Sure. They worship spooks there, right?"

Gordon dropped his head back and laughed. "You are definitely the right one for this story. We need a page-one yarn for our Halloween issue coming up. Don't take the easy route, like going on their phony ghost tour. If there are such phantasms, as some folks attest, I doubt that they're standing around waiting for the ghost tour to come by. Find something edgier that will captivate our readers and leave them wondering who the hell is the guy who wrote this wild story."

"I got it, Flash. It'll be fun."

"You want to include some background on the weird town, of course, but keep it simple. You're not writing a paper on local history."

Actually, I already had an idea. I knew more about Cassadaga than I was letting on. In years past, a handful of costumed Redman students had literally terrorized residents of the spiritualist community on Halloween by racing through the narrow streets, screaming like banshees and dancing and drinking on the graves in the local cemetery. That annual extracurricular activity ended abruptly when one of the old Victorian houses burned to the ground one hallowed eve. The arson was never pinned on any Redman students, but enough suspicion was raised to permanently end the tradition.

Last Halloween, I'd decided the Halloween issue of the *Redman Diary*, as the paper was called, was a good time to look back at the college's strange connection with the spiritualist community. But the administration nixed that one fast. I grudgingly abided and instead wrote a page one opinion piece about the history of college newspapers and the threats against their First Amendment rights by self-righteous school administrators. That didn't go over well either, but they let it pass.

Now a year later, my new editor was sending me to Spooksville. After compiling the obit on old Dan Cummings, a two-term mayor of Deland in the 1970s, I told Gordon about Redman's link with Cassadaga, thinking he would love the local hook. I was wrong.

"Forget that, Tom. That's ancient history. Besides, Delanders don't give a shit about what you privileged private school kids did on Halloween way back when. Like I said, get something current. Or something old and make it current."

Now that I was working on the paper, I had to stop thinking about Deland as Deadland. But ironically, the only people I'd been writing about so far were truly Deadlanders...or soon to be. At least I'd be getting out of town to write about more dead people. "How about a first-person story about a midnight visit to the Cassadaga cemetery? There's a spooky urban legend about that place. It's called the Devil's Chair, and…"

"Stop. Don't tell me any more. Go get the story. I like it already. I want to read it. First person is fine. But don't do anything illegal. You got that? If the cemetery closes after dark, get permission from somebody. Tell them you're on official business from the *Deland Star-Journal*. Show them your new press credentials," he added with a laugh.

"Okay, I'm heading out. I'll text you updates."

"Don't bother. Just get the fucking story. You can text your girlfriend. Or take her with you. And keep track of your expenses."

Not a bad idea, I thought as I walked out to my Prius. Samantha had actually told me once that she wanted to get a reading in Cassadaga. We could get a room in the old hotel and spend the night.

Like my roommates, Sam was a senior at Redman, and lived in the dorm. She was in psychology right now, her last class of the day. I texted her.

Me: *What are you doing this afternoon?*

Sam: *Writing a paper for art history.*

Me: *I got a better idea. A trip to Cassadaga.*

Sam: *Really? I'm in. Call you after class.*

"This is so exciting, Tommy. I've never had a reading. We can get dinner in the hotel restaurant. My friend Darlene said they've got good Italian."

I'd picked her up from the dorm, and now we were just a few minutes from Cassadaga. "Yeah, sounds good." I was glad that Gordon was covering expenses, and I just hoped that included dinner for two...and the hotel room. After all, I would be working late tonight.

"She also said I should get a reading at the house across the street from the hotel."

"Maybe if I can work it into my story, I can get the paper to pay for it."

"Oh, fuck that, Tommy. I don't want you blabbing about my reading in that gossipy newspaper. I'll pay for it myself."

"Sorry. It was just a thought."

She lifted her blond hair off the back of her t-shirt, a habit of hers, especially when she was annoyed. "Yeah, I know, a bad one."

Twenty-five minutes after departing we arrived in Cassadaga, and I drove slowly through the narrow hilly streets lined by old wood-framed houses with picket fences and placards at the gates offering mediumship services. A forest of tall pines framed the town. I pulled into the parking lot in front of the Cassadaga Hotel, a two-story Mediterranean-style structure built in the 1920s. We walked up the steps to the front door and entered a lobby that was right out of another era, complete with antique furniture.

"This is so cool," Sam declared. "What a great assignment for your first article." We peered in at the restaurant, which included a bar, then looked around a New Age gift shop featuring books, crystals, candles, incense, and Cassadaga t-shirts.

"Are you interested in a reading?" the woman behind the counter asked. She wore a billowy purple dress that reached her ankles.

"Not right now," I replied. "Where do we check in to get our room?"

"Right here with me."

Our first-floor room was small and basic with three doors. One opened to a hallway leading back to the lobby, another opened to an expansive porch that stretched the entire side of the hotel, and the third went to our bathroom.

Sam set down her bag and sat on the edge of the bed. She looked around, unimpressed. "I've seen closets bigger than this room." She quickly added: "I want to go get my reading. What're you going to do?"

"Get directions to the cemetery, I guess, and look around some more. Are you going to come with me after your reading?"

"Can't we just relax?" She smiled and patted the bed.

"Sure, later. I want to run over there and get some pictures before dark."

"Okay, fine. But I'm not going there at midnight with you. That's too creepy. I've heard those stories about that Devil's Chair."

"Yeah? What have you heard?" I knew the basics of the

legend, but I wanted to hear what Sam recalled.

"The story I heard is that the chair was built for an old man whose wife and daughter died in a fire. He came and sat in the chair facing their graves for hours every day. They say you can still see his ghost there sometimes."

"So why's it called the Devil's Chair?"

"Because if you're foolish enough to sit in the chair at midnight, the devil will talk to you. And if you come back in the morning, you will see the devil."

"Do you know the part about the beer can?"

"I heard something about it."

I pulled a can of Budweiser out of my pack and held it up. "Supposedly, if you sit there at midnight and leave a can of beer for the devil, in the morning it will be unopened...but empty."

"Well, I'd rather see that beer can than the devil in the morning...or at any time."

We walked out to the porch, and I wished Sam luck with her reading. I hoped she would find someone who was an actual psychic or medium, and not someone playing the role. As she disappeared across the street, I noticed the woman who had checked us in standing near the door to the lobby. She was smoking, holding an ashtray in her hand. I decided to see if I could interview her for my article. After all, I had no idea if I would find anyone in the cemetery to interview—at least anyone who was alive.

"What do you want to know?" she asked as I approached.

"Is it that obvious I was going to ask you something?"

"You look like someone who has questions. Maybe that's what you do, question people. Then you try to make sense out of the answers."

"That's good. You a psychic?" *Or just a good judge of character?*

"I do readings here in the hotel, along with tending the store and checking people in to their rooms. I cover most of the bases here, but I don't wait on tables in the restaurant or make coffee at our coffee bar."

"I'm a reporter for the Deland paper. Can I ask you a few questions?"

"About?"

"Cassadaga, of course."

"Wait."

She closed her eyes and continued to hold her cigarette above her copper ashtray. I pulled my phone out of my pocket and started my recorder. I also snapped a surreptitious photo of her. The ash on her cigarette was lengthening when her head jerked up and the ash fell into her copper ashtray. "No, you want to ask about the cemetery."

Okay. Had she overheard Sam and me talking? Or was she, well, an actual psychic? "That's part of it. I'm writing an article for our Halloween issue. Can I record our conversation?"

"Only if you promise to send me a copy of your article."

"May I use your photo?"

"Yes, but make sure you call me the hotel manager and a practicing psychic-medium."

Whatever, I thought, then snapped a couple more photos of her with my phone. I pulled out one of my cards. "E-mail me at this address on Halloween and I'll send you an attached file."

She held the cigarette between her lips for a moment, took the card, and slipped it into her dress. She exhaled a cloud of smoke. "What do you want to know?

"First, your name."

"Cassandra Carmichael. But you can call me Cassie."

"How did you know I wanted to ask about the cemetery?"

"Stuff pops into my head. Sometimes it's a voice, other times it's an image. I saw you standing by a gravestone. Or actually sitting by one." She shook her head. "What is it about you and dead people? I see them around you."

I shrugged. "I've been writing obituaries."

Cassie frowned. "They're telling me to warn you to be careful, or you might get what you're looking for. Does that make sense?"

"I think so. I'm planning to go to the cemetery tonight at midnight. Will I be able to get in?"

"Sure. If that's what you want. No one will stop you. I'll say this: If you go, you'll have an experience you'll never forget."

It sounded like a warning.

Dinner. The food was good, but I could hardly eat anything. All I could think about was my upcoming midnight journey and planting myself in the Devil's Chair. I was both excited and nervous, remembering what Cassie had told me. Sam was talking about her reading, but I was having a hard time focusing on what she was saying.

When she'd returned to the room from her reading, she'd been unusually quiet. She said she wanted to think about what she'd been told and would tell me about it later. All she revealed was that she'd cried.

We drove to the cemetery, located on a hill outside of town, so I could take a few photos with my digital camera and orient myself. I needed to be able to find the Devil's Chair in the dark. As I'd expected, Sam refused to sit in the chair, but I snapped a few pics of her standing behind it. "That's all," she said. "Let me see them." She slowly swiped through the images, examining each one closely probably to see if there were any spooks lurking in the background. She didn't look happy in any of the photos.

We wandered around for a few minutes, looking at the old graves, some dating back to the late nineteenth century, but Sam was getting more and more uneasy. "Let's get out of here," she said, noting that the sun was low in the sky and she didn't want to be here even at dusk.

We wandered through a grove of trees en route to the car, and both of us abruptly stopped when we heard a sharp screech like an animal under attack. The sound shifted to a howl, then laughter. A man and a woman burst out of the trees. "Gotcha, didn't we!" the woman crowed as they stepped out of the shadows. "Sorry about that. We couldn't help it."

They were a few years older than Sam and me, both slender and dressed in black. Their lips were painted black as well, and they wore heavy eye make up. Their multiple piercings sparkled, and their tattoos seemed to come alive in the warm light of the descending sun.

Sam took a couple of steps back, but I responded in a friendly manner. "Yeah, you got us. I bet you're headed to the Devil's Chair."

They both answered. "How did you know?"

"Hey, mind if I take a couple of photos of you two by the chair?" I told them about my assignment.

"Of course, that's why we're here." Again, they both spoke simultaneously.

That was strange, and it was enough for Sam. "Thomas, give me the keys, please. I'll wait for you in the car."

"Sure. Just don't drive away," I said and squeezed her arm. "I'll be there in a few minutes."

With that, my new companions and I headed for the infamous chair. "Can I get your names?"

"I'm Bela and this is Lugosi."

Great. Bela Lugosi. No doubt Flash would give me a hard time about those fake names, but I'd tell him it fit perfectly for a Halloween story. Lugosi sat in the chair and Bela sat on his lap. I took a dozen shots as they mugged for the camera. "Where are you two from?" I asked.

"Transylvania, Louisiana. It's a real place."

Back in the room. "Hello, Tommy, are you even listening to me? You said you wanted to hear about my reading, and I'm trying to tell you."

"Sorry. I'm just preoccupied with my article. So the reader told you that you were going to dump me for someone else? Is that what she said?"

"No, she said I would find my true love next year. I'm hoping it will be you."

"That doesn't sound very promising to me. Is that what made you cry?"

"No, it was about my relationship with my sister. She nailed it."

I'd heard about the issues between the two sisters and didn't want to get Sam started. "Maybe the reader didn't know that you'd already found love."

"She called it lust."

I choked back a laugh. "Oh, sounds like she tuned in on something."

I could see that Sam didn't find any humor in that comment.

Change the topic, I thought. "Hey, do you want to see those photos I took of that freaky couple sitting on the Devil's Chair? I can pull them up on my phone."

"No, I don't. I've seen enough of them. Did you notice they weren't wearing any shoes?"

"No, I didn't see that."

"Really? How unobservant of you, Mr. Reporter. How did they get there, anyhow? I didn't see any other car."

"Maybe they parked off the main road and walked up."

"Yeah in bare feet. Why would they do that?"

"Who knows? They're weirdos. Hey, you sure you don't want to go back with me at midnight?"

"No way. I don't think you should go, either."

"Seriously, Sam? I'm not afraid of ghosts, because there's no such thing. They only exist in stories."

I arrived at the cemetery at ten to midnight. In spite of what I'd said to Sam, I couldn't help feeling somewhat uneasy walking among the graves. The crunch of leaves and twigs underfoot seemed magnified and made me conscious of the silence and the sleeping bones lost in eternity six feet below. The silver moonlight cast shadows from the gravestones, enhancing the eeriness. I would write about these sensations in my article, while noting that I was a non-believer. That would make my sense of uneasiness more palpable, I thought.

I approached the red brick chair at 11:58. I scanned the graveyard, looking for any shadowy movements or shimmering visions. I couldn't help wondering if those neo-goths were hiding somewhere again, ready to jump out and frighten me the moment I sat down. But the graveyard felt empty. It was just me and all the dead.

I settled into the Devil's Chair, made of red bricks. It had a broad back, a broad concrete seat wide enough for two people. Sort of like a throne, but not really. It was just a local urban legend, I told myself. Nothing was going to happen. I wished it was Halloween tonight. There probably would be some activity here, maybe a few costumed visitors prancing through the graveyard, something to report. But stories about Halloween appeared before the designated day. No one was interested in reading about Halloween events after it was over, unless the reports concerned poisoned candy and razor blades turning up in the kiddies' bags, abandoned houses burning to the ground, or gravestones knocked over and marred with graffiti.

I reached into my pack and pulled out the can of beer I'd brought along. I was tempted to pop it open and guzzle it down. Maybe I would even toast the non-existent devil. But I'd already decided to play along with the legend. So I set it on the arm of the chair.

I should've brought a cushion to sit on. The chair was uncomfortable, and I wondered how the old man had sat here for hours. I adjusted my position and leaned into the backrest. In spite of the hard surfaces, my head nodded after a few minutes, and I was overcome with drowsiness. I'd stayed up reading late last night, and now my shortage of sleep combined with two glasses of wine at dinner was taking its toll.

Voices. I caught my breath, jerked awake. Was it a dream or had I really heard people talking? I looked over my shoulder and saw the same couple entering the graveyard. They each had draped an arm over the other's shoulders, and they were weaving like drunks. I slid off the chair, crouched low, and when I saw they weren't looking my way, I darted over to an old oak tree and ducked behind it.

I would turn the tables and see if I could scare them. As soon as they approached, I would jump out and scream and wave my arms. I imagined they would turn and run or probably stumble and fall. The murmur of their voices grew louder. It was strange that they would come back, but then, that was what I'd done.

"Look, someone left us a beer," Lugosi said.

My back was pressed against the trunk of the tree. They were only twenty feet away. Perfect timing. My heart was pounding. *Do it now,* I told myself. I leaped out, waving my arms, and started to let out what I hoped would be a blood-curdling howl. But I caught my breath and my scream died in a gurgle. The Devil's Chair was empty. I looked around and couldn't believe that they'd somehow managed to move away without my noticing it. I hadn't frightened them away. They were gone before I'd stepped out.

"We're here for you, Tommy." The simultaneous chorus from the two had issued from directly behind me. I spun around, but no one was there.

My phone vibrated. A text from Sam.

Get out of there, Tommy. Those two we saw are dead. They were murdered outside that cemetery back in the mid '80s.

Again, the chorus spoke from behind me: "Stay with us, Tommy. Stay with us."

This time I didn't look back. I raced for my car, and their voices echoed in my head. "Tommy, Tommy. Stay with us. Stay with us."

I tripped over my own foot, stumbled and fell. I crawled on my hands and knees seeking purchase so I could scramble away. I sensed they were directly behind me, hovering over me. A chill raced down my spine. Finally, I bolted up and ran as if death itself was closing in. I heard their voices one more time, both furious now: "TOMMY, STOP!"

Sam and I sat at a table on the porch the next morning with coffee and pastries. We were packed and ready to leave Cassadaga. "Look, I found it, Sam. They were murdered here in 1986, and they were from Louisiana. Here's their picture."

"My god, they look almost the same, except her hair is blue there and he's got a goatee."

"Remember, I told you their names and they said they were from Transylvania. There really is a Transylvania, Louisiana. And her name was Bela and his was Luigi." Close to Lugosi.

"Now you've got a story to write, Tommy. Except you don't believe in ghosts."

"I know. That makes it more interesting. I'm a non-believer— or at least I was—but then I saw something. Too bad there's no proof of it."

"What about the pictures you took of them on the Devil's Chair?"

"Shit, I completely forgot." I pulled out my camera and flicked through the pictures of Sam standing behind the chair and a few others I'd taken. I came to the final ones, and stared at the empty chair. "They're gone. It's just pictures of the chair. So, like I said, no proof."

Sam shook her head. "Let's get out of here."

"Wait. We've still got to go back to the cemetery. I want to see if the can of beer is there, empty and unopened. I still don't believe in the devil, but that would be proof of something."

"Yeah, the devil," Sam responded.

From nearby someone laughed. I look up to see Cassie, who wore a long white dress and held a cigarette and ashtray in her hand again. "I guess you had an experience, Tom."

"Yeah, I did."

She took a deep breath, dropped her head back, exhaled. Her eyes glazed as she stared at me. "The beer can will be your proof, but not the way you think it will."

I thanked her, and we headed on our way. En route, Sam explained that Cassie was the one who had told her about the murdered couple. "She lives in the room next to us. She was smoking on the porch after midnight when I talked to her. She said both of them were shot point blank in the forehead. A handyman who worked in the camp was a suspect, but he committed suicide, and no one was ever arrested."

We walked up to the Devil's Chair for the final time, and the beer was still there and unopened. I rubbed my hands together. "Now to see if it's really empty." I picked it up and was disappointed. "It's still full. It's just an unopened beer."

"Are you sure?" Sam asked.

"Of course, watch." I shook it up several times, held it at arm's length and popped it open, expecting the foamy brew to shoot out.

Instead, a warm red liquid bubbled over my hand and dribbled in front of the Devil's Chair. I dropped the can and looked at my hand. "Shit, it's blood, Sam!"

"You got some on me," she gasped, wiping her arms. "Oh my god, look!"

She pointed at the foot of the chair. Two small pumpkins, the size of softballs, rested in front of each leg, and they were splattered in blood. I picked up one, then the other. Splotches of blood formed two eyes, a nose, and a grinning toothy mouth.

"Wow! I've got to get pictures."

I set the pumpkins on the chair and fumbled in my bag for my camera. But by the time I was ready to shoot the pumpkins, the blood—or whatever it was—had started to fade. I snapped several photos, but when I looked closely at the images, there was no sign of any facial features on the pumpkins, no sign of the blood.

"No! Not again."

Sam reached for the camera. "Let me see."

She swiped through the photos, and caught her breath. "The legend said that you would see him in the morning. Look!"

I peered over her shoulder. To the left of the first photo of the pumpkins was the last one I'd taken of Bela and Lugosi. And now I could see them faintly, ghostly images, and I could see the back of the chair visible through them. Both had a single black hole in their foreheads.

I already knew that Flash was going to call it a double-exposure. It wasn't, but it didn't matter. To me it was proof.

WILD CARD

BY T. J. MACGREGOR

Iam surrounded by toys. A beach ball and a Barbie doll, a stuffed bear with a missing eye, colorful plastic hoops of varying sizes that fit together to form a chain. There's a pretty quilt with frayed borders that's decorated with rainbows, and a little red radio that plays, "It's a Small, Small World."

"Are you comfortable?" Newton, who is in charge of the investigation, asks anxiously, his arms dropping to his sides as he sits forward at his desk. "Would you like some coffee? A Coke? Water? Anything?"

"Coffee would be great." It's three a.m. and coffee is the last thing I want, but I think he'll settle down once he has burned off some of that nervous energy. "With a splash of cream."

He rises quickly, grateful for something to do. His office is no larger than a cardboard box, and he crosses the room in three or four strides. He's a tall man, several inches over six feet, and moves like a bullet. On his messy desk is a photograph in an oval frame, like a locket, of him and his wife and son. The three of them are laughing as though they have shared some private joke. He and his son look like different versions of the same man, both of them with dark hair and eyes and square chins. The wife is blond, blue-eyed, diminutive.

Earlier, he picked up the photograph, turned it over in his hand, thinking. What if... His stake in this has become quite personal.

I have no children. But for me, this process is always personal, even when it fails.

I pick up the brown bear with the missing eye and hug him against my chest. He's soft, of course; little bears always are. But when I squeeze him, he feels almost human. I press my hands to either side of his face. His missing eye seems tragic somehow, that great blank space where the bit of glass should be. The gaze of the surviving eye, that iris like a drop of honey, is fixed, relentless. I start to choke up. I want to heal the bear, protect him, hide him from the bad man.

"Here's your coffee, Claire."

I'm staring at Newman's shoes, loafers, probably from Target. I nod about the coffee but don't let go of the bear. I hear Newman's chair squeak as he sits down. I can smell the coffee. "Something about the mother's boyfriend," I tell him.

A seed of doubt pokes up at the end of that statement. Boyfriend or husband? Why "boyfriend" instead of lover? Does he live with Jessie and her mother?

"What about him?" Newman asks.

I hear his pen scratching across paper. I know he's recording this on his phone as well.

"He tore off the bear's eye to punish her."

I let go of the bear, and he tumbles out of my lap, head over heels, and lands on his back. That singular eye stares up at me, and I want to weep.

The beach ball: Newton passes it to me. He knows the routine. Keep things moving.

The ball's skin is hard, red and white, with a black streak that circles its circumference, a little equator. Jessie loves her ball. Her perfect hands cup and stroke it, explore it like a globe. Now the ball is flying, and she reaches up for it, longs for it, cries for it, and something slams against the side of her head, over her ear. I can feel it. The ball is gone. There is only pain and a terrible silence.

"She's deaf in one ear. Because he struck her. The boyfriend hit her when she cried about the ball."

"Which ear?" Newton asks.

"Left. The left."

We've worked together enough so he doesn't question my certainty on this point. But his job requires that he confirm it.

He pauses his phone's recording and taps out a number. He speaks too softly for me to hear. I release the ball and it bounces away from me, the black equator spinning. It hits the front of Newton's desk and stops. I reach for my coffee. It's thick and rich and still warm. It pools in my stomach, burning like acid, and when I look at the ball again, it is only that, a ball without a story.

I stand, kick off my shoes, and walk barefoot around the tiny room, grounding myself. Outside, it has begun to thunder and lightning. This will be a violent South Florida thunderstorm; the stink of ozone permeates the dark air.

"Okay," Newton says.

As though something is settled. He seems more relaxed now, and I suspect he confirmed that Jessie is, indeed, deaf in one ear and that her mother's boyfriend either lives with them or might as well. I want to ask, but don't. There are certain rules that Newton and I follow. We don't break them. We never even speak of them. When he calls, he merely asks if I'm free, and we both know what that means.

Someday, I may ask him what he thinks of me. But I probably won't like the answer. I make him uneasy. What Newton doesn't realize is that every day he does what I do. He simply has another name for it. Hunch. Instinct. The difference between us is just one of orientation. I read stories with my hands; he reads them in the very air he breathes.

"You feel like taking a dri…" He stops, watching me as I pick up the Barbie doll.

Jessie is three. I don't remember being three, but I remember Barbie dolls. I had two of them. Between them, they had a dozen outfits, a dozen hairdos, a dozen faces. They had furniture and dreams and long talks at slumber parties. They were my friends. This doll is Jessie's friend. She misses holding her, dressing her, sharing with her. Jessie is well and chilled, in a dark, hidden place, and wishes Barbie were with her.

"Claire?"

I realize I'm huddled in a corner of the room, clutching the doll, whimpering and rocking. Distantly, like voices in a dream, I hear a man and woman shouting, arguing about me.

"Claire, hey, listen, I think…"

Yes, I know what he thinks. That we should take a break. That I'm too close to it. His apprehension shows in the lines of his pleasant face, in the way he stands over me, arms folded across his chest as if to protect himself from something. I don't blame him. I'm the X in the equation, the wild card.

I release Barbie and slide slowly up the wall, my heart knotted in my chest. Rain taps the windows. A boom of thunder is followed instantly by lightning that burns a path across the dark wet glass.

"Let's go take that drive, Newt."

We leave by the rear door, like thieves. He has lent me a raincoat, and it flaps at my knees as we sprint across the parking lot to his Honda. The rain is cool and sharp, a sure sign that the storm is ushering in the first cold front of this year's winter.

I don't do this for a living. I couldn't. I sell real estate. It's a seasonal market here in Florida, with our busiest time right about now, in that stretch between Thanksgiving and Easter. But I make my own hours, and when Newton calls, time and sometimes even seasons cease to matter much.

The Honda's wipers whip across the windshield, leaving half-moons of clarity in their wake. I am holding the pretty quilt with frayed borders. I taste the residue of coffee on my tongue.

"Just tell me where to go," Newt says.

Where to go. I press my face into the quilt. The little girl smells make my cheeks ache. My right side throbs and when I breathe, I want to double up in pain. Mommy is worried, probably crying. But I don't care. I'm scared. It's raining, and I'm scared.

I shut my eyes against the quilt, blocking out the rhythmic monotony of the wipers. Static issues from Newton's radio, then a voice. He lowers the volume. The rain falls harder.

Where to go.

"One of her ribs is fractured. He hit her. She ran away. Do you have a map of the area?"

He brings up a map on his cell, but I shake my head. "A physical map."

Newton reaches across my legs to the glove compartment.

He's happily married to his college sweetheart. He has been a cop for ten years. His son is eight. He's a good father and a decent man, uncorrupted by what he has seen in a decade in this business. He isn't surprised by what I just said.

But I know the optimist in him was hoping for some other explanation, a child who simply wandered off and got lost, or a drifter, perhaps, a repeat offender. He knows the nightmare, the monster, is us, but he doesn't want to acknowledge it yet. We are nothing less than the culmination of the choices we make.

I study the map and locate where we are, where Jessie lives, where she was last seen. This would be easier to see on Google maps, with GPS pinpointing our location, but I've found that physical maps usually speak to me more loudly. And I keep clutching the blanket, stroking it, plundering its tales, its brief history. The quilt speaks, but the map does not.

"Do you get anything?" Newton asks.

The conduit is rather like an electrical pulse, connecting me to her, her to me, us to each other. But it isn't consistently clear, and never is it so specific that it offers an address.

"Dark, wet, round, hard, scared."

"Round? What do you mean by round, Claire?"

"Round, I don't know. Something round. Maybe an opening."

"A door? A window?"

"Something hard." I strain, reaching through the wet dark. "A pipe. Yeah, a pipe, that's it. She's in a pipe."

He grabs the map, turns on a light. "A construction site, that's got to be it. There's a new apartment going up about four blocks from where she lives. Does that sound right, Claire?"

"I don't know."

He reminds me that although Jessie's mother reported her missing only several hours ago, she has not been seen for eighteen hours. It means there are no search parties yet, that officially the child isn't even missing. "Please," he says. "Try."

But the pain distracts me. Her pain. It's worse when I breathe. The boundaries between us have long since blurred. Her fingers move, and mine twitch in response. Something wet and sticky oozes from a corner of her mouth; it becomes my mouth.

"She's badly hurt, Newton. I think the busted rib has punctured her lung."

"We'll try the construction site."

He drives too quickly through the wet, deserted streets, speaking to someone on the radio, then on his phone. The boyfriend will be brought in for questioning. The police would encourage the mother to press charges. HRS would get involved. This isn't a pretty story. The most I hope for is that we'll find her and the ending will be better than most.

The wind rises, hurling rain against the windshield, where it smears like spit before the wipers whip it away. Trees crowd the sides of the road, a gang of thugs. The quilt is bunched against my chest, vomiting images of Jessie hiding beneath it, the boyfriend drunk, the mother screaming.

The car screeches into a turn, and a wash of light exposes us like an x-ray: Newton is hunched over the steering wheel, trying to see, and I am huddled against the door, trying to breathe. I'm sure now that what I'm looking at is the opening of a pipe and Jessie is inside it, peering out. But a construction site doesn't seem quite right.

Newton speeds up, the car bounces, the tires spew gravel. Then we are outside, and I have no clear memory of stopping, of leaving the car. We shout her name. Rain pelts the hood of my rain slicker, my face, my eyes. The wind gasps at my ankles and shakes the wire mesh fence that surrounds the construction site. A spill of light from the sodium vapor lamps illumines tractors, trucks, wet dunes of dirt, the shell of an unfinished building. Rods made of steel and iron and blocks of cement are scattered everywhere, like the refuse of a gang war. I see pipes, but none of them are large enough to crawl into.

We keep calling for her, I clutch the quilt more tightly, begging it to give me something vital. But it has nothing more to tell; its story is finished. Pain bursts in my right side, and as I stumble, Newton grabs my arm, steadying me. Black dots swirl across the insides of my eyes, my peripheral vision grows fuzzy, a spasm of coughing eats up my meager reserves of energy.

"What is it?" Newton grips me by both arms, his face so

close to mine I can see beads of water rolling down the bridge of his nose.

"She's fading fast."

And then Jessie offers me something, a small gift of water, of puddles or rivulets from the rain, but water like a river that is standing still. I tear across the dunes and plains of this forsaken place, shouting her name, headed for the canal that runs behind the construction site. Newton races after me. The burning in my side is so deep now, so terrible, it short-circuits everything inside me. I stumble again and sink to my knees in the wet dirt. Newton helps me up, grasps my hand, and we move on.

The light is dimmer back here, little more than a thin varnish the color of nicotine. But it's enough to detect the small hills of dirt and rock that rise along the edge of the can's wall. We lumber like giants, he and I, calling for her, peering over the side into the murky, rain-dimpled waters. I see no protrusions from the wall, no pipes.

I lost her quilt when we left the car and feel I am losing her as well. The borders between us are not as blurred now; she is withdrawing, untangling herself from me. Even her pain is leaving me.

We are just past the building's shell, where the canal turns away from the mangroves on its far side. I spot a shallow slope of dirt and pebbles that leads to a prayer rug of sand. Six inches of pipe jut from the wall. I scramble over the top and land on my knees in the sand. It's soft as a sponge. The beam of my flashlight doesn't reveal much inside the pipe. It's too long, too dark, too wet.

"Jessie?" My voice echoes down the corridor of cement. A spider the size of my palm scampers through the pool of light, the echo of my voice dies, and there's no response.

"Maybe it's not the pipe you saw, Claire."

Maybe: I detest the word. It punctuates the process, breaks it up as a prism does light, sows endless doubts. Six months ago, a *maybe* spelled the difference for a sixteen-year-old girl, a runaway who died in a Miami crack house. *Maybe* is lethal. I'm going in.

"Keep shouting for her," I tell Newton, and crawl into the pipe.

I don't like enclosed spaces. I especially don't like them wet and dark. I move in a squat, one leg, then the other, keeping my hands free. The beam of light seems impoverished in this darkness. The pipe narrows, and I'm forced onto my hands and knees. A spider's web slides across my nose, my cheeks. I jerk back, banging my head on the ceiling. The flashlight slips from my grasp and rolls away from me, clattering, spilling light in thin, pathetic layers.

When it stops four feet later, it illumines an arm, thin and pale, then another arm, then hair tangled like floating seaweed. She is lying where the pipe bends, an elbow of concrete that connects to other elbows, perhaps all the way to the sea. I shout at Newton to get on his phone, call an ambulance. He shouts back.

I quickly unzip my raincoat and lift Jessie against me as I rock back on my heels and settle against the curve of the pipe. Her head lolls against my chest. She whimpers with pain as I pull the sides of my raincoat over her, around her, protecting her as she once tried to protect her little bear.

For a moment that is all too brief, the boundaries between us melt again and her story is *there*, whole and untouched. The boyfriend, the mother, the child, a trinity that is crippled, and here, her pain, her fear, her innocence.

Then we are two again, holding onto each other, the rain as distant as some childhood memory. "It's okay, Jessie," I whisper. "It's going to be okay."

And for her, it will be. Of that much I'm certain.

PORTAL

BY T. J. MACGREGOR

Mary always feels lightheaded after a séance, not quite her-self. It's as if the power of the unseen somehow crosses the invisible threshold between there and here and rides into this world through her.

Right now, she's alone, it's quiet, everyone sleeps. She can hear the distant hoot of an owl as clearly as she hears the beat of her own heart. Her body seems to creak when she moves. Her fingers feel thicker, stubby, and when she flexes them, they don't seem to belong to her. Her skin is damp.

Only once has Mary mentioned this to her husband. In his soft, practical voice, he bypassed the issue of her fingers, of the lightness in her head. He told her that she must put an end to the séances.

But she can't. The séances are her only contact with Willie. And yes, she is sure it's her dead son who comes through, her last born, her precious baby. Her heart aches just at the thought of his beautiful face. When she closes her eyes, she can almost see it, his face, those exquisite features. Willie, who was the most like her.

Mary rises from the bed, body creaking. The lightness shoots through her skull, black stars explode inside her eyes. Water, she thinks. She needs a glass of water.

But before she reaches the basin, the wall directly in front of her seems to burn with color. To glow. She throws up her hands to shield her eyes from the strange, luminous light. Her head pounds, her feet seem to move forward of their own volition, her stomach heaves.

She stumbles and falls into the light. A scream tears up her throat and lurches into the air as a stifled sob. Then the light is everywhere, glowing but dissolving, pulsing yet silent. Mary can't breathe. Mary can't see.

Mary, Mary, quite contrary...

She blinks, her vision clears. She's on her knees, hands gripping the layers of her skirt, her breath heaving in her chest. Directly in front of her is a small child with golden hair, a girl softly singing a song Mary has never heard. *Mary, Mary, quite contrary, how does your garden grow?* She is skipping, her arms swing, her small dainty feet seem to dance against the floor. And then she stops, her eyes grow wide, the song dies in her throat.

"Who...who're you?" the girl stutters.

Mary tries to speak, but her throat closes up. She tries to move, to get up; her legs refuse to work. She and the golden-haired child stare at each other, the moment frozen in time.

"Caroline..." calls the voice of a man Mary can't see. *"Caroline, ready or not, here I come..."*

The girl's head snaps around, she twists her body. *"Daddy!"* She shrieks and runs down the hall toward the man who has appeared.

Mary, Mary...

The light burns around her again, the air pulses, and Mary wrenches back, hands flying to her face.

When she comes to, Abraham is leaning over her, saying her name again. His beard looks odd from where she's lying, sort of fuzzy, with streaks of gray beginning to peek out her and there. "Okay, I'm okay," she says, and presses her palms against the floor, pushing up to a sitting position.

Mary doesn't have to look around to know she is in the room where Willie died, the room where everything has been the same since February 20, 1862. Until today, no one, not even her husband, knew that she has entered this room many times in the months since his death. The rest of her life goes on around her, as though she's merely a spectator at a play. Even though she smiles and shakes hands and does what is expected of her, she knows her real life is here, in this room.

"What were you doing in here?" Abraham asks. "I thought…"

The rest of what he says drifts away from her. Her heart remains in Willie's room. One night, she even fell asleep in here, curled up on the floor near the bed, Willie's voice whispering in her ear. But these secrets are hers and hers alone.

Her husband helps her to her feet and doesn't release her arm even after they've left Willie's room. The hallway is cold, much too dark. The flames of the lanterns flicker along the wall, casting eerie shadows. Mary is suddenly so exhausted she can barely make it into their bedroom.

Her awareness seems to blink off and on, here one moment, elsewhere the next. Abraham, tending to her. Abraham, fixing the quilt over her. Abraham, now speaking in the dark about the trouble in the South. About what he should do or not do.

She realizes he is asking her opinion in that way he usually does, as though he's merely relating events and not asking at all. He wants to know what she thinks because she's from the South, from Lexington, Kentucky, and he seems to have it in his head that her thoughts on the subject reflect the thoughts of all Southerners.

Yes or no for slaves.

Yes or no for intervention.

Yes or no.

Yes.

No.

The last thing she hears is her dead son's voice, whispering that he loves her.

II

It's five days later. She knows because she has counted each sunrise and sunset. She knows because she needs to know. She stands at the closed door to Willie's room. The Death Room. She reaches for the knob, her hand begins to tremble, then to shake. Mary jerks it back and hides it in her skirts, then glances quickly up and down the hall.

No one.

Nothing.

Just the uneasy silence.

Do it, she thinks, and brings her hand out from the folds of her skirt and thrusts it toward the knob. Her fingers brush the metal. *Will, are you here?"*

Mary turns the knob.

The door creaks.

She slips into the twilit room and shuts the door fast, very fast. Then she stands with her back against it, breathing hard, eyes darting left, right, left again. Nothing here. Of course not. There was no séance tonight. There may never be another séance.

Abraham won't tolerate it.

People talk, he says, they think you're odd. You must contain your grief. And oh, he adds, you're spending too much money. The gloves, the clothes….He shakes his head. Too much. Four hundred pairs of gloves and $27,000 on clothes are way too much. Mary fails to understand how these details about her spending habits are connected to the séances.

She doesn't know what to say. She never does. So she presses her hands to her ears to block out the sound of her husband's voice. She catches the scent of Willie's freshly washed hair, of his clean, innocent skin, and her knees buckle and she begins to weep.

III

Mary raises her head. She stands in a room where she recognizes the long, wooden writing table, but nothing else. And yet, she knows she's in the mansion because of the view through the window, a view from the second floor, facing away from the main road. But the rest of it is all wrong.

The writing table is long, cluttered at one end with stacks of paper. Framed photographs adorn it. Of a boy. A beautiful woman. And the golden-haired girl she saw, the girl named Caroline. Between two of the photographs is a rectangle of wood with words engraved on it: *John F. Kennedy.*

Mary runs her fingers over the letters, repeating the name silently to herself, frantically searching her memory for someone named Kennedy. The only name that is the least bit familiar is John, the name of Abraham's secretary.

She hears footsteps, then a door opens and a handsome, oddly dressed man hurries in, flipping through papers, a book tucked under his arm. *"I'll need that file on...."* He glances up and they both freeze.

"My God, what...."

Mary wrenches back. "I...."

The man flinches and the book in his hand crashes to the floor. The noise echoes in Mary's skull, pounds hard and fast, and she charges for the door, running so fast that everything blurs around her. She runs until she can run no more, runs until she bumps into something.

"Mary, what is it?"

Abraham grips her forearms, shakes her gently. She pulls her arms free, runs her hands nervously over her skirt, glances back down the corridor. It looks like home. She laughs quickly, sharply, then looks at her husband.

"The mansion is haunted," she says.

Haunted.

IV

"Mama?"

Mary glances down at her son, eleven years old and as gangly as his father. She doesn't know what he has asked her. "What is it, Tad?"

Tad rolls his eyes, indicating that he has already repeated his question several times. "Papa says that Willie died because he was tired. Do you think that's true?"

Her son's face blurs. She reaches out blindly to touch his head, his hair, wanting desperately to say the right thing, the correct thing. But she doesn't know the answer.

That word, *tired,* bounces against the inner walls of her skull, harder and faster until her head feels as if it will explode.

The June heat pours over her, black dots blast apart inside her eyes, a dizziness seizes her. She stops, leaning against a tree, where the full shade falls over her.

She rubs her hands over her face, smelling summer on her skin. Summer—grass, trees, greenery. But just blocks from here, soldiers lay dying in the hospital. That's where she and Tad are going, to the hospital to visit the wounded, the dying, the victims of the war. Yes, she remembers now.

"Mama?" Tad says softly.

Her hands drop away from her face. "He's not really dead," she replies finally. "We just can't see him."

"Papa says—"

"Papa doesn't understand. Let's hurry now." She grabs his damp little hand and moves quickly forward, toward the hospital and the stink of rotting limbs.

V

The July warmth drifts through the carriage windows, washing over her. Mary shuts her eyes, losing herself in the rhythmic noise of the horse's hooves, clattering in the darkness. She tries to imagine what tonight's séance might bring and hopes desperately for a message from Willie.

She's trying a new clairvoyant tonight, a séance at the woman's house, not the first time she has left the mansion for this purpose. Perhaps this woman can accomplish what others have not, a materialization, an apport, something tangible, something....

Suddenly, the rhythm of the horse's hooves changes and a moment later she's thrown free of the carriage, her body flying through the darkness as though she has sprouted wings. She crashes to the ground, her head slams against something, and the darkness claims her.

When she opens her eyes, she's lying in her bed in the mansion. The excruciating pain in her head has swallowed every other sensation, every thought, every desire. Her body feels as if it's being consumed by fire. She tries to push up on her elbows but doesn't have the strength. When she turns her head slightly, the pain rolls from one temple to the other.

She squints. There. She can just make out Abraham and another man on the other side of the room. The doctor. Abraham and the doctor. With considerable effort, she catches a word, a phrase, of their conversation.

"Infection...delirious...concern...someone with her...."

Mary doesn't want to hear anything else. She wishes the doctor would leave so she and Abraham can be alone. There are things she needs to tell him, the pressing secrets of what she has seen and experienced in this room. She must tell him about the glowing wall, a portal to that other world.

But her husband walks out into the hallway with the doctor. Mary aches with disappointment. He belongs first to other people. It has been like that since she has known him. Even when he comes to her, he brings the multitudes to their bed. He brings the war, the chaos of the country, the needs of the white, the Negroes, the North, the South. And he attends to everyone's needs, but rarely to her needs.

Hot, stinging tears gather in the corners of her eyes and finally spill over. Mary turns her head to the side and squeezes her eyes shut. Distantly, she hears the voices of that other place calling to her. She knows that if she opens her eyes, she'll see the glowing wall. Perhaps Willie lives now in that other place, with the pretty little girl named Caroline.

VI

She wakes suddenly, inexplicably, her nightgown wet with perspiration. She blinks hard and fast against the dark. Why isn't the gas lamp still lit? Why isn't someone in here with her? Where are her sons? Her husband? Why is the mansion so deeply silent?

A scream rises in her throat and falls into the air as a pathetic little whisper. Mary pushes up on her elbows, her heart slams against the walls of her chest, her mouth tastes like sand, is as dry as sand. She may die of thirst.

Or maybe she is already dead.

She drops her legs over the side of the bed, pinches her arm.

Alive. Okay, she's alive. She sits for long moments, motionless, her eyes gradually adjusting to the darkness.

The wall isn't glowing.

She feels her bare feet against the floor.

Water, she thinks, and pushes to her feet. She weaves across the room, toward where she's sure the pitcher and basin are. But the door suddenly opens and the girl with the gold hair runs in, laughing, a little boy trailing after her. The girl, Caroline, sees Mary first, and stops. Her brother slams into her from behind, falls back, hits the floor.

"*I see you,*" Caroline whispers. "*You're Mary Todd. Daddy saw you. I'm not afraid.*"

"You...I..." No, she must be coherent, she must...

"*I'm sorry about honest Abe...I'm sorry...the theater...*"

Her words echo horribly in Mary's skull, she doesn't hear it all. The air quivers, blurs, and she struggles desperately to hold onto the connection between them, the link, the *magic* that allows them to see each other, to speak. And for moments, she sees the girl's face clearly, the promise of extraordinary beauty, the hair like sunlight on snow.

Her arms jerk upward, and she extends them toward the girl, her mouth moving, articulating nothing. Then the little boy cries, wails, "*Ghost, Mommy, ghost!*"

The air ripples again, as though a curtain of shimmering rain lies between them and Mary, and they vanish. Only the light remains. Mary stumbles toward it, toward the light, certain that other people lie beyond it.

But before she reaches it, before the light grazes the tips of her toes, her husband appears, his tall, lanky frame silhouetted in the doorway.

"Mary, my God, you shouldn't be out of bed. The doctor said—"

"The girl, I saw the girl, she said she's sorry about you, about—"

"Ssshhh," he says, and puts his arms around her and helps her back into the bed. "Your gown is soaked. I think your fever has broken." He runs his hands over her face, through her hair, down her arms.

His touch ignites a desire she hasn't known since Willie went away and she pulls him toward her, whispers to him, presses her mouth to his. He tries to pull away from her, but her need is stronger than his resistance and he gathers her in his arms. His body molds against hers. For now, for these few moments, she shares him with no one.

VII

The chill in the mansion surpasses anything she has ever known here. It eats away at her feet, her legs, her hands and face. It slips up her legs, an insidious insect that even the fire in the hearth can't kill.

Tad fell asleep with his head in her lap, and now she lifts it carefully and slips a quilt under it. She doesn't have the heart to wake him. She brushes her mouth to his forehead and he stirs in his sleep, perhaps dreaming of summer.

Mary rubs her hands together and gets to her feet. Abraham is out of the city for the next few days and has taken their other two sons with him. She can't remember exactly where they've gone. Such details elude her more frequently these days. They don't seem to matter as much as the portal in the magical wall.

She lights a lantern and hurries upstairs, through the flickering light of the gas lamps. Already her head feels lighter, the way it has so often since the accident. Her face is damp, too, damp despite the chill in these rooms, and her fingers seem to be shorter, thicker. She has come to recognize the symptoms, to realize they have recurred every time she has traveled to that other place. In moments, as soon as she crosses the threshold into Willie's room, her body will no longer feel as though it's her own.

She pauses outside the room, her heart drumming, beads of perspiration rolling down the sides of her face. She digs into the pocket of her skirt for the key, slips it out. Her hand is so unsteady she drops the key. Its clatter against the floor seems to echo endlessly in the shadowed, cavernous hall. She gets the key in the lock, turns it. The door swings open, creaking softly.

Mary just stands there, unable to step into the room, but

unable to move away. She holds up the lantern, trying to illumi-
nate shadows in the distant corners, to make out the foot of the
bed, the shape of the water pitcher. But the light doesn't reach.

Go.

Can't. Abraham wouldn't like it.

He isn't here.

Can't...can't...

Go.

Mary squeezes her eyes shut and hear the whispers of that
other world. She steps quickly into the room and only then do
her eyes flutter open. The whispers cease.

She pushes the door shut with her foot and forces herself to
move toward the magical wall. She passes the darkened windows. Then, a foot short of the wall, she stops, sets the lantern
on the floor, and sits beside it. Now, she thinks. Now she will
wait.

Mary waits for a long time, her body motionless on the floor,
the lantern's flame tossing light and shadows against the magical wall. Nothing happens. Her eyes begin to burn, her spine
aches, her stomach knots. Maybe what they're saying about her
is true, that she's a little crazy, not all there, that Willie's death
and the fall from the carriage months ago affected her mind.

She fights back a wave of despair. Silence clamps down over
her, a thick, terrible silence. But then, in the heart of it, she hears
something. Voices. Weeping. Drum rolls.

Her head snaps up. Willie's room is gone. The darkness is
gone. She finds herself at the edge of a crushing crowd outside a
tremendous cathedral. Everyone around her is weeping, watching the front of the cathedral. Mary slips through the weeping
throngs, certain Willie is here somewhere, that he's hiding from
her. She calls his name, panic swelling in her chest, and hurries
as fast as her legs will carry her.

She reaches the front of the crowd and stops. There, a few
feet from her, stands the girl with the golden hair, Caroline.
And the young boy. Between them is the lovely woman from
the photograph, her body draped in black, a thin black veil covering her face. She's holding her children's hands. But as a cas-
ket is carried from the cathedral, the boy releases his mother's

hand and brings his fingers to his brow, a solemn salute.

Their sorrow washes over her, a crippling tide, and she runs away from them, from the mother and her two children, from the endless crushing tide of sorrow. She trips, she falls, she scrambles on her hands and knees, her sobs slapping the quivering air. Darkness clamps over her, a thick, terrible darkness in which she hears a voice say, *"The President…shot in Dallas…"* Then, another voice: *"On board Air Force One…Johnson was sworn in…"*

Her head explodes, and her hands fly to her skull, gripping it as if to contain blood and bone. The room spins, the crowd blurs, the light dims, then everything goes black.

VIII

"I saw…I heard…Johnson as president…"

She stammers, chokes, sobs what she has seen, what she has heard, what she has experienced. And although Abraham listens intently and holds her tightly, she glimpses something disturbing in his eyes.

Only later does she realize he blames himself for these "episodes," that's how he refers to them. *Mary's episodes*, like the title of a chapter in a book about his life.

Perhaps it's guilt that urges him to suggest a séance. It catches her off guard, the way he utters it so quietly over dinner, when it's just the two of them at the table. *"I think we should try to talk to William…"* But maybe it isn't guilt at all; maybe it's just a need he has never spoken aloud until now, the need of a father who has lost a son.

And of course she arranges it, secretly thrilled that his desire is so close to her own.

The clairvoyant who conducts the séance is the one Mary was to see the night of the carriage accident. The room where they sit is crowded with mementos of her childhood in Kentucky. Candles flicker. A cat slips in and out of the eddying shadows, its movements so graceful that Mary isn't quite sure whether it's real or not.

They sit, the three of them, at a round table in the center of the twilit room. The clairvoyant's hands cup the sides of a large glass ball in front of her. A breeze blows through an open window, filling the curtains like sails. Now and then, some noise from the street reaches her. Or Abraham shifts in his chair, as restless as a child. But mostly, it's quiet in the room, peaceful.

Mary watches the glass ball, mesmerized by the reflection of the flickering flames. Her eyes get heavy, she can barely keep her head up. Abraham leans over closer to her and whispers, "I think we should go, Mother. Nothing is going to happen here."

She shakes her head, unable to speak because now images are forming in the glass ball, clear, crisp images that flicker through the sea of glass like pieces of a dream. She wants to wrench her eyes away from the glass, but she can't. Her mind seizes the images, clarifies them.

A stage, she sees a stage. She sees a man and a woman watching a play, sees them from the back, the man in a rocker, the woman close beside him. She realizes they are in a private box in a theater. And there, farther back and deep within the shadows, she sees a crouched figure moving slowly and silently toward the man and the woman. He has a gun.

Mary struggles to shut her eyes, but her lids refuse to close. She begs her feet to move, demands that her body rise from the chair, screams within herself to get out now, to get out and not look back. But her body doesn't hear her pleas. Something inside her has broken down, she is frozen to this chair, her eyes riveted to the glass ball.

An explosion echoes through the room, a gunshot, chaos erupts. She screams. And screams.

IX

Then, suddenly, the world goes still again. She moves through a corridor, through an exquisite silence, and sees the golden-haired girl playing with a doll. The girl looks up, eyes wide and startled. Her delicate mouth forms an O shape; she hugs her doll tightly to her chest. This time, Mary speaks first.

"Your father, you need to warn your father...He cannot go to..."
"Daddy and Mommy went to Dallas..."
Too late, it's too late. *"You must get word to him..."*
The child frowns. *"About what? I don't understand."*
"Danger, he's in danger in Dallas..."
But the child is gone.

X

The windows in her bedroom are thrown open to the April night, to the fresh, green scents of spring. Mary hums as she dresses for the theater, the air like a promise of dreams to be fulfilled.

She really doesn't want to go to the theater tonight but Abraham insists on seeing, "Our American Cousin." And because he thinks it's good for them to get out, she consents to go. After all, if she resists, Abraham will think that her madness has returned, that she's holding séances, that she's stuck back there in the black miasma of so many months ago. He needs to believe she's better now.

So they are escorted out to the carriage by men from Company K, the men who guard her husband when he is in the mansion or at the Old Soldiers' Home. They enter the carriage alone, just the two of them, and tonight Abraham sits next to her and takes her hand in his and kisses the back of it and whispers, "You know I love you, don't you, Mary?"

And she touches the side of his face, drawing him toward her, and kisses his mouth, a kiss that deepens, that will last forever.

ABOUT THE AUTHOR

Rob & Trish MacGregor reside in South Florida. They write fiction and non-fiction. Both have won the Mystery Writers of America Edgar Allan Poe Award. Trish's latest novel is Apparition. Rob's latest novel is Time Catcher. Their most recent non-fiction book is Aliens in the Backyard: UFO Encounters, Abductions & Synchroncity. They also co-authored The 7 Secrets of Synchronicity and Synchronicity and the Other Side. Trish is also the co-author of Power Tarot (with Phyliss Vega) and Rob is the author of Psychic Power and co-author of The Fog (with Bruce Gernon) and The Rainbow Oracle (with Tony Grosso).

Curious about other Crossroad Press books?
Stop by our site:
http://store.crossroadpress.com
We offer quality writing
in digital, audio, and print formats.

Enter the code FIRSTBOOK
to get 20% off your first order from our store!
Stop by today!

www.ingramcontent.com/pod-product-compliance
Lightning Source LLC
Chambersburg PA
CBHW060437180626
46817CB00007B/2863